# Hope Ignites
## Jaci **BURTON**

**headline**
ETERNAL

Published by arrangement with Berkley,
a member of Penguin Group (USA) LLC.
A Penguin Random House Company.

First published in Great Britain in 2014
by HEADLINE ETERNAL
An imprint of HEADLINE PUBLISHING GROUP

1

Cataloguing in Publication Data is available from the British Library

ISBN 978 1 4722 1537 6

Offset in Times by Avon DataSet Ltd, Bidford-on-Avon, Warwickshire

Printed and bound by CPI Group (UK) Ltd, Croydon, CR0 4YY

Headline's policy is to use papers that are natural, renewable and recyclable
products and made from wood grown in sustainable forests. The logging and
manufacturing processes are expected to conform to the environmental
regulations of the country of origin.

HEADLINE PUBLISHING GROUP
An Hachette UK Company
338 Euston Road
London NW1 3BH

www.headlineeternal.com
www.headline.co.uk
www.hachette.co.uk

*To the toughest, and also the most honorable, the most gentle, and the most loving man I've ever known— my husband, Charlie. Thank you for being the calm in the rough waters of my life, my shoulder to cry on, and for giving me the love I've always needed.*

# Hope Ignites

# Chapter 1

LOGAN MCCORMACK HAD to have been drunk or out of his goddamned mind to have agreed to let a movie crew film on his ranch.

Why he thought it had been a good idea was beyond him. But Martha, the ranch cook and house manager, was starstruck, and when she'd heard who the lead actress was—some name Logan had already forgotten, alongside some freakin' hunk of the month as her costar—Martha had gone all melty and told him it would be good for business.

Plus, the production company had offered a buttload of cash, and he wasn't the type to turn down extra money. Since they'd be filming on the east side of the property, which was mostly hills and grassland and nowhere near their cattle operation, they'd be out of the way. So at the time it had seemed like a good idea.

They'd come in a week ago, a convoy of semis and trailers and black SUVs. Logan had been working the fence property and had seen them driving in. Hell, it was a Hollywood parade. It looked like the whole damn town had showed up at the gates to the ranch to witness it. He'd gotten all the gossip about it when Martha had served up dinner. She'd talked it up nonstop, her voice more animated than he'd heard in a long time.

"I'm pretty sure Desiree Jenkins and Colt Stevens are on our property as we speak," Martha had said as she'd laid the salad on the table. "Are you going to go check it out, Logan?"

"Why would I want to do that?" he'd asked, way more interested in eating than he was in the goings-on at the east property.

"You rented them the land. It's your responsibility to make sure they're settled in."

He'd said no, and Martha had argued. And when Martha argued about something, it was best you just do whatever she wanted because she wasn't the type to let a topic die.

"I'll go see about it in a few days." That few days had turned into a week, and Martha had been nearly apoplectic that he hadn't stopped by the movie set yet. Which could affect what she served for dinner, since Martha in a snit meant she could take to her room with some kind of mystery ailment, and he'd end up eating baloney sandwiches for dinner instead of a hot meal.

So after he was done with his work the next day, he climbed into his truck and drove over to the site. Crews had already finished building the set for . . . whatever movie it was they were filming. Some post-apocalyptic-futuristic something or other, supposedly set on another planet. The sparse vegetation, scrub, and hills of the east property would work just fine for it, he supposed. He'd signed the contracts and deposited the check, but hadn't bothered to pay attention to the name of the film. He wasn't much of a moviegoer. To go to the movies meant heading into town, and he'd rather sit on the porch and have a beer at night. He liked the quiet. If he wanted to see a movie, he had a television and one of those subscription accounts. That was good enough for him.

Martha was right. It already looked like they'd built a

small town on some of the flatlands out there. He parked his truck on the rise, popped open the beer he'd shoved in his cooler, and leaned against the hood of his truck to watch the hustle of people moving back and forth. Trailers had been set up as living areas, though these trailers looked way more expensive than anything Logan could ever afford. They were more like big houses on wheels. Probably what the stars lived in while they shot the movie.

An SUV came up the road, dust flying behind it. It stopped in front of Logan's truck and a couple of sunglass-wearing burly guys who looked like a more casual form of the Secret Service dressed in black camos and black T-shirts rolled out of the vehicle and stalked toward him.

This should be good.

"This is a closed set," one of them said, trying his best to look menacing.

Unruffled, Logan stared at them. "Okay."

"You aren't supposed to be on this property."

"I own this property."

One of the guys in black frowned at him. "You're the property owner?"

"Yeah."

"Got ID?"

Logan let out a short laugh. "I'm not about to show you my ID. Like I said, I own this land and you're renting it."

"We'll still need to see ID," burly guy number two said.

Logan folded his arms. "Yeah, and you can kiss my ass."

His attention turned to a slight woman—a girl, really—running up the hill. Technically she appeared to be jogging because she wore tight pants that went just past her knees and a sleeveless top that hugged her slender body. She had raven black hair pulled back in a braid, and the guys suddenly stepped in front of Logan as if he were about to pull a gun on the woman.

When she reached them, she stopped, drawing in several deep breaths.

"What's up, Carl?"

"Saw this guy parked up here and came to check it out. He says he's the property owner, but he won't show ID to prove it."

She finally straightened and stretched her back. "Is that right? And are you the property owner?"

"So it says on the ranch deed."

She looked him over. "I don't see any cameras on him. Do you?"

The one named Carl shook his head. "No. He was just leaning against his truck drinking a beer."

"Then he's probably the property owner." She walked over and held out her hand. "I'm Des."

Logan shook her hand. "Logan McCormack."

"Nice ranch, Logan."

"Thanks."

"Have you been down to watch filming yet?"

"Why would I want to do that?"

She quirked a smile. "I don't know. I thought maybe you'd find it interesting."

"Are you working on the film crew, Des?"

Her lips curled into a smirk. "You could say that."

One of the big guys stepped forward. "Miss Jenkins?"

"It's okay, Carl. You and Duke can take off."

Carl shook his head. "Not a good idea."

She shot him a look. "And I said I'm fine."

With another serious death glare, the guy named Carl and the other one got into the SUV and drove back down the hill.

"Are those your bodyguards?"

She laughed. "Sometimes."

"So you must be the star of the show."

She shrugged. "Well, I'm the lead. I don't know about star."

"What are you doing out here?"

"Taking a break. And getting some exercise."

"Not really a gym on-site for you to work out in, is there?"

"No. This is better. A lot of hills to run in. You must love it here."

"It's home."

She leaned against the front of his truck, grabbed the beer from his hand, took a long swallow, and handed it back to him. "Thanks."

"I don't recall offering it to you."

She turned to her side. "You're not very friendly, are you, Logan?"

"I try not to be."

"Yeah? And why's that?"

"It keeps people away."

"Oh, so you don't like people."

"I didn't say that."

She laughed, and he liked the gravelly, raspy, sexy sound of it. Which he shouldn't.

"Do you have any more of those?" she asked, eyeing his beer.

"I might."

When she cocked a brow, he added, "Front passenger floor of the truck. There's a cooler. Help yourself."

She went around and grabbed a beer, bringing him one, too. "Yours looked about empty." She popped the top and took a long swallow.

"You sure you're old enough to be drinking those?"

There went that laugh again. "I'm sure." She gave him a sideways glance. "Are *you* old enough to be drinking them?"

"Funny." He popped the top on his and took several long drinks, wondering why the hell he was standing here next to—what was her name again?

Oh, right. Desiree. Des.

She leaned next to him and looked out over the valley. "Just how big is this ranch, Logan?"

"It's pretty big."

She shot him a look. "Pretend I'm smart and just tell me."

"It's a little over forty-five thousand acres."

"Holy shit. That's a lot. No wonder you could afford to lend us a small piece of the pie."

"I didn't lend it. I'm renting it to your moviemaking company. Which means I make money. Working a ranch is a costly business."

"I'm sure it is. Though honestly, I wouldn't know."

He took another swallow of beer as he studied her. "City girl?"

"A little of that, and a little country. I've been around. Never lived on a ranch, though."

"Where are you from?"

"Just about everywhere."

"Military?"

She tilted her head and looked up at him. "What makes you think that?"

"I don't think anything at all. Just guessing."

"Good guess. Yeah, my dad's Army. We moved around a lot."

"So you've seen the world."

She didn't smile this time. "You could say that."

"You probably still see a lot of it, being an actress."

"Sometimes a lot more than I want to." She took a couple drinks of her beer and kept her gaze focused below, where the movie was being filmed. And she stopped talking.

Logan didn't know what to make of Desiree Jenkins. She couldn't be more than in her mid-twenties at best, which put her firmly in the close-to-ten-years-younger-than-him category. Scrubbed of makeup, she looked like a teenager, but there was a worldliness in her eyes that made her seem a lot older.

She sure was pretty with her long dark hair and wide eyes that he couldn't quite get a handle on, color-wise. Every time she shifted position, so did the color. At first they seemed blue, but now they were more like a brownish green, with little flecks of gold in them.

"You're staring."

He frowned. "Huh?"

"You're staring at me. Do I have dirt on my face?"

"No. I'm looking at your eyes. The color of them."

"Oh, yeah. They're like a chameleon. They shift with my surroundings. Pretty cool, huh?"

"Huh. I guess so."

She leaned back against his car again. "Not much impresses you, does it, Logan?"

"Nope." But her eyes did.

"So tell me about your ranch. What do you do here?"

"Work."

"Wow, so descriptive. I'll bet you're a great conversationalist at parties."

"Don't get to a lot of parties around here."

"Maybe you don't get invited to a lot of parties."

"Can't say that breaks my heart any."

She rolled her eyes. "Anyway, about the ranch?"

"We work cattle. We also have horses, but they're wild mustangs so we don't mess with them except to make sure they're fed and have water."

"Okay. Do you raise the cattle for beef?"

"Yeah."

"You didn't strike me as a dairy farmer."

"Really. And what does a typical dairy farmer look like to you?"

She shrugged. "No idea. Not like you. You're more the rugged, work-the-land type, not milk-the-cows type."

He wasn't sure whether to take that as a compliment, or whether she'd just insulted dairy farmers. Either way, it was obvious she had no idea what she was talking about. Then again, he didn't know shit about moviemaking. But he wasn't spouting off about it, either.

"Well, I gotta go."

She pushed off the truck and handed him the empty beer can. "Thanks for the drink. You should come down and watch filming."

"No, thanks. I'm plenty busy with my own work."

"You might find what we do utterly fascinating."

"I'm interested enough in what I do."

She cocked her head to the side, revealing a soft column of her neck. He didn't want to be interested in her neck, but he was.

"Afraid you might linger a little too long? Maybe get bitten by the acting bug?"

He laughed at that. "Uh, no."

"Then come on down and watch us work."

Martha would have a fit if he'd gotten an invite and he didn't say yes. "My house manager is a big fan."

"Bring her down to watch a day of filming. We're doing a big dramatic scene tomorrow. She'd probably love that."

"She probably would."

"I'll have to warn you, there's a lot of standing around and waiting in between takes, but I promise you the end result is always worthwhile. What's your housekeeper's name?"

"Martha."

"You and Martha come on out to the set. I promise it'll be fun."

There were a million reasons this wasn't a good idea. But then there was Martha, and he hated the thought of cold sandwiches. "What time?"

"I'm usually in makeup by six a.m., so we should start shooting by eight."

"You get up that early? I thought all you movie stars slept 'til noon."

"Now who's funny? I'll let the crew know you're coming." She lifted her arms over her head, stretched, then kicked off into a run, waving at him. "See you tomorrow, Logan."

Why the hell he'd agreed to that, he had no idea. He had more than enough to do, and losing a day would put him behind.

But at least Martha would be happy.

DES MADE IT back to the film site and ran straight into Theo, her director.

"Des. Where'd you run off to?"

"I took a run to get some exercise. Did you need me for something?"

"Yes. We need to do a reshoot of one of this morning's scenes. I told you not to disappear."

"Sorry. I'll head over to makeup and hair."

"Too late now. I've already dismissed the crew for the day, and the lighting isn't right. We'll pick it up later." He walked with her as she headed to her trailer. "I wanted to go over tomorrow's scenes with you, though. How about dinner tonight? My trailer?" He put his arm around her shoulder.

Her skin crawled and she immediately wanted to shrug him off. Theo was a notorious, disgusting, very married womanizer, who liked to hit on his leading ladies, especially on location. But he was also a brilliant director, so one had to take the bad with the good. "I need a shower after my run, Theo. And I've already made plans to run lines with Colt over dinner. You're welcome to join us, though. We could knock out discussion about tomorrow's scenes then."

Theo paused, then shook his head. "No, that's all right. We'll do it in the morning during prep. I'll see you then."

"Okay. See you tomorrow, Theo."

She stepped up her pace before Theo came up with any more pervy ideas.

"Cornered you, did he?"

She smiled at Colt Stevens, her costar. "He did. Why weren't you loitering nearby to save me?"

"Sorry, babe. I was on the phone. I saw Theo hook on to you as soon as you got back on set. Did you have a good run?"

"I did. Did you have a good phone call?"

His eyes gleamed. "I did."

Des looked around to make sure they were alone. "And how is Tony?"

"Pining away for me, as always. I wish he could be here."

"I wish he could, too." Des wrapped her arm around Colt's waist. "Why don't you just come out of the closet and be done with it already?"

They'd reached her trailer. Colt opened the door for her, and Des stepped in. Colt followed and shut the door. "Oh, right. Smokin'-hot movie star who gets all the sexy, romantic roles comes out as gay."

Des shrugged. "So? It's the twenty-first century, Colt. And you kiss better than any leading man I've ever worked with. I doubt any of your future leading ladies would be deterred."

Colt sat on her sofa, stretching out his long legs. "Thanks, babe. Tony thinks so, too."

She laughed. "Seriously, though. We have chemistry through the roof, and it shows on-screen. If you can pull that off, who cares who you love offscreen?"

"Well, I sure don't. And you don't. And probably most of America doesn't give a shit, either. But my management team does care. And they say no to coming out."

She plopped onto the sofa next to him. "I'm sorry. You should be able to live your life freely and not have to parade around with a bunch of women you don't care about while Tony is stuck loving you behind the scenes."

Colt let out a sigh. "I know, love. But it is what it is, and I guess it's going to stay that way for a while. Maybe someday we'll be able to change that."

She pushed off and stood. "Hopefully sooner rather than later. I want you to be happy."

"I want you to be happy, too."

She gave him a smile. "I am happy. I'm living my dream here."

"Sure you are."

"Did you get dinner ordered?"

"Should be here in about fifteen."

"Pop open a bottle of wine for us, then. I'm going to hop in the shower."

Des stripped and got into the shower, washing away the

body makeup from the day's scenes and the sweat from her run. She thought about Colt. They'd known each other since before either of them had even gotten their first part in film, when they'd bunked together in a one-bedroom apartment in Hollywood. They'd become fast friends and had stayed that way. She'd found out right away that Colt was gay—hard to hide that kind of thing from your best friend and roommate. And when they'd started getting roles together, they'd bonded and supported each others' careers. Fortunately, they'd also been lucky enough to score roles in films together. Which, of course, made love scenes sometimes awkward to film, because as close friends, it was hard to play lovers. But they were professionals and they were actors. And because they were so close, they had a natural chemistry that lent itself well to the camera, so they worked at using that chemistry. They were comfortable together and lit up the screen. They were often linked together in the gossip circles, which Colt found hysterical.

So did Des. She didn't mind bearding for him, and often went to premieres and out to dinner with him to give him a cover when he didn't feel like playing the role of a straight guy with some other woman.

Until she'd met James and had started a relationship with him.

Which had recently gone up in flames. But she wasn't going to think about him anymore. He'd already wasted enough of her time. She was never going to have a relationship with another actor.

Now she was free to hook up with Colt again. At least on the surface.

She got out of the shower and put on a pair of shorts and a tank top. The smell of dinner made her stomach clench. She was hungry, so she hurriedly combed out her hair and went into the main room of the trailer, where Colt was laying out forks and plates.

"Chinese food?"

"Yeah."

"All that salt. I love looking puffy in front of the camera."

Colt grinned. "You couldn't look puffy if you tried. Sit down and eat."

They ate, sipped wine, and roughed out tomorrow's scenes in between bites.

"I met Logan McCormack, the owner of the ranch, today," she said as she grabbed a fortune cookie.

"Yeah? What's he like?"

"Incredibly sexy, in a brooding, loner cowboy sort of way."

"Really. Would I like him?"

She laughed. "I think you'd love him. And Tony would kill you."

"Hey, I'm devoted and madly in love and you know that. Doesn't mean I can't ogle."

"I invited him to the set. He said his house manager is a big fan, so he's going to bring her tomorrow."

"Hmm."

She looked at Colt. "Hmmm what?"

"You're interested. Now I really can't wait to meet him."

"I didn't say I was interested in him, only that he was interesting."

"Same thing, isn't it?"

"Not at all." She cracked open her fortune cookie and popped a piece into her mouth as she unfolded the fortune and read it.

*Your life is about to change in new and exciting ways.*

She'd believe that when it happened.

# Chapter 2

"HOW'S MY HAIR?"

Logan looked over at Martha as they rode toward the set. "What?"

She smoothed down her hair and checked herself in the mirror. "My hair, Logan. It's humid out here. What if I get to take a picture with Desiree or Colt? How does it look?"

"It looks fine."

Martha shot him a glare. "That is not a helpful statement."

"Your hair looks nice, Martha. Definitely pictureworthy."

"Too late. Just drive."

Logan shrugged, not understanding why this whole thing was such a big damn deal. But he loved Martha, so he'd endure it for her.

There was a designated parking area, and he gave his name to security, who checked him off the list and gave Martha and him a day pass, which irritated the crap out of him.

"Why the hell do I have to have a pass to walk on my own goddamned property?" he grumbled as they were led through a gate.

"Oh, quit complaining," Martha said, her eyes wide as she soaked it all in.

"This isn't freakin' Disneyland, you know. It's McCormack property. You've been here before."

"Oh, no, Logan. To me, it's Disneyland. By way of Hollywood. Look at the set, all the people running around. They've turned the land into something magical."

When he'd told her yesterday that he'd run into Des, she'd squealed, dinner forgotten as she asked him the celebrity version of twenty questions. What was Desiree like? Was she nice? What had they talked about? Was she as pretty in person as she was on the screen? Had Colt been there with her?

Damn, but the woman had been incessant. And when he'd told her Des had invited them on set, her eyes had grown wide as saucers, and he thought he might have had to hold her up. She'd gripped the counter and told him he was lying. When he'd assured her he wasn't, she'd abandoned dinner and gone home, claiming she had to figure out what she was going to wear. Good thing dinner had been ready so all he and Martha's husband, Ben, had to do was serve it up.

"This is amazing," Martha said as they wound their way onto the set.

Didn't look amazing at all to him. It looked like someone had taken piles of rocks and blown them up. There were plenty of trees and hills, but a lot of it was scrub. He supposed it was stark and desolate enough for their movie, though he had no idea why they didn't film it in the desert in California.

He'd asked them that question and they'd told him there were no clouds out there, not the right kind of scenery for the location they required. Here, there were plenty of clouds to give them the gloomy feel for the shoot. Plus, it could potentially rain, and they needed that. They'd given him a lot of explanatory bullshit about this being the ideal location, Also, it was private property, which meant they could keep the movie secret from the media.

Whatever.

He had to admit they'd done a lot in the short time they'd been here. There were buildings and caves, all painted and kind of impressive. On the north end there were giant, steel-like structures painted gray and forbidding, which resembled some kind of futuristic metropolis.

Maybe it was supposed to look like that. Though only half of it looked like the set. The rest of it was cameras and what appeared like a train track and equipment and a hell of a lot of people.

"You must be Logan." A young dark-haired woman came over, wearing capris and a tank top. She also had on a headset and carried a phone, a clipboard, and a digital notebook. "I'm Jessica, Desiree's assistant."

Logan shook her hand. "Nice to meet you. This is Martha."

Jessica shook her hand. "Des told me you were coming today. We have chairs already set up for you to watch the filming. Follow me."

Jessica led them to two chairs with a clear view of the set. "Right here. Is there anything I can bring you? Would you like a drink?"

"I'm fine," Logan said.

"Me, too. Thank you, Jessica," Martha said, smiling so wide Logan was afraid her face was going to break.

"Des will be out shortly to greet you, but then she'll have to get right on set."

"Fine with me. Thanks," Logan said, hoping they could just watch a scene, Martha would be placated and then they could get out of there. He had work to do. Cows didn't exactly manage themselves. And while his crew would work fine alone, he didn't take days off. It wasn't in his nature.

"This is so exciting," Martha said, nearly wriggling in her chair. She really had gone all out, getting dressed up in her fancy slacks and Sunday blouse. She'd even put on makeup, something Martha did only for church and special events.

He supposed, for Martha, this was a special event.

Logan had worn what he always wore. Jeans and a T-shirt. And his boots. It was just as hot and dusty out here as it was on the rest of the ranch. Besides, he saw no reason to get dressed up for these movie people. They were just regular people like him, right?

"You two look comfortable. You ready for the day?"

Martha clutched his arm as Des appeared from behind them.

She sure looked different from yesterday. Instead of her scrubbed, clean look, she was dressed in tight cargo pants and a black tank top. They had her hair mussed, her face streaked with dirt, and what looked like a bloody gash on her arm. She wore a strapped thigh holster and some kind of mean-looking futuristic weapon tucked onto her hip, another longer, rifle-type one slung across her back. And some very kickass boots with laces and buckles that even Logan had to admit looked sexy as hell on her.

Martha slid out of her chair and held out her hand. "Good morning, Miss Jenkins. I'm Martha Fleming. Thank you so much for letting us come to your set today."

"Hi, Martha. I'm so pleased to meet you, and I'm glad you could make it today." Des gave Logan a wide smile. "Nice to see you again, Logan."

Logan nodded. "Des."

"Are you ready for an action scene today?" Des asked them.

"They sure have you made up, don't they?" Martha asked, looking at Des. "How long does that take?"

"Not too bad for today. About an hour and a half in hair and makeup. I'm going to get a little more roughed up, but Colt will take the worst of it, so unfortunately for him, he'll have to sit longer in the chair than I will after this scene."

"How exciting." Martha was practically vibrating.

"They're ready for you, Des," Jessica said.

Des nodded. "I'll be right there." She turned back to Logan and Martha. "I hope you enjoy it. The scene is fairly short, so I'll be back to check on both of you after."

She walked away and was soon joined by a tall, sandy-haired man dressed similarly to Des.

Martha gripped his arm again. "Oh, my Lord. That's Colt Stevens. Isn't he handsome?"

The guy was muscular, for sure, showing it all off in his half-ripped sleeveless top. Colt and Des smiled at each other as they got into position. The director—or Logan guessed it was the director—started calling out something. Des pulled her weapon and crouched down behind one of the buildings, Colt right next to her in a similar position. Several other actors dressed in black combat gear and wearing some type of creature makeup were on the other side of the buildings. They were armed, too. It looked like it was Des and Colt against an army of at least a dozen.

When the director called "Action," Des and Colt started talking. It appeared as if they were trying to strategize an escape, but the guys in black made the first move, firing their weapons. Des and Colt fired back. No sounds came from the guns. Logan assumed those sounds would be dubbed in later. The firefight lasted only about a minute, but Logan had to admit he'd leaned forward, getting into the action, especially when Des and Colt bolted from their position of security, the aliens advancing on them. When her gun was out of imaginary ammo, she holstered it and slung the rifle over her shoulder and began to fire.

Logan smiled at the way she held the rifle. Des needed some lessons on rifle fire. If it were an actual shoot-out, she wouldn't hit the broad side of a barn with that thing. Then again, this was all make-believe, so it didn't matter.

She was hit, presumably in the leg, because she dropped her weapon and went down, clutching her thigh. A bright burst of red came from her thigh and the aliens advanced on her.

Des was captured, dragged away through the dirt by one of the taller men. Colt started to come for her, but he was jolted back as if he had been hit by gun or laser fire, though, of course, there was no gunfire sound.

Des screamed out, arms flailing, yelling for Colt to run, not to come for her. Colt hesitated, special effects smoke billowing all around them.

Nice. It was over in a minute or two, the director yelled "Cut" and everyone got up.

"That was a good take, everyone," the director said. "We'll regroup for scene seven in thirty minutes."

Des brushed herself off and went over to Colt. Heads bent in conversation, gesturing and pointing over the scene they'd just shot, Logan studied the two of them as they talked. The connection between them was obvious. The smiles they shared and the way Colt touched her made it seem as if they were intimate. He wondered if they were dating.

"Wasn't that exciting?" Martha asked.

"It was interesting."

"Interesting?" Martha nudged him. "I barely breathed the entire time."

"Okay, it was a pretty good scene."

"Look, she's bringing Colt over." Martha straightened her blouse, and Logan rolled his eyes.

"You gonna leave Ben for this guy?"

Martha shot him a look. "Of course not. Colt's young enough to be my son. He's younger than you, for heaven's sake."

"Then I don't think you need to primp."

She slapped his arm. "You're a mean man, Logan McCormack."

"How did you like the scene?" Des asked.

"Oh, my," Martha said. "It was amazing."

Des waited.

"It was good," Logan said.

"Logan, Martha, this is Colt Stevens."

Colt gave them a genuine smile and shook their hands. "Pleasure to meet both of you. And, Logan, thanks for the use of this ranch. I'm hoping to get out and explore, that is, if you don't mind."

Logan was predisposed not to like Colt, but he was friendly and not arrogant. "Do you ride?"

"Some. I spent time on a ranch in my errant youth, but I'm a little rusty."

"Oh, you have to come over to the ranch. In fact, you and Des should come for Sunday dinner." Martha frowned. "What do you eat around here, anyway?"

Des wrinkled her nose. "Either takeout from town or whatever catering gives us."

Martha crossed her arms. "Which is?"

"Nothing edible, that's for sure," Colt said with a laugh.

"Then you definitely have to come for Sunday dinner. I make home-cooked meals every night, and it's not that far. It sure beats takeout and whatever your catering truck is going to fix for you."

"We wouldn't want to put you out, Martha," Colt said. "We're used to eating in our trailers."

"Nonsense. You'll come for dinner. I insist. Besides, it'll be a treat for me. I'll get to pick your brains about the movie business."

Des looked at Colt, who then grinned at Martha. "Sounds like a win-win to me. Besides, I'd really like to get back on a horse again, provided Logan doesn't mind."

If he said he minded, Martha would likely kill him. "I don't mind. Come for dinner, like Martha said. The more people Martha can cook for, the happier she is."

"This is true," Martha said with a smile. "Sunday dinner is my specialty."

"Sunday dinner it is, then," Des said. "And thank you. If I never see a Chinese-food box again, I'll be happy."

When the bell rang, Des and Colt had to leave to get ready for their next scene. Colt was talking to Martha, and Des moved in next to Logan. "You sure you're okay about us coming to the ranch house for dinner?"

"Hey, I'm not the one cooking. If Martha wants you, consider yourself invited."

"Still, I'd hate to intrude."

"You're already here on the land. A couple extra people at the house won't make any difference."

She patted him on the chest. "That's what I like about you, Logan. So warm and inviting." She tilted her head back, and he was caught again by her ever-changing eyes. "See you later."

"What was that about?" Martha asked after Colt and Des left.

"Nothing."

"I think she likes you."

"I think she likes Colt."

"And I think you know nothing about acting. Or women."

"That much is true." What he did know was they were going to have guests for dinner on Sunday. And one of them was Des, a woman he didn't understand at all. Not that he understood any woman, but her in particular.

And when she'd touched him, he'd felt something, which bothered him.

He liked the type of woman he could categorize—the kind you took to bed and the kind you stayed away from.

He'd like to stay away from Des.

He'd also like to take her to bed. She had a smart, sassy mouth, a sexy smile, and an attitude a mile long. But he figured that Colt guy was her boyfriend, and he didn't get in the middle of a relationship, so he planned to steer clear of her.

He was good at staying away from women, had lived thirty-four years without tangling himself up in a woman.

He had enough trouble just managing the ranch, which was enough to handle.

Women were a lot more work.

A woman from Hollywood? No way in hell was he tangling with that.

# Chapter 3

———

"THIS ISN'T EXACTLY a Hollywood premiere, Des. Let's get a move on."

Colt paced impatiently in Des's trailer while she put the finishing touches on her hair, which had decided not to cooperate today. Damn Oklahoma humidity. Her hair was flat and uncooperative and looked like a mop. Ugh.

Not that she was trying to impress anyone or anything. That someone she was definitely not trying to impress would likely not even notice her, anyway, so why would she even bother? She was only going over there for the home cooking.

She finally gave up and pulled it back in a high ponytail, slipped on her boots and came out of her bedroom.

"I'm ready."

Colt gave her the once-over. "You look cute."

She looked down at her dark blue short-sleeve button-down shirt, shorts, and boots. "Not too casual?"

"No. It's cute."

She leaned into him. "And you look hot." Then again, he always did, even in jeans and a button-down shirt.

"What do you think about the boots? Too city-boy-trying-to-look-country?"

"Not at all. Your boots are scuffed, and you're not a city boy."

"Tell that to my house in the city."

She laughed. "Let's go. I'm seriously craving some home cooking."

They made the drive over to the main ranch house. Des stared out the window at all the land. Stuck in L.A. all the time, where space was at a premium, she gaped at the free expanse of land here, couldn't fathom what it must be like to look out your front door and know the land as far as you could see was yours.

She rented a condo and she could hear her neighbors argue. She made good money, but she invested it. One of these days she'd like to have property somewhere remote, where she could be alone . . . like this. Someplace to call her own, where she could establish roots and never have to pick up and move again.

"You're quiet."

She turned to Colt and smiled at him. "I'm enjoying the view. Isn't it magnificent here?"

"It's pretty damned awesome."

He pulled into the driveway and parked. Dogs suddenly appeared and started barking, their tails wagging furiously back and forth. And, oh my, there were a lot of dogs.

"Oh, my God, they have dogs," Des said with a wide grin. She opened the door and slid out of the SUV, suddenly surrounded by yips and wagging tails as the dogs greeted her. She crouched down to pet them, all various breeds and shapes and sizes.

"Hi there, cuties."

"I see you've met the dogs."

Logan's voice was deep and entered her senses right

away. There was just something about him that got to her. She lifted her head and smiled up at him. "I have. What are their names?"

He stepped down off the porch and gave a low whistle. In an instant, the dogs ran to him.

"Sit."

It was like magic. They all sat at his feet, clearly knowing who their master was.

She stood and followed while he pointed down the row. "This is Whip, Duke, Maisie, Sally, Cinder, and Punk. We have a couple of cats around, too, but they're harder to spot. They like women, though, so they might come out today to see you."

Des crouched down to pet them again, shoving her face in their fur. "They're gorgeous."

In the meantime, Colt went over to shake Logan's hand. "Thanks for letting us come over today."

"You can thank Martha for that. She'd have invited the whole crew if I'd let her."

Des looked up at him. "I take it she likes to entertain."

"She thinks everyone needs a home-cooked meal."

Speaking of Martha, she opened the screen door. "Oh, you're here. Welcome. What are you doing in the dirt? Dogs, shoo."

They must listen to Martha, too, because the dogs all took off. Logan held his hand out for Des. She slipped her hand in his and he hauled her to her feet.

"You'll get dirty down there on the ground," he said.

She met his gaze and her stomach fluttered. "I don't mind getting dirty."

His gaze held hers, and it was like something she'd never felt before—an instant connection, something hot and primal that she'd just love to explore with him—in the dark, just the two of them, alone. But just as quickly as it was there, Logan looked away.

"Come on inside. It's hot out here."

The house was magnificent. Old, but in great shape, with its two-story charm, and, oh, rocking chairs on the front porch to enjoy that amazing view. She loved all the flowers pouring from pots on the porch. The added color was a burst of sunshine, as well as the gardens growing off to the west side of the house. She wanted to investigate . . . everything.

Inside was just as charming as out, with polished darkwood floors and a pretty damned amazing kitchen, with high-end appliances, everything so modern in contrast to the old-country charm of the home.

"It smells so good in here," Colt said. "If it tastes as good as it smells, I might never go back to the set again."

Martha's cheeks blushed pink. "I can guarantee it's better than takeout."

"I'm sure it is," Des said. "Thank you again for inviting us."

"I'm thrilled you're here. Logan, show them the house. Provided you'd like to see it."

"I'd love to see it." Des looked to Logan.

"I'll let Martha show me around later," Colt said, pulling up a chair at the island. "I'm going to sit here and filch some of these corn bread muffins from her. I'm starving."

Martha laughed and grabbed a plate, setting it in front of Colt. "All right. Logan, show Des around."

Des figured Logan was about as excited at giving her a tour as he would be at having makeup put on for a scene. But he nodded and led her out of the kitchen and into a very expansive living area. He stood in the doorway. "This is the family room."

She walked in and perused the furniture, some modern, such as the flat-screen television, but there was a sprinkling of antique furniture, too, no doubt handed down by generations of family. She went and got a closer look at an old cabinet. She loved that it was scarred, wondering about the history of the piece.

"I love old furniture," she said.

"It's been there as long as I've been alive. I think it was my great grandmother's."

She nodded, sliding her hand across the old wood, then moved her way to the fireplace, admiring the stonework. She studied the photos sitting on top of the mantel—three young boys posed in an older photo. She picked it up, then turned to Logan.

"One of these boys is you."

"Yeah. And my brothers."

She tapped the child on the left. "That's you?"

"Yes. The one in the middle is Luke, who's the second oldest, and the youngest is Reid."

"So just you three boys?"

"Yeah."

"Do they all live here on the ranch?"

"No. Only me."

She rolled her eyes. Getting information out of Logan was like digging out an impacted tooth. "Where do they live?"

"Luke lives in town. Reid lives in Boston."

"They're not ranchers like you, then?"

"No."

She sighed. "And what do they do?"

"Luke's a cop. Reid's an architect."

She moved out of the room and joined him in the hall. "Why didn't they want to be ranchers?"

He moved down the hall. "Not in their blood."

"Like it's in yours?"

"I guess. There's a mudroom this way that leads out to the other entrance, and the laundry room, and a bathroom. Not much to see here. And just bedrooms upstairs. And a couple bathrooms."

When she didn't start back to the kitchen, he said, "I suppose you want to see those."

"That'd be nice. Unless you didn't make your bed and you don't want me to see it."

He gave her an exasperated look. "Come on."

They went up the stairs. There was a long hallway, with doors on either side. She stopped at the landing. "Does Martha live up here?"

He shook his head. "No. She and Ben, her husband, have their own house a little ways down the road."

"You live here all alone?"

"Yeah."

"Big house for just one person."

"It suits me fine."

She peeked her head into the first couple of rooms, all neatly maintained, then continued down the hall. "Which one's your room?"

"The master at the end of the hall."

"The biggest room, then."

"Yeah. It used to be my parents' bedroom."

"And where are your parents now?"

"My dad died a while back. My mom's . . . gone."

She stopped. "Gone?"

"She took off after my dad died. Remarried a short while after. Decided ranch life wasn't for her."

He said it so matter-of-factly, but Des knew it must have hit him hard. It probably still hurt. "That must have sucked."

"It did. We survived it."

"Obviously you did since you seem to be doing well for yourself. I'm sorry about your dad."

"Thanks." He opened the door to his bedroom. "See. Just a plain room. Nothing special."

And he didn't want her in his bedroom. Which made her curious, so she stepped in.

Typical guy's room. Huge bed, dresser, and a chair. Big window. "Oh, there's a deck." She turned to him. "Do you mind?"

He looked like he minded, but he said, "Go ahead."

She opened the French doors and walked out. "Holy shit, Logan. What a view."

Land as far as she could see. Rolling hills, trees, cattle wandering the hillside, it was the most amazing thing she'd ever seen. Two chairs sat on the deck, too. She could already imagine herself popping open a beer at night or having a glass of wine and settling in to watch the moon and the stars. "This far outside the city, the stars must be amazing at night."

He'd stepped outside next to her. "I wouldn't know. I don't sit out here."

She turned to him. "Are you serious? Why not?"

He shrugged. "I don't know. When I come upstairs, I go to bed. Not much time to sit out here and watch the stars."

"Dude. You're living all wrong. You have to take the time to enjoy life's beautiful moments."

He finally cracked a half smile. "Is that a line from a movie?"

"No. Consider it a life lesson. How could you not want to sit out here? Bring a woman up to your bedroom and seduce the hell out of her with a bottle of wine and this view?"

He stared at her, and she stared back.

"Is that a request?" he asked.

"I don't know. Are you inviting me to your bedroom?"

"No."

And that was a quick response. "Too bad. I'd like to sit out here by moonlight. And I'm damn good in bed, too, so your loss."

She walked away and out of his room.

Let Mr. Silent and Moody suck on that one for a while.

LOGAN STAYED ON the deck and pondered what the hell had just happened.

Had Des propositioned him?

And had he really turned her down?

Well . . . yeah. Hell, yes, he'd turned her down. First, she was way too young for him. Second, she was an actress and out of his league. And Colt was likely her boyfriend. And again, she was too young for him.

And gorgeous. And sexy as hell in her short-shorts and boots and, God, those legs. Tanned and long, and he could already imagine them wrapped around him.

And she was trouble. Capital *T*, capital *R*, and all the rest of the letters thrown in, too.

Bring a woman up here and seduce her in the moonlight. What the hell kind of woman said shit like that?

He stared out the doorway and into his bedroom, already imagining a tangle of sheets and legs and Des, sprawled naked on his bed, her long dark hair spread across his pillow.

His dick went hard.

Shit. He dragged his fingers through his hair and tried to think about something else besides Des naked.

He liked his sex uncomplicated, and he knew plenty of women who could give him that. Des was going to be spending time on his property. He'd have to see her again and again, and to him, that was a whole lot of complicated.

He walked off the deck and looked for Des, but didn't see her, so he went downstairs. He found her in the kitchen, bent over the counter while she chatted with Martha and Colt. He tried not to stare at her ass and legs as he walked in.

"Oh, there you are, Logan. Desiree and Colt were telling me about the scenes they'll be filming while they're here at the ranch. Apparently, much of the movie takes place on the planet, so they're going to be here two months."

Logan reached into the refrigerator for a beer. "Isn't that great."

"It is. And I told them they could come over for dinner whenever they'd like."

Logan popped the top on his can of beer, then perused Martha's gleeful expression. "I know you'll enjoy that." He looked over at Des and Colt. "And so will the two of you. Once you taste Martha's cooking, you'll never want takeout or whatever the catering truck makes you again."

"That's what I'm afraid of," Des said.

They moved into the dining room to eat. Ben came in and Martha made the introductions.

"Sorry to be so late," Ben said. "I was working on the truck." He looked over at Logan. "I thought it was the starter, but looks like it needs a new alternator. You want me to run into town tomorrow?"

Logan shook his head. "No. We need to work the calves over on forty-two, and we have two extra hands coming in for that. You can handle them. I'll head into town and pick up a new alternator."

"Okay," Ben said.

"Actually, Colt has scenes all day tomorrow. I have an early scene in the morning, then I'm done for the day," Des said. "If it doesn't conflict with your schedule, would you mind if I went into town with you?"

Logan looked at her, then shrugged. "That'd be fine. Is there something in particular you want to do?"

"Not really, but I'd like to see Hope, and since I don't know the town, maybe you can give me a tour."

"We need more of that medication Emma put Maisie on. Her rash has mostly cleared up, but she's still scratching," Martha said. "If you're going to town, maybe you could also stop by the vet clinic."

Logan sighed. "I can do that. Make me a list of what else we need for the dogs."

"Glad you're going to town and not me," Ben said with a grin.

Yeah, Logan figured Ben would say that. Ben hated making a lot of stops. Logan didn't get into Hope all that often, so it wasn't that big of a deal for him to run errands while he was there.

"You should see what Luke's up to while you're there, too," Martha said. "Maybe you can have lunch."

"Luke's likely working and won't have time."

Martha gave him a look. "He's gotta eat, same as you."

Since arguing with Martha was pointless, he nodded. "I'll text him."

"Though Fourth of July is coming up. He and Emma will be coming over for that, and we'll all get to see them then." Martha turned to Des and Colt. "Will you two be heading back to L.A. for the holiday?"

Colt shook his head. "No. Since it falls in the middle of the week, we'll just hang out here."

"We have a big spread on the Fourth. Tons of food, and family and friends come visit. If you don't mind the ogling of the locals, we'd love to have you. Logan buys the biggest and best fireworks and we have a blowout."

"Sounds fun," Des said, eyeing Logan.

"You're both welcome to come," Logan said. "It's definitely a party."

"We'd love to," Colt said. "Thanks."

"And invite whoever you'd like to, if you have people nearby," Martha said.

Colt gave Des a look. She smiled back at him. Logan had no idea what that meant.

After they finished eating, they carried their dishes to the sink and Martha tried to shoo them out of the kitchen, despite both Des and Colt's protests that they wanted to help clean up.

"You might as well give up. She never lets guests help wash the dishes," Logan said.

Des, however, refused to budge. She made herself at home and started scrounging through the cabinets looking for containers for the leftovers. Logan leaned back and watched with amusement as Martha sputtered that a movie star should not be crating leftovers in her kitchen.

"First, I'm hardly a movie star. Being an actress is just my job. Second, my mother and father both would kick my butt if I just walked out on someone who had fixed a meal for me without helping to clean up. So you can forget it. I'm not leaving."

Colt pitched in, too, nudging Martha aside to scrub the roasting pan for her while she dried some of the pots and put them away.

"It's not like we have servants doing our dishes at home," Colt said.

Martha dried her hands on the towel. "You don't?"

Des laughed. "Not quite. I live in a two-bedroom condo. No room for anyone but me in my small kitchen."

"I would have thought you'd have some big house in the hills or maybe on the beach."

"They ask ridiculous prices for homes out in California. And a house on the beach?" She laughed. "There's no way I'm shelling out good money just for a beach view. I'm still renting. I'm on the road half the time making movies, anyway, so why buy a big house I can't enjoy? Eventually I'll buy a place, but right now I'm saving my money."

"Smart girl," Martha said.

"I have a house, but it's a small one in Sherman Oaks," Colt said.

Des smiled. "It's a charming older house with two bedrooms."

"Big enough for my needs. I just got sick of condo living. I wanted a yard. Not quite as big as your backyard, Logan, but in L.A. terms, it'll do."

"You make do with what you have," Logan said.

Colt nodded. "Exactly. And speaking of your wide-open spaces, how about a ride on your horses?"

"You up for that?" Logan asked Des.

Des shook her head. "No, thanks. I'm too full to go bouncing around on the back of a horse. But I'd love a look around. Unless that's too much trouble."

"I can take Colt out for a ride on the horses," Ben said. "I need to check on a few things anyway. He can come with me."

"Great," Colt said. "I'm excited to get back on a horse again."

Logan was hoping to tell Des no, but it looked like he was out of options. "Fine. Let's go, Des."

"Martha, do you want to come along with us?" Des asked.

"Oh, thanks, but no. I'm in the middle of a really good book, so I'm going to put my feet up and relax for a while. You and Logan go ahead."

Logan gave Martha a look, and she smiled sweetly at him.

Martha was up to a bit of matchmaking, which wasn't going to work.

For a lot of different reasons.

DES PICKED UP her pace alongside Logan's long stride, excited about seeing the land. She was certain Logan wasn't thrilled about being anywhere near her or taking her anywhere.

Which made her want to annoy him even more.

Who knew this location shoot was going to be so much fun?

"Where would you like to go?" he asked.

"How about we just start with a walk? I'm stuffed after all that food, and I need to walk off a few hundred calories. You can show me what you do around here."

"All right."

While she hadn't always lived in a big city, it had been a long time since she'd seen so much land. The smell of dirt and cattle, while not exactly pleasant, wasn't a turnoff for her. It smelled of hard living and muscle, the kind of work that had nothing to do with makeup and looking pretty for a camera. There was no acting involved in that kind of work.

They'd moved past several barns and stopped at one of the penned-in pastures where a herd of cattle roamed. The cattle moved lazily about, some eating, some standing around, and some huddled in the shade of several tall trees.

Des climbed up on the fence and straddled it. She looked down at Logan.

"What is your typical day like?" she asked.

"There really isn't a typical day. It depends on the season. There are always calves to work, moving cattle from one part of the land to another, separating grown calves from their mamas and putting heifers in with the bulls to make sure they're impregnated. There are cattle to take for sale, getting them weighed in and sold off. In the winter months we have to supplement the feed and make sure the ponds aren't frozen so the cattle have access to water. We do inoculations, castrations, and assist with births if they're needed, though most of the cattle do just fine on their own, birthing-wise. Weather and cattle health may come into play."

She stared at him. "I think that's the most you've ever said to me at one time. You really love what you do."

And then he clammed up and stared out over the pasture.

She hopped off the fence and they started walking again.

"So is it me you don't like, or women in general?"

He kept his gaze straight ahead. "I like women just fine."

"Then it's me." She quickened her steps to stay up with him. "And why is that?"

He stopped, turned to face her. "Shouldn't you be out riding with your boyfriend?"

She studied him. "You think Colt and I are in a relationship?"

"Sure seems that way."

"Based on what, exactly? That we're starring in a movie together?"

"I've just seen the way you interact."

She laughed. "First, I'm an actress. If our chemistry comes across when we act together, I guess that means we're doing a damn good job. Second, Colt and I have been friends since we were eighteen years old."

"Which was what? Two years ago?"

Des rolled her eyes. "You're kind of a dick, Logan. I'm twenty-five."

"Oh, all worldly and mature, aren't you?"

"And you're still being a dick. Anyway, for the record, Colt and I are not now nor have we ever been involved with each other romantically."

"So you're just sleeping with him."

She rolled her eyes. "Oh, my God. Do you work for the tabloids or something?"

"No."

"Well, you sure have a way of twisting my words around. No, we are not having sex. We've never had sex. We're friends. We've been friends since we first started out in the business. I rely on him and he does the same with me. And in this business, it's hard to find people you can trust."

"And you trust Colt."

"With my life."

His lips curved.

He was so irritating. "What?"

"You movie people are so dramatic."

She turned and walked away from him. He caught up to her easily.

"And here I thought you were tough."

"I'm plenty tough. But you're an asshole."

He didn't seem offended. "Not the first time I've heard that."

She stopped and turned to face him. "Then tell me, Logan. Exactly what does it take to warm you up? Because I've been nice. I've been friendly. I've invited you to the set of the movie. And yet I'm getting all this hostility from you and I don't understand why."

"Was I being hostile? I thought we were just bantering."

"You call that bantering?"

"I would. Obviously, you wouldn't. I guess I'm used to my brothers and the ranch crew. We regularly hurl insults at each other. If I offended you, I'm sorry."

She wasn't buying it. "So you insult Martha?"

"Martha's like a mother to me. I would never insult her. Besides, she might seem sweet on the outside, but she takes no guff. She might beat me over the head with a cast-iron skillet."

Des could see that about Martha. "So you treat women differently, then."

"Of course."

"But not me. Or did you just not notice I was a woman."

"Oh, I noticed, all right."

"At least you're not blind. I was beginning to wonder about you, Logan."

He'd walked off the gravel road, and they'd ended up under a shady group of trees near a lake. She headed toward the copse of trees. Her feet were tired so she grabbed a spot under one of them and sat down.

He looked down at her. "Now what are you doing?"

"Sitting." She patted the spot beside her. "You should try it."

"I don't think so."

"I don't bite. Honest." He might enjoy baiting her, but she really enjoyed his discomfort around her.

"I'm fine standing."

"Suit yourself." She pivoted around to look out over the lake. "Are there fish in there?"

"Yeah."

"Do you go fishing?"

"Sometimes."

"I know how to fish."

"Seriously."

She tilted her head up to find him looking at her. "Yes. Seriously."

"When have you gone fishing?"

"Lots of times, though not in a long time. When I was a kid, my dad would take me fishing whenever we were stationed somewhere near a lake."

"And you liked spending time with your dad, even if that meant learning to fish."

"Exactly. And hey, I was an adventurous sort of kid. Fishing never bothered me."

He crouched down and pulled up a piece of grass. God forbid he should actually sit. That might make him comfortable.

"Anything else you can do in that lake?" she asked.

He frowned at her. "Like what?"

"I don't know. It's hot here. Maybe skinny-dipping?"

"No."

She laughed. "Why not? Are there alligators or eels in there?"

"No."

"Then you're missing out on another opportunity to get a woman naked."

"I don't miss out on opportunities to get women naked. I just don't skinny-dip."

"Today might be your lucky day, Logan."

She stood, and so did he. When she began to unbutton her shirt, he grabbed her hands.

"Stop."

"Why? Afraid to see me naked?"

"No. But unless you're an exhibitionist, you're going to be baring yourself to a half dozen of my hands."

She turned and looked in the direction of his gaze. Sure enough, several ranch hands were working the fence line north of them. She hadn't even noticed.

"Well, shit." She hurriedly buttoned up her shirt.

Logan cracked a smile. "I'm sorry to have missed that show."

"You might have mentioned those guys to me."

He shrugged. "We had some fence come down and several of the guys are replacing it today."

"Asshole." She turned and walked away, Logan's laugh ringing in her ears.

She didn't say a word to him on the walk back to the house. Instead, she went inside and found Martha in the kitchen pouring a glass of iced tea.

"How was your tour?"

"Interesting," Des said, gratefully accepting a glass from Martha. "Thank you."

Ignoring Logan, she visited with Martha for a while, asking her questions about her duties on the ranch. Martha was a great conversationalist, and talked pretty much non-stop about ranch life and her daily routine.

She was obviously a hardworking woman, just like everyone who worked the ranch.

Colt and Ben eventually showed up. "How was the ride?" she asked.

Colt grinned. "It felt great to be on a horse again."

"The kid's good," Ben said to Logan. "We can put him to work anytime."

Colt laughed. "Thanks. It's nice to know I could potentially have a backup career in case this whole acting thing doesn't work out."

Martha let out a snort. "Considering your box-office draw, young man, I don't think you have anything to worry about."

Colt leaned over and kissed Martha on the cheek. "Thanks for that."

"We should get going," Des said, having had enough of Logan's attitude for the day. "We've taken up enough of everyone's day."

"You did no such thing," Martha said. "I loved having you here. I don't get a lot of female company. You're welcome anytime."

She hugged Martha and so did Colt.

They walked outside and toward the vehicle they'd arrived in.

"Do you want me to come to the set to pick you up tomorrow?" Logan asked.

Des nodded. "That would be great, thanks. I appreciate you taking me with you."

"No problem. I'll see you in the morning."

She climbed into the car, wishing they hadn't been

interrupted at the lake. She wondered what would have happened if there hadn't been a crew there when she'd unbuttoned her shirt.

Would Logan have stopped her from undressing? Or would he have joined her?

Now there was some fodder for her fantasies.

They drove away from the house and back toward the set.

"How was your alone time with the hot rancher?" Colt asked.

"Fine. How was the ride?"

"It was good. Makes me want to do a lot more riding. I hadn't realized how much I missed it."

She shifted in her seat. "I'm sure they'd let you come over and ride. They'd probably put you to work."

"And I'd probably enjoy it. So would Tony."

"Are you going to try and sneak him out here for the Fourth of July?"

"If I can. His movie finishes the end of June, so he'd be clear."

"That's dangerous talk for someone whose management team is all over him about staying in the closet."

"You could invite him."

"I could, couldn't I? I could invite several of our friends so it would look more like a group thing. I know Martha would enjoy that."

"She probably would. I'm not sure Logan would, though."

"I'm not sure I care what Logan likes or doesn't like."

Colt grinned. "I think you're smitten in a big way."

"And I think you're full of shit."

Colt's laugh rang out in the car.

"You're very irritating."

"And you're very transparent, Des. Just jump him and get it over with. You know you want to."

That was the problem. She was very attracted to Logan, but she wasn't sure it was because she wanted him, or because he kept trying so damn hard to push her away, while at the same time giving her the kind of looks a man gave a woman when he wanted to get her in bed.

He was confusing. And irritating. And sexy as hell.

Which meant she was determined to get to know him better.

And unravel the mystery that was Logan McCormack.

*Chapter 4*

LOGAN GRABBED HIS phone and checked the time, tapping his boots on the dirt as he waited for Des.

He should have known better than to agree to take her into town with him. Even though she'd promised she only had one scene this morning, she'd been in the middle of it when he'd arrived on the set, which meant she was still in full costume and makeup. Which was fine. He didn't mind waiting for her to finish up.

Jessica had seen him and invited him to watch. It was an indoor scene today, taking place inside some dark, dusty, prison-like set they'd built. Colt and Des were chained together, the two of them in ragged, torn clothes.

Des's character implored Colt's not to give himself up for her sake. It was very emotional, the two of them sharing a kiss at the end of the scene. A really long, passionate kiss that looked damn real to Logan.

But then the director had claimed the scene wasn't quite right, and needed to be reshot, so they'd had to start over.

More emotion. More kissing. By the time the director

JACI BURTON

42

decided they'd gotten the scene just as he'd wanted it, Logan's irritation had reached the boiling point.

After the kiss, Des and Colt broke apart. Colt smiled when he saw him.

"Hey, Logan. How's it going?"

"Fine," he said, trying to disengage his clenched jaw.

"I'd love to stay and talk, but I've got to jump right into the next scene. Catch you later?"

"Sure."

Des came over, too. "I know, I'm so sorry I'm late. Come on with me to the trailer. It'll only take me a few minutes to get ready."

And just like that, the passion he'd seen between Des and Colt had seemed to fizzle.

Maybe it had just been acting. Sure didn't seem that way to him, though.

He walked with her the short path through the set construction to the back lot where the trailers were housed. He stepped inside, wowed by the luxury of Des's trailer.

She was toeing off her boots and pulling off her socks when she reached for her tank top.

"I think I'll wait outside."

She grinned. "I wasn't going to get naked in front of you, Logan," she said, revealing another tank underneath. She paused, looking at him. "Unless you'd like me to."

He narrowed his gaze at her. "Don't push it too far, Des."

She put her hands on her hips. "Or you'll what? Walk away?"

He didn't say anything.

She laughed. "That's what I thought. I'll be right back."

She closed the door to the bedroom and shortly thereafter he heard the sound of water.

Damn woman. She pushed all his buttons and he knew she did it deliberately. What was she after, anyway?

Maybe she was an exhibitionist and she just liked getting naked in front of people. Then again, if she was, the appearance of his guys at the lake yesterday wouldn't have deterred her.

So she obviously just wanted to get a rise out of him.

It was working. He pushed back thoughts of what she was doing in the shower and wandered around her trailer. Her touch was all over the place, from books—she liked thrillers—to scripts, DVDs, and video games.

He picked up a few movies—not her own. She liked action movies, comedies and horror, all of which were movies he'd choose. He was surprised by her choice of video games, mostly those bloody games of war and fantasy.

"Those are for Colt," she said.

He looked up to find her standing in the doorway in some kind of silk robe, no doubt naked underneath, though thoughts of her naked made his dick hard, so he should think of something else. The smell of something sweet— her shampoo or soap or something—wafted toward him, and he couldn't help but take a deep breath.

Which didn't help the erection thing he had going on, because now he had thoughts of licking her neck.

"You don't play the games?" he asked, figuring that was a safe, nonsexual subject.

"Of course I do. And I watch the movies and read the books. On a movie set there's a lot of down time. It gets very boring. That's why I'm happy to have a chance to see your hometown today. With nothing on tap for me, I'd have spent the day in here reading or watching movies. I'll just be a few minutes."

After she closed the door, he stood and adjusted the crotch of his jeans, deciding to grab a glass of cold water.

This was a bad idea. He was a walking hard-on around Des, and being near her was bad for him—mentally as well as physically.

When there was a knock at the door, he turned to the closed bedroom door. "Des?" he asked.

"It's probably Colt," she yelled from the bedroom. "You can open it."

He did, but it wasn't Colt. It was some older guy with a salt-and-pepper beard. He remembered seeing him on the set. The guy frowned and stepped into the trailer.

"And who might you be?"

"Logan McCormack. And you are?"

"Theo Winfield. I'm the director."

"Ah. Des is getting dressed."

Theo sized Logan up, looking suspicious and maybe a little jealous and protective, like a boyfriend would. Hell, for all Logan knew, maybe he was.

Des came out in a pair of jeans and a T-shirt, her hair loose and flowing around her shoulders. She wore a pair of tennis shoes and very little makeup.

She looked pretty. And she was frowning. Logan could tell instantly that Des wasn't happy about Theo being there. But then she covered it with a smile. "Oh, hi, Theo."

"Desiree. I was unaware you were entertaining."

"I'm not. Logan is the ranch owner. He came by the other day to watch a scene being filmed."

"Oh, I see." Theo's tone instantly changed and he smiled at Logan. "It's a great location, perfect for the film."

"I'm glad it's working out for you," Logan said.

Theo turned to Des. "I have some free time while they're setting up the next scene. I was hoping we could have a chat about some upcoming scenes."

"I'm afraid not, Theo. Since I don't have anything filming the rest of the day, Logan has graciously offered to take me into town with him."

"Are you sure that's a good idea, Des? What about exposure?"

Des grabbed her purse and slung it over her shoulder. With a shrug, she said, "Hope's a small town, Theo. I'll take my chances."

"I still advise against it. The paparazzi have been stalking the gates of the property, hoping for pictures of you, especially after your breakup with James."

She stepped out of the trailer. Logan and Theo followed.

"Then I'll guess they'll get some. But I'm not going to hide."

"Des—"

"I've already made Logan late today, Theo. We need to run. I'll catch up to you later, okay?"

"We need to talk, Des," Theo said, making it sound urgent.

"Oh, I know. I'll for sure come find you when I get back."

She grabbed Logan's arm and dragged him away.

"He's kind of persistent," Logan said as they headed to the parking area.

Des rolled her eyes. "You have no idea."

"And overly protective. Like a father figure?"

She snorted. "Ha. No. More like a pervy, married lech who'd like to get me alone so he can try and get in my pants."

Logan stopped and turned to face her. "Seriously?"

"Yes. He's an awful bastard and I hate being alone with him. Colt usually tries to have my back, but it's not always possible. So I have to do this little dance of avoidance around him."

They reached the truck and Logan opened the door for her. She slid inside, and he came around and got in, then started it up. "So why do a movie where he's the director?"

"One, because he's a great director, despite his proclivities for hitting on his leading ladies. And two, because I'm a big girl and I can take care of myself. I know how to say no, and I make sure I'm never alone with him."

"He sounds like an asshole who needs to have the shit kicked out of him."

Des smiled. "I'd like to see that day come. Unfortunately, no one does that to a big-time director. People like Theo get away with bad behavior because they carry a lot of weight in Hollywood."

What a crock. "I'd be happy to knock him on his ass if you'd like me to."

Her lips curved. "I'll keep that in mind. Thanks."

What kind of a shithead cheated on his wife and hit on young actresses? Granted, Logan didn't know anything about these Hollywood types, and maybe that kind of thing happened all the time. Des didn't seem too upset about it, and she'd handled Theo easily, but it pissed him off. If he'd known about it, he'd have been tempted to take Theo behind the trailer and teach him some goddamned manners.

He gripped the steering wheel hard and tried to concentrate on the road, but his thoughts kept coming back to the way Theo had looked at Des.

"Are all directors like him?"

"Like Theo? No. Some are very nice and work hard to get the best out of their actors. Others are narcissistic, arrogant dickheads, but they're not trying to sleep with every actress they direct, if that's what you're asking."

"Yes, that's what I'm asking. Have you come up against directors like Theo before?"

"There are always people like Theo in our industry, people like casting directors or producers who expect you'll have sex with them in order to get a part."

"And?" he asked, glancing her way.

"And I've never once had sex with someone to get a role in a movie. I made a vow a long time ago that if I couldn't get a part based on talent alone, then I obviously wasn't good enough to be in this business."

"Good for you. Some people are fucking scumbags."

She laughed. "Amen to that."

As they drove through the gates, Logan noticed the throng of people with cameras hanging out at the entrance to the property.

"Your fans?"

She wrinkled her nose. "Paparazzi, hoping to get some advance shots of the moviemaking. It's great that we're filming on private property, so they don't have access. I think that was another of the reasons they found this location so attractive."

He pulled out and Des turned her head as the paparazzi started shooting. There was a sudden rush as people ran off to jump into their cars.

"Now you're screwed. They'll follow you into town, which isn't at all private."

"I know, but I really want to see Hope."

"Not much to see. It's a typical small town. Surely you've seen a lot of them."

"But I haven't seen this one. So your brother's the sheriff?"

"City cop."

"Oh, that's right. He's probably going to hate me for causing a stir."

"I doubt that. He likes to stay busy."

Logan kept an eye on his rearview mirror. They had definitely acquired an entourage of cars behind them. Des didn't look into her mirror once, just kept her gaze firmly planted on the windshield in front of her.

"It's so remote out here. Your nearest neighbor must be miles and miles away."

"I guess so."

"I'm so used to living in a big city with people all around, I have a different perspective. You can't move or breathe without someone knowing every move you make. You could probably step out on your back porch or on your deck at night in your underwear—or even naked—without anyone seeing you."

"I could."

She took a deep breath and let out a sigh. "That would be so great."

"You could buy a place that's remote, so you could get away."

"I could. I plan to, someday."

He glanced at her. "When is that someday?"

"When I feel like settling down. When I find the right place."

"And when is that?"

"I don't know. I haven't felt like settling down before."

"You're still young. You probably crave all that travel and adventure."

"I liked it at first. But now—"

She didn't say anything more, and he didn't want to pry.

Des looked out the window, ignoring the convoy of cars she knew were behind them. She'd taken a big risk leaving the safety of the ranch, but she really did want to see the town.

They'd been stationed in small towns before when she'd been a kid, and they'd always been her favorite places. Always tight-knit communities with the best people. Not that she got to hang out with the locals all that much—not until she was a teen and got her driver's license. She'd always lived on base, in base housing, with all the other army people. Her dad had always insisted on living on base, and had required her to go to school with all the other army kids.

Which had made sneaking out and getting to know the local towns and kids that much more fun.

She liked Logan, and she knew he was from a small town. She'd done a little research on Hope before she came to the location, and it was a beautiful place set in northeast Oklahoma. She'd never been to Oklahoma before. She'd already decided she wasn't going to spend all her time holed up in her trailer, even if the paparazzi stalked her.

Though what they were looking for, she had no idea. It wasn't like she was all that interesting. But she was young, and she and James had had a high-profile romance, so they always thought there was dirt to dig up.

It took about fifteen minutes before she saw the sign that they were entering the city limits of Hope.

She saw the high school first. It was one story, but it

seemed to go on forever, with two buildings that faced each other and a big football field behind it.

"Oakdale High. Is that where you went to school?"

"Yeah. There are two high schools in Hope. This one serves a lot of the kids who live outside city limits. Hope High School is in town and serves the rest of the city."

"Interesting. I wouldn't think a town as small as Hope would support two high schools."

"There are also all the county residents. The population is larger than you'd think."

It looked so small. Then again, as they drove farther into town she saw more and more businesses and side streets filled with homes. She supposed she had had this mental image of a one-stoplight town like she often saw in movies, but Hope was nothing like that. While it was a small town, there were miles of it, including a community center, medical and dental facilities, urgent care centers, several restaurants, and what appeared to be a lot of impending expansion.

"Your town is growing."

"Uh-huh."

She switched her gaze over to Logan. "Which is why you like living on the ranch?"

"I like Hope just fine, but it's a lot bigger now than it was when I was a kid."

"Progress isn't a bad thing, you know. It's good for your town to grow."

"So they tell me."

He pulled into an auto parts store. Des smiled. She was just sure the paparazzi were going to find this riveting.

"You want to come in?"

She released her seat belt. "Oh, definitely."

He gave her a funny look, but shrugged. "Okay."

Out of the corner of her eye she saw the entourage of cars pulling into the parking lot, and she smiled. They wouldn't come inside—it wasn't in their nature, and besides, hordes of photographers tended to upset customers and store owners, and that usually led to police getting called and photographers getting arrested. Instead, they lingered outside and took pictures.

Of Des, inside the auto parts store. She couldn't help but laugh at that. No doubt the paps had already conjured up Des rendezvousing with some secret lover at the auto parts store, so she might as well give them their money's worth. While Logan headed over to the parts counter, she busied herself wandering up and down the aisles, scanning air filters, socket wrenches, and various types of motor oil.

"Excuse me, but aren't you Desiree Jenkins?"

She turned to find an older man wearing a polo shirt emblazoned with the name of the store on it. "I sure am." She read his name tag and stuck out her hand. "And you're Bill."

Bill shook her hand. "I sure wish my wife was here. She's a big fan of yours. We both really enjoyed that movie you were in, *The Heart of Sunrise*."

"Thanks so much, Bill. I liked making that movie. It was one of my favorites."

"Sorry you had to die at the end, though."

She laughed. "Yeah, me, too."

"Would it trouble you too much if I ask for an auto-graph? And maybe a picture?" He pulled out his phone.

"Not at all."

Bill led her over to the counter, where Logan was checking out.

"I've got a pad of paper here. If you could make it out to DeeDee, that's with two sets of double *E*s, my wife would be tickled."

"Sure, Bill." Des wrote out an autograph to his wife, then Bill handed Logan his phone.

"Hey, Logan, would you mind taking a picture of me and Des?"

Logan cocked a brow. "Didn't know you were a fan, Bill."

"Oh, DeeDee and I go to the movies all the time. She's going to be so mad she missed the chance to meet Desiree."

Des got close to Bill and smiled. Logan took the picture and handed the phone back.

"Thanks a lot."

"You're welcome."

"You sure have a lot of picture takers out front," Bill said.

"Yes, unfortunately I do."

Logan grabbed his bag. "Are you ready?"

"Sure."

She ignored the photographers outside, and their barrage of questions about who Logan was and what she was doing in Hope today. Fortunately, Logan had parked right out front and he opened the truck door for her. She slid inside and she could tell when he came around and got inside the truck, he was pissed. He put the truck in gear and pulled out in a hurry, paying no attention to the photographers scattering all around them.

He didn't say anything as they drove down the road. At least not for a few minutes, but his jaw was clenched.

"I'm sorry about that," she finally said.

"It's not your fault they swarm on you like scavengers." He shot her a look. "You get that all the time?"

She nodded.

"Jesus Christ. What are they after?"

She shrugged. "Something newsworthy."

"And the auto parts store in Hope is newsworthy?"

"They camp out in airports and take pictures of celebrities coming off and going onto airplanes."

"Why?"

"I have no idea. To see what they're wearing or who they're with or where they're going. Then they sell the photos to the highest bidders. Me being here for a movie shoot is, I guess, newsworthy."

"I don't find it hot news. No offense."

Her lips lifted. "None taken."

He pulled out his phone and punched a number. "Hey, are you on duty today?" He shifted his gaze to hers as he listened. "I'm in town, and I've got Desiree Jenkins with me."

Des wondered who he was talking to.

"Yeah, the movie star . . . Because she wanted to come with me, that's why." He rolled his eyes as he drove. "No, idiot, we're not."

And now she really wanted to know who he was talking to.

"Listen, those damn photographers are swarming her. Think you can do something about that while we run some errands?"

Ah. Likely his brother Luke.

"Thanks. We'll be stopping at Emma's place next. Meet us there."

He clicked off.

"Does this mean we get a police escort?"

"Something like that."

The Hope Small Animal Hospital was a charming one-story that looked a lot like an oversize house with a huge parking lot. A full parking lot, too, which now contained two police cars at the parking lot entrance.

Logan pulled in and rolled down the window. A tall, extremely good-looking cop who resembled Logan strolled over to the window with a fierce but adorable German shepherd in tow.

"Causing trouble?" Luke asked.

"Yeah, that's me. Des, meet my brother Luke."

Luke tipped his hat. "Ma'am."

"Hi, Luke. Call me Des. And thank you for running interference. I'm sorry about the paparazzi."

"I'm sure there's not much you can do about them, but we'll try to keep them out of your way."

"I'd appreciate that."

"We'll try to get out of town as fast as we can," Logan said.

"Don't be so fast. I told Emma you were here with Des, and she wants you to stick around and have dinner with us tonight. We can do it at the house so there's no ruckus at one of the restaurants."

Logan looked at Des.

"I'd love to," she said.

"Sounds good," Logan said.

"Good. Emma closes up at six, so you'll have to kill some time."

Logan nodded. "I'm sure we'll find something to do."

"Great," Luke said. "I get off at five, so we'll see you at the house."

Logan pulled into a parking spot and turned off the ignition. "I suppose you're going to want to come in."

"There are animals in there. And Emma, who I suppose is dating Luke?"

"She's his fiancée, so yeah."

"Awesome." She took off her seat belt. "Let's go."

Luke and another officer had put a halt to the photographers parking in the lot and were waving their hands for them to move along. Des couldn't resist a laugh.

"They must be hating that," she said.

"What?" Logan asked, then looked. "Oh. Your photographers? Yeah, probably. And it's likely making Luke's day."

They stepped inside and all activity stopped. There were a few people in the waiting room, and Des caught the stares. Not that she wasn't used to being stared at, but it was always a little disconcerting.

And small-town stares were always a little different.

"Oh. My. God. Desiree Jenkins." A young girl with short dark hair and glasses stepped from around the counter and held out her hand. "I'm Rachel and I'm a big fan."

"Hi, Rachel. Call me Des."

"Oh, my God. So excited you're here, Des." Rachel looked around the waiting room. "Hey, everyone, did you know Desiree Jenkins was in town? She's just so awesome."

Des actually felt herself blush, which almost never happened. She gave everyone a wave. "Hi."

Rachel turned to Logan. "Oh, hey, Logan. Martha called ahead and told us what you needed. I already have it at the counter."

Logan cracked a smile. "Thanks, Rachel. Is Emma around?"

"She's checking on a surgery patient, but you can go on back."

Logan put his hand on the small of Des's back and propelled her forward. "Come on, movie star."

She met Leanne on the way back, who she found out was one of Emma's assistants. Leanne was sweet and super-friendly, but then had to run because she had a cat who needed inoculations and another one who needed a nail trim and a bath. Leanne was a talker, but Des liked her.

They found a stunning brunette back by the kennels. Wearing scrubs with her hair up in a ponytail, she sat on the floor near an open kennel, her ears plugged with a stethoscope as she listened to one of the dogs, who looked to be out cold.

"You'll be fine, Pally," the woman soothed, stroking her hand over the dog's fur before closing the kennel door. "And you'll be going home later today."

She pushed off and stood, then her eyes widened when she saw them. "Oh, crap, Logan. I didn't see you standing there."

"Sorry, Emma."

Emma stopped at the sink to wash her hands, then came over and hugged Logan. "It's okay. I was just seeing to one of our patients who had surgery this morning." She held out her hand. "You must be the famous Desiree everyone in town's been buzzing about."

Des shook her hand. "I don't know about famous, but yeah, that's me. Call me Des."

"So nice to meet you. How's the movie shoot going?"

"Pretty good. I was happy to get off the set today so I could come see your town."

Emma paused to pick up a couple of charts, then led them down the hall and into her office, where she was immediately bombarded by two adorable dogs, one a yellow Labrador retriever, the other a white-and-brown pit bull. She leaned down and petted them.

"Okay, girls, calm down. We have visitors. Des, this is Daisy and Annie."

Des crouched down to greet the dogs. "Hi there, girls. Aren't you just the sweetest things?"

The dogs came over, sniffed her, then leaned into her for some love. Des's heart swelled. She looked up at Emma. "They're so cute."

"Thank you. I've had Daisy for a while, and Annie's still a puppy, though you could never tell by how big she's gotten."

After petting them for a few minutes, Des stood.

"Please, have a seat. Would you like something to drink? I have water and pop."

"I'd love some water," Des said. Logan declined.

Emma grabbed two waters from her mini fridge in her office, handed one to Des and opened one for herself. They sat in her office and Emma leaned back.

"Long day?" Logan asked.

"Yes. Two surgeries this morning. One was a twisted bowel, so it was complex and took longer than I wanted it to. And the other was a knee surgery on a rather young canine." She hunched her shoulders, then relaxed them.

"Sounds like you could use a spa day," Des suggested.

Emma laughed. "Mmm. A spa. Exactly what Hope needs and doesn't have."

"Oh, that's too bad. I know a few people who would love to set one up in a town like this."

"And I know several women—myself included—who would make use of it regularly."

"Sounds like a match made in heaven."

"We should definitely talk. Speaking of, Logan, did Luke ask you about dinner tonight?"

"He did. We're all set."

"Awesome. We'll have chicken or something simple since it's a workday for me. I hope you don't mind simple, Des."

"That sounds great to me. Thank you for the invitation."

"You're welcome. And I hate to be a lousy host at the moment, but I have patients to get back to."

Des stood. "It was great to meet you, Emma."

"Here, too. I'll see you both tonight."

Des followed Logan to the front of the clinic, where Rachel handed him a bag.

He took out his credit card and paid, and she said goodbye to Rachel and Leanne.

Photographers had parked in the lot next to the clinic, but Luke was doing a good job of keeping them from stepping onto Emma's lot.

"How does he do that?" she asked.

"I think Boomer scares the shit out of them."

Des frowned. "Oh. His dog?"

"Yeah. He has a mean growl. I'd bet none of those photographers would want to test him."

She laughed. "Probably not. I should get a dog like that. Maybe I'd have fewer cameras stuck in my face."

They climbed into the truck. "A dog for protection wouldn't be a bad idea, especially if this whole paparazzi thing is the norm for you, even when you're on location."

"Traveling as much as I do would be a hard life for a dog."

"Dogs that are trained for protection services get used to the travel."

She looked in the side mirror to see all the cars following. "I suppose they would be. It's something to consider. And I do love dogs."

"Are you hungry?"

"I am, actually. I'd hate to bombard some poor restaurant with the paps, though."

"I think Bert's can handle it. They'd enjoy the free publicity."

"If you say so." The restaurants in L.A. hated it, though she refused to stay holed up in her condo all the time. So she went out. Then again, it wasn't this bad in L.A., because the media hounded other, more famous people than her. She might have someone with a camera follow her when she went out to eat, but it wasn't a horde of photographers like today.

Thankfully.

He drove down the road and they ended up in front of a very charming restaurant at the side of the highway. Since they'd gotten a late start it was actually past the lunch hour, so the parking lot was nearly empty. It didn't take long once they got out of the truck and headed inside for the procession of vehicles to pull into the parking lot, though Des noticed that Luke and the other police car pulled in, too, and came inside.

"I didn't know you were so popular, Logan," an older woman said once they got to their table.

"Yeah, the ranch is a real hot spot for photographers these days. Anita, this is Des."

"Oh, I know who you are, Miss Jenkins. I've seen a few of your movies. Nice to have you in town."

"Nice to meet you, Anita. And call me Des."

Anita handed them menus. "We're glad you stopped in. I recommend the club sandwich today. And Bert, he owns this place, makes the best fries in the state. Charlotte, his wife, also makes the finest sweet tea you'll ever taste."

Des laid her menu aside. "No sense in me looking any further. I'll have sweet tea and the club sandwich. With fries."

"Same here," Logan said, handing off the menus to Anita.

In the meantime, Des met Bert, the owner, who looked like a holdover hippie, with his long ponytail of gray hair.

Charlotte's hair was gray, too, but she styled it short. Both were very nice to come over and greet her. They told her they were happy to have her in their restaurant, and if there was anything she wanted, not to hesitate to ask. Then they hurried off behind the counter to fix lunch.

They didn't even pay attention to the photographers pressed against the window. They did stop to pour coffee for Luke and the other officer, and, of course, to pet and fuss over Boomer, who was obviously welcome everywhere he went.

"Nice people here."

"Yup."

Anita brought their tea, and true to her word, Des smiled when she took a sip. "This is heaven, and so much better than anything from catering."

"You can't beat a glass of homemade sweet tea."

"On the movie set they give us this fancy flavored stuff, overbrewed and tastes like crap. Same thing with coffee. It's always some new flavor every day. I just like a basic cup of coffee."

"I like that about you."

"What? You like something about me? I'm shocked, Logan."

His brow furrowed. "I never said I didn't like you."

"Oh, but you try really hard to act like you don't. Secretly, I think you burn for me, and you desperately want to get in my pants, but you're trying hard to act like you don't."

He stared at her for the longest time, then looked out the window. "I sure as hell hope someone out there doesn't have long-range microphones. If they pick up this conversation, they'll have one hell of a story."

"As far as I know, there's no story to tell about us." She pinned him with a look. "Yet."

He gave her a look right back as he leaned toward her. "Do you make it a point to do this with all the men you meet?"

"Actually, no. But there's something about you that gets under my skin. Maybe it's your lean, chiseled looks, or those stormy gray eyes and the way you track me with them. I also like the way you walk."

"You like the way I walk."

"Yes. It's not deliberate or calculated. But it's damn sexy."

She watched him swallow, then he took a long drink of his tea.

It was suddenly very warm in the diner, and her nipples hardened, rubbing against the material of her bra.

She had no one to blame but herself for the way she was feeling. But he'd asked, and she figured she might as well be honest with him. He was either going to go for it or not.

She kind of hoped he would, though. She liked this man. He might be a little on the quiet side, but underneath?

There was a fierce storm brewing in Logan McCormack. And she'd like to be in the middle of that when it burst.

Logan was getting decidedly uncomfortable, especially under the table, where his jeans were tightening. He'd never met a woman like Des, one so blatantly honest in her assessments and the way she approached men. All the women he knew were more . . . subtle. They might look at you a certain way or say something that let a man know she was interested.

Des was just . . . out there. She wanted him, and she made no bones about letting him know it.

He just didn't know what the hell to do about it.

Nothing. That's what he was going to do about it.

Nothing at all. Because of all the reasons he'd decided the moment he'd met her. She was too young for him. She was a movie star, and out of his league. She said she and Colt weren't involved, but now there was this ex-boyfriend thing he'd heard about, and he didn't need that kind of entanglement. Plus, there were all these goddamned photographers. At least they weren't allowed on the ranch.

He didn't know how she dealt with them, but she seemed oblivious as Anita brought their sandwiches. She dug in and ate as if hundreds of cameras weren't focused in on every bite she took.

"How do you do that?" he finally asked.

She paused, mid-bite. "How do I do what?"

"Ignore all those cameras monitoring your every move."

She shrugged. "I can't do anything about them. After my first couple movies were critical successes and I started having paparazzi follow me around, I was freaked out. That loss of anonymity can be overwhelming. But I had some friends in the business who helped me through it. Eventually, you get used to the paps who stalk you and take photos of you every time you're in public and you learn to ignore them. As long as they don't breach your personal space, everything's okay."

"And if they do?"

She looked up and met his gaze. "It hasn't happened yet."

"Are you prepared for what you'll do if that does happen?"

"Not really."

"Maybe you should hire a bodyguard. Just how popular are you, anyway?"

She looked over her shoulder. There were at least twenty-five photographers out there. "You tell me."

"I guess you're pretty damned popular. I'd hate it."

"I did, too, at first. But it's part of the business."

"I don't think I'd like your business."

"With all that land you have, all that space to be alone? No, I don't imagine you would."

He finished off his sandwich and fries, keeping one eye on the photographers. Though Luke and Evan seemed to have them well in hand. And Boomer had taken up residence near the front door. Patrons coming in greeted Boomer with a pat on his head. Locals were used to seeing Boomer around. Logan knew that without a command, Boomer was a house pet. The photographers, on the other hand, seemed to have one eye on Des and the other on Boomer, as if they expected the giant German shepherd to go crashing through the front door and take off after them any second.

That made him smile.

Anita finally brought their check.

"I can get this," Des said, reaching into her purse.

Logan frowned. "Seriously?" He took out his wallet and paid Anita.

"I'll be back with your change."

"Caveman mentality. Women pay these days, you know," she said.

"Not when they're out with me, they don't."

"Okay, then. Thanks for lunch."

"You're welcome."

When they got up, so did Luke and Evan. Boomer, on instant alert, stood by the front door.

"We'll clear them out," Luke said, as Logan and Des approached.

"I feel bad you have to take time out of your day for this."

Evan smiled. "Are you kidding? This beats the hell out of sitting at a speed trap. If something comes up, dispatch will radio."

They pushed through the front door and moved the photographers back, Boomer making an imposing figure. The photographers obviously didn't want to tangle with a police dog whose hairs were raised, so they complied and headed toward their cars.

Des looked at Logan. "I really like it here. The police in L.A. aren't so accommodating."

"I'm sure the police in L.A. have a lot more to do."

They climbed in the truck and Logan started it up, then grabbed his phone to check the time.

"Any more errands to run?" she asked.

"No. And some time to kill before we're due at Luke and Emma's place for dinner."

"How about you drive me around and show me the town?"

He looked at her. "We drove through it."

"Yeah, through the main highway. I want to see the town."

"That was it."

She cocked her head to the side. "It was not."

He put the truck in gear and backed out. "Fine. I'll show you the town. That should take about five minutes."

"I think you underestimate Hope, Logan."

He pulled out of the parking lot. "And I think you overestimate it."

But if she wanted to see Hope, he'd show it to her. Every damn block of it.

# Chapter 5

LOGAN STOPPED AT the end of the driveway and rolled down his window. Luke came over. "Des wants a tour of the town. Think you can stop the procession for a bit so we don't disturb the residents?"

Luke nodded. "I can do that. Y'all have fun."

"Thanks."

He pulled out and Luke and Evan halted the progress of the other vehicles.

"That is awesome," Des said, feeling as if she were part of a stealth operation. Hell, any time they could beat the paparazzi, it was a win in her book.

"He won't be able to hold them long, but maybe we can lose them." Logan turned down a side street, then hit one of the blacktop highways, pushing the gas pedal to hit maximum speed. When he got to the nearest exit, he turned left across the railroad tracks, then right again.

"I'm so confused right now with all these turns you're making. I have no idea where the main highway is, or where we are," Des said.

Logan slowed as they entered a residential section. "The best part is, neither do those photographers."

"So . . . where are we?"

"This is one of the older sections of town, one of the first ones built when Hope was incorporated. The houses are smaller and closer together."

Des loved the little one-story homes, even if some were a little run-down. There was history here with the painted mailboxes and bikes in the yard. It felt safe and like home.

He made a few turns and they reentered the highway. A few miles down the road, he turned into another residential neighborhood. Here, the houses were a little larger, with well-kept yards and even a park and a man-made lake.

"This is so pretty," she said.

"It sold out pretty fast, too. They even built a school within the subdivision."

"Oh, that's handy."

Logan drove out of the subdivision and down the county road. The road curved and trees grew thicker, lining the road. She felt as if she were someplace else, each turn taking her to a different place. Suddenly there were wide-open spaces, a golf course, and much, much bigger homes with a lot of land. She even spotted deer hiding amid a grouping of trees.

"This is beautiful. There's such a variety here."

"Just about anything you could want. Smaller homes with little patches of grass and tiny yards, medium-size houses, or a whole hell of a lot of acreage. There's something for everyone here."

"And this is all Hope?"

"Yeah."

"Wow."

When he made another turn, there was Hope High School, a beautiful tan brick building with bright red colors on the school sign.

"Oh . . . there's play practice after school today. What

time is it?" Des took a quick look at the dashboard clock. "It's three o'clock. What time does school let out?"

"Two forty-five."

She slanted him a look. "Can we stop?"

Logan frowned, but slowed the truck down. "What for?"

"I'd like to go in."

"Again. What for?"

"To see the students practice for the play. They're doing *Much Ado About Nothing*. I love Shakespeare."

Logan shook his head. "Whatever." He pulled into the back parking lot and turned off the car, then turned to her. "You really want to go in and watch some kids practice Shakespeare?"

"Absolutely. Do you think they'd let us in? I know you can't just walk into a high school."

He opened the door. "They'll let us in. I went to school with the principal."

Des smiled. "I love small towns."

She slid out of the truck, excitement making her shiver despite the oppressive heat.

"Do I look okay?" she asked as they headed toward the front door.

"What? You look fine. It's a high school, Des, not a movie premiere."

She laughed. "You're right. I'm nervous. I haven't been to school since . . . well, since I was in school. I cut my acting teeth on Shakespeare. God, I love it so much."

He gave her a look. "Obviously. You do realize this is a high school play, not Broadway, right?"

"Yes. But I loved the drama club in high school. It's where I discovered I wanted to become an actress. These kids are so full of joy and love of the craft."

Logan didn't say anything, just held the door for her and led her to the office. A young woman stood behind the counter. She was very attractive, with short blond hair and pretty green eyes.

"Hi, Logan."

"Hi, Serena. Is Daryl in?"

"He sure is." She picked up the phone and pushed a button. "Hey, Daryl, Logan McCormack is out front to see you. And he's got Desiree Jenkins with him," she added in a very excited voice.

Des grinned.

She listened for a moment, then hung up. "He says to go on right into his office."

"Come on, Des." Logan led her past the desk and toward the back of the room where a sign on the door said "Daryl Tucker, Principal."

A tall, blond-haired, very good-looking man wearing a red polo shirt and khakis stood behind the desk. He came around and shook Logan's hand.

"What's up, Logan? And you must be Desiree Jenkins. I'm Daryl Tucker."

Logan smiled. "Hey, Daryl. You're looking all principal-like."

Desiree grinned at that. "Nice to meet you, Principal Tucker."

"Oh, please. That makes me feel old. Call me Daryl."

"I will if you call me Des."

"Have a seat." Daryl leaned against the corner of his desk. "So what brings you two to Hope High?"

"Des saw the sign about drama club practice today, and she was hoping she could sit in and watch."

Daryl's brows rose. "Really? Margaret Penfield is our English teacher and head of the drama club. She'll be thrilled. So will the kids."

"Oh, great," Des said. "I'm a big fan of Shakespeare. I actually did *Much Ado About Nothing* in high school myself."

Daryl pushed off his desk. "Then let's not waste any time. I'll take you to the performing-arts center."

Des walked next to Logan, listening to him and Daryl catch up. Apparently Daryl had gotten married last year to a teacher from Oakdale High. The two were expecting their first baby in a few months.

"How's Patty feeling?" Logan asked.

"Complaining about teaching on her feet all day and her ankles being swollen because it's so damn hot. Sorry for cursing, Des."

"Nothing I haven't heard before, Daryl," she said as they made their way outside and across the lawn.

The performing-arts center was beautiful and looked new. It was a round building; she couldn't wait to see what it looked like inside. As they took the cement steps leading up to it, everything about her high school years came rushing back to her.

She'd been lucky they'd been stationed in one place that long, so she got to do at least two years of high school in North Carolina. It had been hard to insert herself into an already established group, but she'd done it anyway because she'd loved drama, had loved being in the plays and musicals. Though she couldn't sing for shit, whenever there was a musical she'd at least try to get minor roles or work on set design. Anything to be a part of the production.

As they stepped through the double front doors she could already hear the cast rehearsing the familiar words, lines that she still remembered. They walked toward the stage and Des's nerve endings tingled. She wanted to leap up there and start reciting Beatrice's dialogue.

Instead, she grasped Logan's arm midway down. "I'll just grab a seat here."

"Why not go all the way down?"

"I don't want to disturb them."

He shrugged. "Suit yourself. We're going to sit here, Daryl. Des doesn't want to stop the practice."

"Okay. I'll just let Margaret know you're here, then I'll get back to work."

Daryl headed down to the stage where he stopped to talk with a curvy redhead. It was dark in the audience section, but the woman looked their way, then nodded at Daryl, who waved in their direction and headed out a side door.

The acoustics in the theater were great, so while Margaret led the students through their scenes, Des leaned forward and listened. They were rehearsing the festival scene, when Beatrice was ranting about Benedick to a man she thought was someone else, when it was, in fact, Benedick himself in disguise. A delightful scene and the teens were doing a great job. She laughed at Beatrice's over-the-top performance and Benedick's responses.

"What's this play about?" Logan asked.

She turned to him. "You've never seen it?"

"Not much for Shakespeare, though I had to read *Julius Caesar* and *Romeo and Juliet* in English class in high school. Didn't care for it. Hard to understand."

She laughed. "It can be. But it's also rich with language and interpretation and such a delight for an actor to play. So much tragedy, and in the case of *Much Ado*, comedy."

"So this is supposed to be funny."

"Yes."

He leaned back in his chair. "Huh."

"Just watch, and listen. You'll get the hang of it."

"I doubt that."

Des could tell Logan was confused, so she sat back and explained the basics of the plot to him.

"So everybody lies to everybody else. Not only about what they feel, but about what they're doing."

"Pretty much."

"That doesn't make any damn sense. If they all just said how they felt, none of this would happen."

She rolled her eyes. "And then there'd be no point to the play. Deception and holding of truths is part of the plot. Benedick really does love Beatrice, and she feels the same, but there's a certain amount of pride, neither of them daring to admit to the other how they feel. And Hero's crushed that Claudio so easily believed the lies told about her. He has to prove his love to her."

"See? If everyone was just honest, none of that game-playing would be necessary."

"And all that honesty happens in real life, right? People always tell each other exactly how they feel."

He just looked at her. "I guess not."

"I thought so." She wondered what would come out of his mouth if he was honest about his feelings—about anything and everything. Maybe at some point she'd just ask him. But not right now.

For now she was content to sit back and listen to the young dramatists play out their scenes.

"Okay, everyone, you're hitting your marks just fine," Margaret said. "I do want to tell you that we have a very special guest sitting in the audience watching us today. She didn't want to interrupt rehearsal, but I know you'd all like to meet her. She's in town for a movie shoot, and I hear she's a big fan of Shakespeare. Miss Desiree Jenkins is in the house today."

Oh, crap. And she thought she'd just sit and listen for a while, then sneak out. But a chorus of squeals went out, followed by applause.

"I guess you should go say hello," Logan said.

"I guess so." She stood. "Come on down with me."

"I'm fine right here."

She nodded, and headed toward the stage.

LOGAN HADN'T THOUGHT Des would be able to hide for long. He stayed in his seat and watched as she was surrounded by a throng of both male and female fans. She shook a lot of hands, then phones came out and she took pictures with people, never once seeming tired or irritated by the number of photos.

"Hey, Logan, can you come down here for a minute?" she yelled from the stage.

He pushed off and walked down.

"Logan, I didn't see you up there," Margaret said.

"Hi, Margaret." Living in a small town meant you knew pretty much everyone. Margaret had gone to Hope High, but she'd married Ed Penfield, one of his high school buddies from Oakdale.

"Could you take a picture of all of us with Mrs. Penfield's camera?"

"Sure." He took Margaret's camera, and Des gathered close with everyone while Logan snapped off a bunch of shots before handing the camera back to Margaret.

"Thank you, Logan," Margaret said. "This is going on the wall in my office."

"I'd love a copy of that," Des said. "I'll give you my e-mail address."

Margaret blinked. "Okay. I'll be sure to send you one."

Des grabbed Margaret's notebook and jotted down her e-mail.

"Miss Jenkins," one of the students asked. "How old were you when you first started acting?"

"Call me Des," she said, and grabbed a seat on the floor of the stage. "I actually started in high school, doing plays like this. That's where I first fell in love with acting. I did the same play you all are doing, as a matter of fact."

"You did?" one of the girls asked, her eyes wide.

"I did, though I only had a minor role."

"How did you get on television?"

"A lot of it is simply luck and timing. When I was eighteen, I made my way out to Hollywood to try my luck at acting. I made some friends and we worked multiple jobs to pay the rent. When I wasn't working, I took acting classes and went out on auditions. I managed to snag some roles in commercials and was lucky enough to book a few guest spots in television shows."

"And your first television part was as a street hooker in an episode of *Law and Order: SVU*," one of the boys said.

Des laughed. "That's very true. I was so excited to get that role. All twenty-four seconds of it, before I was strangled and tossed behind a Dumpster. That was the high point of my life at the time."

They all laughed.

"And then your breakout movie role was in *Elizabeth's Dawn*. You died in that one, too," someone said.

Des smiled. "Yeah, it's great to get a death role. Those always have some meat and give you a chance to show what you can do. Dying on film is not easy, kids."

"Is there anything you'd do differently if you could?"

That question came from Margaret.

"Honestly, I try not to live with regrets, because I can't go back and fix anything I screwed up. I can only look forward. So anything I do differently I'd have to do in the future. I do try not to repeat the same mistakes I've made in the past. Does that make sense?"

Margaret smiled and nodded. "It does."

"Like . . . what mistakes?" one of the girls asked.

"That's a good question." Des took a deep breath. "Don't get close to people who are bad influences on you, no matter how cool they seem or what they offer you. Sometimes that inner voice you have that tells you something is bad? It's there for a reason. Listen to it. It'll never steer you wrong. I didn't always listen to that voice, and now I always do."

"That's very good advice, Des," Margaret said.

Des had an easy rapport with the teens. She answered all their questions honestly. She admitted to some mistakes she'd made along the way and gave them sound advice. She was honest about the industry and didn't make it sound like it would be a dream come true for all of them.

"Oh, man, my roommates and I ate a lot of ramen noodles for a very long time. Listen, this business is harsh. It's filled with rejection, and for every one of us who is successful, there are thousands who aren't. You have to be really tough, and you have to take rejection well. I still get turned down for roles I really want badly."

One girl's eyes widened. "You do?"

"Of course. You know *Shot Down*, the blockbuster last year that starred Suzanne Lachelle?"

All the kids yelled yes.

"I wanted Suzanne's role so badly. I auditioned six times for it, and it was down to the two of us. I didn't get it. And you know how successful that movie was. But Suzanne was brilliant in that movie, and when I saw it, I knew they had made the right choice."

"So you aren't mad that she got the role and you didn't?" one of the girls asked.

"Well, to be honest, initially, I was really pissed."

They all laughed.

"But you aren't going to get every role you try out for. That's not realistic. And like Suzanne in the role in that movie, some actresses are better suited for a part than you are. Acceptance is a large part of the industry, and there aren't any guarantees. All I can tell you is that if you want it badly enough, go for it, but be prepared to fail."

She went on and answered every question they asked, until Logan looked at his phone. "I'm sorry, but we need to go."

Des stood. "I'm sorry, too. We took up all of your rehearsal time. But I had so much fun talking to all of you."

She said good-bye to the kids and Margaret walked with them to the entrance. "This was worth giving up half a rehearsal day. The kids learned a lot from you."

"I'm not sure I gave them anything useful."

Margaret took her hand. "You gave them honesty. That's more than they'll get from a lot of people, especially someone in your industry. Thank you for that."

"I enjoyed it. They're great kids, Margaret. Talented, too. I'll be back to see the production in a few weeks, if you don't mind."

"I'd love that. The kids would, too."

"Great. I'll bring Colt with me, too. He loves this play as much as I do."

They headed outside to the truck, and since Logan had parked it between two of the school buses, they were still well hidden from any of the photographers who might be wandering around looking for them.

"You did good in there," Logan said.

She looked at him. "Complimenting me again? I might think you like me, Logan."

"Don't go getting any ideas."

She climbed into the truck and put on her seat belt. "Oh, I have a lot of ideas where you're concerned."

He shook his head. "I don't know what to do with you, Des."

She laughed. "Don't worry. I know exactly what you can do with me."

# Chapter 6

STAYING TO THE back roads and winding through neighborhood streets, Logan drove them a few miles away to a one-story home in a beautifully landscaped neighborhood. The house was an older model, but Des could tell it had been recently repainted a lovely green with white shutters. The lawn was well kept, and there were colorful flowers in pots lining the front porch. The garage door was open, and Luke was outside. He motioned for Logan to pull into the garage. When he turned off the engine, Luke pushed the button and closed the door.

They climbed out and Luke grinned. "I figured we'd hide you from the photographers, who've been burning gasoline all over town looking for you two for the past several hours."

Des laughed. "Hey, that's good for Hope's gas stations, isn't it?"

"It's nice that they're helping our local businesses, even if they don't want to be. Come on inside. Emma's not home yet."

They walked in to a nice living area with the kitchen and

dining area behind them. It was open and sunny, with a large window in the living room and a sliding glass door off the kitchen. Boomer came to greet them, so Des crouched down to pet him.

Des looked up at Luke. "Has Boomer seen a lot of police action?"

"He's a great police dog, and, yeah, he's caught quite his share of perps. He took down a suspect last spring that was breaking into pharmacies and medical offices to steal drug supplies."

Des scratched Boomer's ear. "Good dog."

"Come on in and take a seat. Would either of you like a beer or a soda, or maybe some water?"

"I'd love a beer," Des said.

"Same for me," Logan said.

Luke went to the refrigerator and grabbed three beers, opened them and handed them out. They went into the living area and Des pulled up a nice comfortable spot on one of the chairs.

"What did you do this afternoon?" Luke asked.

"We went to the high school. Des talked to the drama students."

Luke looked at her and gave her a smile. "Bet they enjoyed that."

"I'm pretty sure I enjoyed it more than they did. They're doing one of my favorite plays, so I wanted to stop by and watch them practice. And how did your day go? Did you and Boomer catch any bad guys?"

"Nothing eventful went on today. A couple fender benders and some speeders. Pretty routine day."

"Sounds great to me. Whenever I'm in L.A., it seems like you can't turn on the TV without seeing a televised police chase on the freeway."

"Big news out there."

She took a long pull of her beer, swallowed and nodded. "Yeah. And a lot of crime. A town like Hope is a nice break from having to have bars on your windows."

"I imagine it would be."

"You don't have to live in L.A., do you?" Logan asked.

"No. A lot of actors keep homes outside of the L.A. area. I just haven't gotten around to buying one yet. And I only spend half the year or less at my condo there since I have a busy shooting schedule. Maybe when I get married and have a family, I'll buy a place somewhere remote. With big dogs and less crime."

Luke laughed. "That sounds like a great plan."

The front door opened and Emma came in with Daisy and Annie. It was wild chaos, with dogs scrambling around sniffing each other, tails wagging.

The dogs came over to greet her. "Hi, girls. It's so nice to see you again." She bent to pet them.

"Oh, you're here. I didn't see your truck, Logan."

Luke went over and gave Emma a kiss, then took her bag. "I had them park in the garage. The photographers are still trying to hunt them down."

Emma's gaze panned over to Des. "You poor thing. It must be hell to be hounded like that."

"I'm used to it. I'm sorry for the disruption, though."

"It didn't disrupt me at all, and Luke tells me it was fun for him today." She turned and wrapped her arms around Luke. "How was your day?"

"Uneventful. Yours?"

"It was good. Did you get the food?"

"I did."

Des watched the interplay, the way Luke and Emma only had eyes for each other. So that's what it was like to be madly in love with someone. She felt the intensity of it all the way across the room. Her gaze slid to Logan, who was watching her, not his brother and Emma.

She felt the zing, and everything inside her heated.

"Are you two hungry?" Emma asked.

Yeah, she was definitely hungry, but not for food. She shifted her gaze to Emma. "Sure."

"Great. We're having barbecued chicken kabobs for

dinner along with some rice. I hope that's okay for you."
Emma paused. "I'm sorry. I didn't even think to ask if you
were a vegetarian or something."

Des laughed and stood. "I'm not, and it all sounds awesome. What can I do to help?"

"Let me take a quick shower, then we'll get started."

"I'll go get the grill fired up," Luke said.

Alone with Logan, she moved over toward him. "Hungry?" she asked.

His eyes went stormy dark. "Yeah. You?"

Edging closer, she felt the power of him, the way his
gaze tracked her as she nearly touched him. "Starving."

He smelled good, and it had been a really long time
since she'd been with a man. And she'd never been with a
man like Logan. All the guys she'd slept with before had
been actors, and honestly? Not exactly tough guys.

She'd just bet Logan McCormack had never had a manicure in his entire life. She'd bet his hands were rough, worn
with calluses. She'd love to feel his work-roughened hands
gliding over her skin. There would be no refinement in his
touch, no practiced moves that she'd wonder if he'd learned
them on a movie set.

She swallowed, and his gaze tracked to her throat. She
watched his lips, and really wanted his mouth on her neck.

"Des."

"Yeah?"

"Stop."

"Stop what?"

"Whatever it is you're doing."

"I'm not doing anything."

"Yes, you are."

She cocked a brow. "What is it that you think I'm doing,
Logan?"

"Looking at me."

"And that's bad?"

"Here it is."

"So . . . you want me to look at you somewhere else?"

The back door opened and Logan stood. "Anything I can do to help?"

Luke took a look at them and grinned. "No, I think I can turn on a gas grill by myself. Anyone need a beer refill?"

Logan finished his off in one swallow. "Yeah, I definitely need another."

She played with the dogs while the guys talked.

Emma came out of the bedroom a short while later, her hair still wet. She had thrown on a pair of capris and a tank top. "I feel so much better now. How about we get started on that chicken?"

Logan followed his brother outside. She washed her hands and helped Emma slice up the chicken and skewer it onto the rods, along with vegetables and pineapple.

"I have this supersecret sauce I marinate the kabobs in," Emma said.

Des watched her add ingredients to a container. "Supersecret, huh? I have to admit, I love food, but I'm never home enough to do more than grab takeout."

"You don't like to cook?"

"I love cooking. Or at least I'd love to learn to cook. Whenever I'm home, I dabble with cookbooks. But I'm just not in one place long enough to get the hang of things, which is why I do the whole takeout thing. Obviously I don't have a lot of patience—or time."

Emma laughed. "I know how that is. I ate a lot of frozen meals before Luke moved in. But now that there's the two of us, we both like to experiment on the food front, and I find myself cooking more than I used to. Plus, this marinade is easy."

She showed Des the ingredients she used.

"You're sharing your supersecret recipe with me?" Des asked.

"Well, you do need to do more cooking, right? It's only fair I give you a leg up on the easy stuff."

Des grinned. It wasn't all that difficult to make, and Emma laid the skewers in the marinade.

"Now we'll let those settle for about fifteen minutes, and we can start the rice cooking."

"You're right. That wasn't hard at all. You're really good at this."

"I've failed at a few things, but Luke is nice enough not to say anything. It's mostly a learning experience."

"I guess I'll have to practice, since food is one of my favorite things, and I'd like to cook more."

Emma reached into the refrigerator and grabbed a bottle of wine. She opened it, then pulled two glasses from the cabinet. "Come on, let's grab a seat. The guys can take it from here."

Emma peeked her head out the door to let Luke know the kabobs were in the fridge and marinating, then led Des into the living room. They took a seat, and Emma poured the wine.

Des took a sip. "This is very good."

"I'm sure you have great wines out in California, with all the wineries out there, but, you know, we have liquor stores out here," Emma said with a grin.

Des laughed. "It's all the same thing, right?"

"I guess so. And as far as cooking, I'm sure it's hard for you with all the travel you have to do."

Des leaned back. "Honestly? It's a little tiring. I mean I love the work, and I want to do as many movies as I can while I'm still popular. But the lifestyle is rough."

Emma nodded. "I can imagine it is."

"I don't want to sound ungrateful. I know there are thousands of actresses out there who would kill to be in my shoes."

"But it's exhausting, right? I don't know how you do it. You released . . . what? Four films last year?"

"Yes. And thank you for knowing that."

Emma's lips curved. "I'm a fan."

"Thank you. And like I said, I'm so grateful for being able to do what I do. I've had countless opportunities, and the chance to work with amazing directors."

Emma looked at her. "But?"

"I don't know. It's almost like I feel if I stop, the offers will dry up. And at the same time, I've been working non-stop since I was nineteen. That's seven years, which I know isn't a lot, but I'm ready for a break, which sounds awful."

"I don't think it sounds awful. I'm not an actress, but I went through veterinary school for four years, then immediately started working with a group of doctors in South Carolina. I had intended to do that for several years, but the opportunity to buy my own practice here came up last year and I jumped at the chance, even though it was going to be a huge financial burden. The past several years have been intense. So I understand what it's like to feel as if you're running nonstop without taking a breath."

Des liked Emma. Emma didn't judge her or treat her any differently just because she was an actress. She even understood where she was coming from. Work was work, no matter what type of job you had. She was so grateful Emma understood that.

Des didn't often talk about her feelings, figuring no one would really understand how she felt. She worked long days a lot of the time, and she was often on location, moving from state to state or country to country, losing track of time—and time zones. She'd often wondered what it would be like to settle somewhere permanently, to have a home instead of a rented condo.

"But now you're feeling more settled?" Des asked Emma.

Emma took a glance over her shoulder, smiling. "Yes. Definitely more settled. But it wasn't easy getting here. I had some . . . issues with my past that had to be dealt with, and Luke has been very patient with me."

"He's very hot."

Emma laughed. "Yes, he is."

"And a cop, too. That must be nice for you."

"It is. Though I like to think of myself as extremely independent—and trust me, I fought very hard to gain that independence—it's still nice knowing the hot cop with the gun sleeps next to me at night."

Des smiled. "I'll just bet it is. And he has the handcuffs, too. Imagine the role-playing."

Emma laughed, hard. "Oh, I like you, Des. My friends would like you, too. Please tell me you're going to be around the ranch for the Fourth of July shebang."

"Martha invited me."

"Great." Emma studied her. "You mean Logan didn't invite you?"

"Logan keeps his distance from me."

She half-turned on the sofa and took a glance out back. "So what does that mean? Do you like him?"

"I do like him. But I think he's afraid of me."

"Really." Emma's brows arched. "Real-l-l-y. That's so interesting. Logan is so quiet and mysterious, especially about women. I never know what to think about him."

"Me, either. I know he likes me, though."

"Is that right? How do you know?"

"Come on, Emma. You're a woman. You can tell by the way a man looks at you that he's interested. And the way Logan looks at me? He's definitely interested."

"Oh, so he looks at you *that* way."

Des nodded. "Yes. So what he says and how he feels are two different things. I just have to get his mind aligned with his body."

Emma's lips curved. "If anyone can bring Logan to his knees, Des, I'm sure it's you."


LOGAN WAS ONLY half-listening to Luke talk about work while he grilled the kabobs. His gaze kept tracking Emma and Des, and he wondered what they were talking about. All he could make out was their two heads huddled together in the kitchen, but he'd occasionally hear laughing. And then Emma would poke her head around and look at him.

He knew damn well Des was talking about him. What

the hell did she have to talk to Emma about that had to do with him? Now movies, that he could understand. Luke had told him that he and Emma had movie-night dates once a week because Emma liked going to the movie theater in town. So he knew Emma and Des had a lot to talk about there.

But he knew when women were whispering secrets, and that they had nothing to do with talking about the latest movie.

"These are done," Luke finally said, taking the kabobs off the grill.

They went inside, where Emma and Des were still in the kitchen, huddled together like they'd been best friends for years.

"I'm leaving the dogs outside," Luke said.

"That's fine. I'll put their food out there," Emma said, grabbing their bowls.

"I'll help you." Des grabbed one of the bowls while Emma scooped up the food.

"Those two made friends fast," Luke said, standing next to Logan while they washed their hands in the kitchen sink.

"Yeah, they did."

"Table's already set, so grab something to drink and have a seat," Emma said after they came back inside.

Emma and Luke took their regular seats on one side of the table. Des took a spot across from Emma. It would have been awkward for Logan to pull up one of the end chairs, so he grabbed the spot next to Des.

The food was great, and he told Emma so.

"Thanks. It was easy enough to make. I mentioned that to Des, who apparently wants to take up cooking."

Logan slanted his gaze her way. "Yeah? In your big fancy on-set trailer?"

"Hey, there's a stove in there. I could actually cook if I wanted to. Or had time. Or access to a grocery store."

"It probably beats that crap they feed you."

"You're right there. And now that I know Emma's secret-marinade recipe, I have something to fix."

"No way. Emma showed you her recipe?" Luke looked at Emma. "Even I don't know that recipe for your infamous marinade."

Emma leaned her shoulder against Luke's. "Well, I'm sorry to tell you this, honey, but Des is kinda special."

"Ouch," Luke said.

Des laughed. And ate a fantastic dinner. And drank wine, and very much enjoyed the company of Emma and Luke. Even Logan seemed relaxed, and she got to listen in to some ranch talk as Logan filled Luke in on the goings-on. Though she didn't understand some of it, because they talked stock and sales and inventory, it was still fascinating to hear a rancher talk about his passion.

Luke listened and nodded, and if Logan asked a question, Luke would defer to him and tell him the ranch was his to operate and Luke was fine with any decision he made.

"So tell me about your movie shoot, Des," Luke asked as the topic changed from ranch talk to movie discussion.

"It's going fine, I suppose. Logan got to watch a couple of scenes being filmed."

Luke arched a brow. "Is that right? And?"

Logan shrugged. "They were good. Surprisingly better than I thought they'd be."

"Gee, thanks," Des said with a laugh.

"Though your aim is off."

"Excuse me?"

"When you used your longer gun. You need better training."

"I've had weapons training."

He scooped rice up with his fork and took a bite.

"Are you saying it doesn't look authentic when I shoot?"

"You're unwieldy with that weapon. You're not firing it with authority."

Des grabbed her glass of wine and studied him. "And you think you can make me look better."

"I can make your aim better, that's for sure."

"You do realize we're not firing live rounds out there."

He gave her a look. "Uh, yeah. But that doesn't mean you shouldn't be aiming and shooting like you mean it."

"Fine. Next time I'm at the ranch you can show me. And next time you're on the set, I'm putting you to work as an extra."

Logan frowned. "I don't think so."

"Hey, you said realism was important. I think it's also important for you to see what it's like to be an actor."

Luke snorted. "She got you there."

"No way in hell am I dressing up like some freakin' alien."

"Oh, Logan. You'd make a great alien. You have the build for it."

Des turned to Emma. "He does, doesn't he?"

"I am not going to be in the movie."

"I think I'll ask Martha if she wants to be in it, too. The two of you could be together. Like an alien family."

Des could almost see the smoke blowing out of Logan's ears.

"Martha would eat that up, wouldn't she, Logan?" Luke asked.

"Yeah, she would. And she can definitely do it. I'm not gonna."

Des quirked a brow. "Are you afraid to spend a day as an alien?"

"No. I'm just not interested. And I don't have the time."

"Oh, come on, Logan," Luke said. "It's the opportunity of a lifetime to say you were in a movie. Make the time."

"Luke's right," Emma said. "If I had someone to cover for me at the clinic, I'd do it in a heartbeat. And Martha will love it if you do this with her."

Luke and Emma stared at him, and Des smiled. She had him, and he knew it.

"Fine. I'll be an alien."

Des took a sip of her wine and smiled at him over the rim. "This is going to be so awesome."

"And then we'll work on your rifle skills," Logan said.

"Can't wait."

With that settled, Logan looked over at Luke. "You and Emma coming for the Fourth?"

"Wouldn't miss it," Emma said. "Martha said we don't come around often enough, and she misses all the dogs."

"That's her way of guilting you into coming over for Sunday dinner."

Luke nodded at Logan. "Martha has a way with that guilt. And we'll definitely be there for the Fourth. I wouldn't want to miss the fireworks."

Logan's lips curved, and, oh, he was sexy when he allowed himself to smile. "It's the best part."

Luke grinned. "You just like blowing shit up."

"Well . . . yeah."

"Like that time you shot that rocket off and set the grass on fire."

Des looked to Logan, who shrugged. "It was a science experiment."

"Bullshit," Luke said. "You bought that rocket at the model store, built it, and thought you could send it to space."

"I sent it up, didn't I?"

"Yeah. And right into the dry grass. Man, Dad was pissed about that fire."

Des caught the hint of a smile on Logan's face. "He was."

"Uh-oh," Emma said. "You were in trouble, Logan?"

Luke laughed. "When you have to bring the water truck out to contain a grass fire in the middle of the dry season, trouble is an understatement. I thought for sure our dad was going to have to call the fire department."

"It's a good thing he got it contained with the water truck, or my ass would have been as burnt as that field."

"So, your father was a little mad, huh?" Des asked.

"Oh, more than a little mad. I was shoveling cow shit for a month."

Des laughed.

"Oh, poor Logan," Emma said.

"Don't 'poor Logan' him," Luke said. "He deserved it. And then there was the time you hid all of Mom's makeup in the barn."

"Now that was someone you didn't want to piss off." Though Logan's lips curved when he said it.

Des grinned. "You hid her makeup in the barn?"

"That stuff was like liquid gold to her. She put it on as soon as she got out of bed every morning. I thought she was pretty enough without it, and I told her that. She said no woman is beautiful until she has her hair and makeup finished."

"Apparently you disagreed," Emma said.

Logan nodded. "So one morning in the summer, I got up early, snuck into her bathroom and gathered up all her makeup into my school backpack, and hid it in the barn."

"You could hear her screaming all the way from in the kitchen," Luke said with a smile.

"How old were you?" Des asked Logan.

"Seven or eight, I think."

"She came after you like you were the devil himself," Luke said, pride in his eyes as he looked at his brother. "And even better, Logan played dumb, said he had no idea where her makeup was."

"Yeah, but she knew it was me."

"She always blamed you for shit."

"Mostly because I was the one to blame for most of it."

Luke laughed. "That's true."

"Did you get in trouble for hiding her makeup?" Des asked.

"She sent me to my room for the day. Which for a kid that age is like being in hell."

"And if I recall, Dad thought it was pretty funny when Mom complained about it over dinner. He told her Logan was right and she did look pretty without makeup. Which set her off all over again."

Logan nodded at Luke. "Yeah. And then I got sent back up to my room after dinner."

"She was mad at you for about a week over that," Luke said.

"It was worth it."

They both laughed.

Des leaned back in the kitchen chair. "Makeup seems like kind of a silly thing to get so upset about."

"You didn't know our mother," Logan said. "No sense of humor."

He left it at that, and Luke didn't elaborate, so Des didn't probe any further, but she really wanted to know more about the woman who raised him. He'd mentioned her once, but only to say she was gone, and she'd remarried. His voice had been flat and she hadn't wanted to ask. But she was curious.

After dinner, they all took their dishes into the kitchen and helped Emma clean up, then settled into the living room with drinks. Logan had switched to soda, but Des enjoyed another glass of wine. She had an early call tomorrow, but she didn't want to leave. She'd so thoroughly enjoyed this day that she wanted it to go on as long as possible.

"We're just so happy you're here in our town to film. It puts a lot of revenue in Hope's coffers," Luke said.

"Yes. All your local motels filling up with the paparazzi, right?" she asked Luke.

He laughed. "Yes, and they're eating at our restaurants, too. Thanks for that."

"My pleasure."

After about an hour of chatting, Logan stood. "Dawn comes early at the ranch, so we need to move along."

Des stood, too. "Thank you all so much for having us over for dinner. I really enjoyed being here with you. And the excellent food and wine."

Emma hugged her. "You're welcome any time you need a break from the set."

They said their good-byes and climbed in the truck.

It was a nice ride back to the ranch, especially since there wasn't a procession of paparazzi behind them.

Logan was quiet, his gaze focused on the road.

"Thanks for taking me out today—and tonight," she said.

"You're welcome."

"I know how busy you are running the ranch and all, and you have that part to get the truck fixed. If I hadn't been with you, you probably would have just run into town and come right back."

"Yep."

"So . . . why did you bring me with you?"

His gaze slid to hers. "Because you asked."

Okay, so he was back to quiet. She leaned back and looked out at the scenery. Once they left Hope city limits, there was more grassland, and fewer houses.

"So where did you go to park when you were in high school?"

He frowned. "Park?"

"You know. Where did you take a girl to go make out?"

"Didn't need to take a girl anywhere. There's miles of property on the ranch. Plenty of places to hide out there."

"Is that right? You didn't feel the need to get away from the possible prying eyes of your family?"

He let out a short laugh. "Not with that many acres. All we had to do was get in the truck and drive out to one of the ponds, or head out a few miles to someplace remote. My dad always went to bed early, and my mom didn't much care what we were doing, as long as we didn't bother her."

Again that thing with his mom. She caught the tinge of resentment in his voice. "I'm getting the impression—and correct me if I'm wrong—that you and your mom weren't always on the same side."

"She hated the ranch, hated being married to my dad, and didn't think very highly of having children. So in answer to your question, I didn't think much of my mother's skills as a wife or as a parent. Within the first year of my dad's death, she remarried, left Oklahoma, and I haven't seen her since."

Des just sat there, stunned into silence for a few seconds while she absorbed what Logan had told her. "God, Logan, I'm so sorry. How long ago did your father die?"

"When I was twenty-two. Reid, my youngest brother, had just turned eighteen. She probably would have left as soon as my dad died, but Reid wasn't of age yet. And she hadn't gotten her hooks all the way into her new husband yet. But she'd been mentally and emotionally gone for years before that, so her physically leaving didn't much matter to us anyway."

"And you haven't heard from your mother in all these years?"

"No."

"Well, what the hell is wrong with that woman? She has three children and she just . . . abandoned them?"

"Yeah."

"That sucks."

Logan just shrugged.

Des couldn't sit still on her side of the truck. She was furious on Logan's behalf. Mothers didn't just up and leave their children. It simply wasn't done. Okay, so maybe it did happen, but what the hell was wrong with Logan's mother? Did she not have a maternal bone in her body?

"So, she didn't like the ranch. Couldn't she have moved to Hope? Or into Tulsa? That way she would have still been near you and your brothers."

"She didn't like small-city living. She wanted to be in a big city, and Clyde—that's her new husband—offered that to her. She was out the door in a hurry, and never once looked back."

"Sonofabitch." If she had been within distance of Logan's mother, she would've slapped her. Hard. She reached across the truck and laid her hand on his shoulder. "I'm so sorry she did that to you and your brothers."

"I was over it—and her—a long time ago. Don't feel sorry for me."

"Clearly, I have no reason to feel sorry for you. You're better off without her. And you have Martha, who is obviously a fine mother figure and a more fit role model than your mother ever was. But I'm pissed, Logan. No woman should abandon her children. I'd like to smack your mother and maybe tear a few strands of her hair out."

That got a quirk of a smile out of him.

He pulled onto the property and headed down the dark roads. Here, there were no lights from the city. She was glad he knew where he was going because she couldn't see anything but the headlights from the truck. It wasn't like there were streetlights out here on these roads, and other than the main house and barns, which they'd passed, there was . . . nothing.

She turned to him. "Take me out to one of those ponds or lakes you mentioned earlier."

He slowed down so he could glance her way. "What?"

"You know, those places you used to take girls when you wanted to be alone."

She saw him let out a breath, then he shook his head. "Not a good idea."

"Why not?"

"You know why not."

"So, are you just not into me, Logan, or are you afraid of what might happen if you and I are alone together?"

"We're alone right now."

She shot him a look. "And you're evading the question."

"What was the question again?"

"Never mind." She shifted in her seat, deciding all men were assholes, and she was giving up on this one. Clearly, he wasn't interested. "Just take me back to the set."

LOGAN SHOULD HAVE breathed a sigh of relief that Des had finally quit pushing about getting him alone.

Though for some reason he still felt unsettled, and then for some stupid reason he took a left at the fork in the road instead of the right turn he should have made that would have led them back to her movie location.

And before he knew it, he'd stopped the truck in front of his favorite part of the ranch—the cabin and lake house.

"Where are we?" Des asked, already opening the truck door and sliding out.

He got out, too, and followed her. It was late, and it was still so damn hot you could feel it every time you drew a breath. But at least the bugs went away at night, as long as there were no lights. And here, it was as dark as it could get.

"I come here to go fishing, and whenever I want to get away."

She turned to face him. "So, this is where you used to bring your women?"

"Girls. I brought girls here. I bring women to the house."

Des took a few steps forward, closing the distance between them. He could smell her shampoo, her skin, and everything he wanted, but shouldn't.

"And what does that make me, Logan?"

"Trouble."

He couldn't see her eyes here in the dark, but he felt her, could swear he heard her heart beating. Or maybe that was his. He'd never been shy about women—or about sex. He always made sure both sides knew what they were getting into. And he never made any promises, so there'd be no regrets later.

He wasn't a promises kind of guy, and not a forever kind of guy, either. He'd seen the havoc created when a woman hated the life he lived, and he'd never bring that down on a woman. Or on himself. So, sex? Hell yeah. Relationships, or, God forbid, love? Not for him. He'd never go through the hell his father had.

He knew the kind of women to choose.

Des, on the other hand, was the wrong kind of woman

because he didn't know a damn thing about her, or what she wanted.

"If I'm trouble, what are you doing here with me?" she finally asked.

"Damned if I know. Showing you the lake, I guess."

"Come on, Logan. I think you know what you want. And what I want."

"Why?" he asked.

"Why what?"

"Why do you want this?"

She cocked her head to the side. "Do you really want me to spell it out for you?"

"Maybe."

He caught her smile. "I thought it was women who needed all the sweet talking and reassurances."

"And you don't?"

"No. I just want to have sex with you." She moved in closer, their bodies brushing against each other. "I think you're very attractive, and there's something about you that gets to me, in a moody, brooding-cowboy kind of way."

He was an honorable man, and he had resistance down to an art form, but there was only so much he could take. And Des was hot, she smelled good, and she'd damn well spelled out for him what she wanted—and what she didn't.

He'd be a damned fool to walk away from that.

And he was no fool.

He wrapped his arm around her and jerked her against him. "You sure this is what you want?"

She tilted her head back. "Yes."

"Okay, then."

He cupped the back of her head and brought his mouth to hers.

## Chapter 7

DES'S WORLD EXPLODED as soon as Logan's mouth met hers.

He wasn't gentle. There was no finesse in this kiss, no artful, choreographed slow exploration. There was just a hungry passion of melding lips and searching tongues. It was what she'd expected, what she'd craved from him, and oh, damn, was it powerful.

And when he cupped her butt and lifted her in his arms, she felt the dizzying heights of nirvana like she'd never felt before. His strides were quick and sure, his mouth still fixed on hers as he walked. She had no idea where he was taking her, and she sure as hell didn't care, because his hands were on her butt and her breasts were smashed against his chest.

When she heard him walking up the steps, she pulled her mouth from his. "Where are we going?"

"Into the cabin."

"And here I thought we were going skinny-dipping."

"Too many mosquitoes. Besides, there's a bed in here."

"What? No roughing it and getting naked out on the ground?"

"I don't like mosquito bites on my dick."

She laughed. He kicked the door shut and released her, but kept his arm wound very possessively around her. She slid down every delicious hard-muscled inch of his body, listening to the rough sound of his breathing. In the dark like this, she couldn't make out his features, but she could hear every sound he made, from his labored breathing to his groans when she cupped the center of his universe in her hand.

"Des."

"Yeah."

"I like your hands on me."

That's what she'd waited so long to hear—that he actually liked something.

She intended to rock his ever-loving world tonight.

She dropped to her knees and started to undo his belt. "Then you're really going to like my mouth on you."

Logan hadn't expected this. Or maybe he had, and that's what had held him back because he sure as hell knew he was going to get a handful of wild woman when he took on Des.

And now, she was on her knees, unzipping his jeans and taking out his cock, putting her hands on him and blowing his world apart as she took charge.

Not that he minded a woman taking charge, especially as it related to his dick. But he wanted . . .

Hell, as he looked down at her, and she tilted her head back and offered up a saucy grin, he didn't know what the hell he wanted. Only that she not stop.

And when she put her mouth on him, he tilted his head back and closed his eyes, concentrating only on the sensation, the way the heat and wetness of her mouth and tongue surrounded him.

She made him shudder, made his knees weak. And she was damned relentless, so if he didn't put a stop to this now, he was going to show her just how long it had been for him.

"Damn, woman. You drive me crazy." He reached for her, pulling her up and taking that incredible mouth of hers in a hard kiss, unable to get enough of her. She moaned against his lips and he drove his tongue inside, licking against hers.

She reached down and grasped hold of him, and he nearly lost it as her smooth, soft hands surrounded him and began to stroke. She was like a demanding wildcat, and it was time he took control. He pulled her ponytail holder out and threaded his fingers into the thick softness of her hair, then wound it around his hand and tugged her head back so he could lick along her neck.

He thought he'd distract her from the stranglehold she had on his cock. Instead, she tightened her hold, gripping him tighter, stroking him deeper.

"Des, stop."

She let go and lifted her head to stare at him. "Why?"

"Because you're too damn good at that, and I don't want to come before I'm inside you."

Her lips curved in a sexy little smile he wanted to kiss right off her face. "Well . . . good to know." She wrapped her hand around the nape of his neck and drew his mouth toward hers.

She was demanding, and he liked that she wasn't shy at all. He scooped her up and carried her to the bedroom, depositing her onto the bed. She slipped off her tennis shoes and popped the button of her jeans, while he toed off his boots and shrugged out of his jeans.

He liked watching her undress, the way she shimmied out of those tight jeans she wore, leaving her in just her shirt and underwear. And then she made quick work of her top, which left her wearing only her matching very sexy black bra and panties.

He took off his socks, pulled off his shirt and dropped his boxer briefs, then climbed onto the bed, pushing her onto the mattress.

"Hey, I'm not naked yet," she said as he loomed over her.

"I know." He bent and pressed a kiss to the swell of her breast, his lips lingering over the softness of her skin. Then he went lower, grasping the material of her bra into his mouth, taking her nipple with it.

"Oh," she said, arching into his mouth. "This would be so much better if we took my bra off."

He ignored her, sucking the material—and her nipple—into his mouth. He nibbled with his teeth, a little harder than he normally would if there hadn't been the barrier of satin and lace.

Des moaned, and cursed.

"Dammit, Logan."

His name floated out as a whisper as she grabbed his head and pulled it up.

"Yeah."

"Let's get this bra off. I want your mouth on me. On my skin, sucking my nipples."

Again, that blatant honesty of hers that seared him, that made him desperate to possess her in the most primal of ways.

He lifted her only long enough to undo the clasp on her bra. He pulled the straps down her shoulders—with her help, since she seemed to be in a big damn hurry to get the bra off.

God, she was beautiful. With only moonlight streaming in from the window of the cabin, her skin shone a pale silver glow, her nipples dark against the light of her skin. Her breasts were small, and as he cupped them in his hands, his thumbs brushing over the peaks, she lifted into his touch.

"Yes. That's exactly what I wanted."

He leaned over her and took her nipple into his mouth. She was like silk, and seemed so fragile, so small next to him. He tried to be gentle, but that's not what she wanted.

"More," she whispered, her tone breathless as he

grasped her breast in his hand and deepened the draw of her nipple between his lips. Her answering moan was his gratification. Passion made him slip his hand behind her back and use his teeth to tease her.

"Oh, God, Logan. Do that again."

Her nipples were sensitive, and that rocketed him to new heights. He was hard, heavy, and ached to be inside her. But he loved the feel of her skin, the way her nipples beaded and tightened inside his mouth. He loved the way she writhed against him with every flick of his tongue across the taut buds. And when he laid her down flat on the bed and kissed his way along her ribs, making his way down her very tight stomach, she leaned up on her elbows to watch him.

Des was ever curious, and so present, not content to be passive. Whenever she could, she reached down to touch him. And when he kissed her hip bone and began to pull her panties down, she drew in a breath.

Here, she was beautiful. Hell, everywhere she was beautiful. How could he have ever thought she was too young? She was most definitely a woman. And as he spread her legs and put his mouth on her, she cried out like a woman, arching her sex against him, demanding he pleasure her.

She tasted sweet and tart, and he licked the length of her, listening to the sounds of her moans that made his cock turn to steel and his balls draw up. He watched her every move, listened to every sound she made, taking her in as she shuddered.

He was going to explore every inch of her tonight—over and over again. And then he was going to slide inside her, and he already knew it was going to be as damn good as he'd been imagining since the first time he met her.

Des's breath caught. She felt like she was in space, weightless, hovering above the covers. Yet every nerve ending was so tight with tension she felt as if she might burst at any second. Logan had one very talented tongue, and he used it to tease and torment her right to the very edge of reason.

She grasped the sheets, holding on tight as Logan mastered her. She was so close, but the sensations were so delicious she held back her impending release, wanting to savor every second.

The beard stubble on his chin was rough—delicious as he rubbed it across her sex and thighs. She had known it was going to be like this. These were no practiced moves by an actor. He was a real man who was going after what he wanted. And what he wanted was to make her come.

She tried to resist, to enjoy these sensations that bombarded her senses, but Logan was relentless, and she couldn't hold back the tidal wave of her release as it swept her away, catapulting her over and over until she cried out with the sheer pleasure of her orgasm.

And when she fell, completely satiated, Logan was there, gripping her hand as he kissed his way up her body, still possessing her in a way that had taken her breath away.

Her face was flushed, her entire body fused with heat as she smiled up at him. "You're very good at that. I might want you to do that to me four or five or maybe six more times tonight."

His lips curved. "I can do that."

"And I hope to God you have condoms somewhere here in this cabin, because you need to be inside me right now." Her body pulsed with need, still so very aware of him and what she wanted to do with him.

"Yeah, I have condoms. I wouldn't have brought you here otherwise." He went into the bathroom and came out with a box of them.

"Well, aren't you prepared?"

"Like a boy scout."

"So . . . you bring a lot of women here?" she asked as he opened the box and pulled out a condom.

"Nope."

Surprisingly, she believed him, and she didn't believe

the crap slung by most of the men she knew. Logan didn't seem like the kind of man who lied. He was too straight up and brutally honest.

She lifted up on her elbows and watched as he tore open the wrapper and fit the condom over his cock, the whole time his gaze roaming over her body.

She'd never thought her body was anything spectacular. She kept in shape by running, knew she had to look good in front of the camera, so she worked out. Fortunately, she had a good metabolism, but otherwise, she didn't care much about her appearance. But the way Logan looked at her made her feel deliciously sexy. And when he grabbed her ankle and dragged her to the edge of the bed, his hands sliding over her legs, she'd never felt more like a woman. A woman desperately wanted by a man.

There was a raw hunger in his eyes she wanted to tap into, that barely leashed passion she'd seen the first time he'd looked at her. She tried to sit up, wanted to kiss him, but he pushed her back down on the mattress.

"Not now. I need to be inside you."

Okay. Obviously a take-charge kind of man in the bedroom. She lay back as he crawled onto the bed and pushed them both to the middle of the mattress.

Then, he kissed her, tunneling his fingers into her hair and covering her body with his. And when he slid inside, her breath caught. He took it slow and easy, framing her face with his big, rough hands, tangling his fingers in her hair and moaning against her lips until she wanted to die from the pure pleasure of it all.

It was an onslaught of sensation, and she didn't know what to appreciate first—the way he moved so expertly inside her, the way his tongue mimicked his movements, slowly, so deliberately sensual, or the way it felt to feel his strong, steely body on top of hers. All she could do was wrap her legs around him, lift into him and hang on for the ride of her life.

She swept her hands along the corded muscle of his

forearms, moving up toward his shoulders. He was hard—everywhere—and as he broke the kiss and stared down at her, she felt his strength as he moved within her, as he lifted his torso from her and used his lower body to grind against hers in a way that caused her to gasp.

She dug her nails into his arms. "Oh . . . that's good. Do that again."

He did it again. And again, rolling against her, using his body to give her the ultimate pleasure.

"You'll make me come if you keep that up."

His lips curved into a wickedly sensual smile. A smile that made her reach up and trace her fingers across his bottom lip.

"That's the idea, Des. For you to come."

She shuddered and lifted against him, demanding more of that sizzling delight that arced through her like a compelling drug.

She could easily get addicted to the way he made her feel, to this languorous sensation that drove her to dizzying heights.

But as his thrusts deepened and her breath caught, she couldn't hold back. He nestled down on top of her and cupped her butt, drawing her closer to the magic that entwined them together, that made them one. She swept her hands over him, held on tight and released with a gasp, drowning in the waves of pleasure that swamped her over and over again.

That he went into the abyss right after her only served to prolong her orgasm, as if she was riding the crest, only to be flung into the crashing waves once again with Logan. The way he gripped her, his mouth fused to hers as he shuddered with his release was the sweetest ending to this amazing dance.

They stuck to each other, both sweat-soaked as they caught their breath. He kissed her neck and swept his hand across her ribs, gripping her hip and clenching it like a lifeline.

Yeah, she needed a lifeline right now because that had been amazing. She had known it would be good with Logan, but this whirlwind had been unexpected. That he didn't immediately get up and create distance between them, that he instead drew her to his side and leisurely explored her body with his fingers? Now that was a surprise.

"Well . . . that was okay for a start," she finally said.

He let out a deep laugh and cupped her breast, using his thumb to brush across her nipple. "Good to know there's room for improvement."

Her breath caught, surprising the hell out of her that any part of her was capable of renewed arousal. Apparently, she was more than ready for round two. And judging from the erection poking at her lower back, so was he.

He was like . . . superhuman.

"What time do you need to get back on set?" he asked while nuzzling her neck.

She shivered. "I have an early call. Like six a.m."

"Me, too. I have to work cattle at dawn."

She wriggled her butt against his quickly hardening cock. "So we have plenty of time for round two then."

He turned her over to face him. "Don't you need to get some sleep?"

"That's the makeup department's problem tomorrow. Don't you need to get some sleep?"

He grinned down at her. "I've been riding horses since I was four years old. I can do that with my eyes closed."

"Then I guess it's no sleep for either of us tonight." She wound her hand around his neck and pulled him closer for a kiss.

*Chapter 8*

---

"YOU LOOK LIKE shit."

Des followed Colt off the set after finishing their scene. "Thanks, Colt. I know."

After their third scene of the day, and she couldn't even count how many takes Theo the dictator had put them through, Des was exhausted. No sleep the night before hadn't helped, either.

Not that she was going to complain about that. At all. And okay, they'd finally fallen sleep around four a.m., after several bouts of some very robust, very intimate lovemaking. Logan had cradled her against his chest, telling her he needed a few minutes to recover and then they'd go for round five. Or was it round six? She'd lost track somewhere around the time they'd headed into the tiny kitchen to grab something to drink and he'd ended up bending her over the counter.

Her body quivered as she remembered the fast and furious way he'd taken her, or how quickly she'd climaxed as he'd touched her while he'd been buried deep inside her.

She'd never been so passionately tuned in to a man the way she had with Logan. And he might be quiet and uncommunicative when they were together, but sexually? Holy crap, the man could sure communicate just fine that way.

"And you're sweating or something. Your face is all red. You should have makeup do something about that. I know it's hot as fuck out here."

Yes, it was, but it wasn't the heat that was causing her face to turn red, it was the recollection of all the sex she'd had last night.

"Yeah, I'll stop by the makeup trailer to have myself repaired."

They walked side by side on their way to the trailers. "Are you all right?"

She stopped and turned to Colt. "I'm fine. Why?"

"You've been so quiet all day. Normally we're chatting like a couple of teenagers. Not today, though."

She shrugged. "I'm just tired. I didn't get enough sleep last night."

"I knocked on your door around ten, but you didn't answer. I figured you'd gone to bed early."

"I wasn't in my trailer at ten. I was still with Logan."

Colt's brows rose. He looked around, then grabbed her arm and pulled her up the stairs and into her trailer. The blissful air-conditioning immediately began to cool down her heated skin. She pulled off the leather vest and dropped it onto the chair, then went to her fridge and got a bottle of water.

"You were with Logan? Why didn't you tell me this? I want details, Des. In detail."

Ignoring Colt, she unscrewed the cap on the water bottle and drank half of it before taking a breath. Releasing a sigh of relief, she took a seat at the table. "There's not much to tell, really."

Typically she and Colt talked in depth about their relationships. But there was something so intimate about what she and Logan had shared, as if it had been more than just a fun night of sex, that it felt somehow . . . sacred to her.

Which was ridiculous, of course. She and Logan were worlds apart. There could be no relationship between them, and when he'd dropped her off at the set this morning, he might have given her a smoking-hot, lingering kiss, but then he'd driven away without looking back.

He likely wouldn't even think about her today. He'd gotten laid. So had she. It had been fun. She was always logical about sex and relationships. They rarely, if ever, lasted, and she wasn't looking for one, anyway, especially not with an Oklahoma rancher. What were the odds of something like that lasting? Like a million to one.

"Des. You're not talking." Colt went and grabbed a water for himself. Now he slid onto the bench across from hers in the kitchen and was giving her his most probing gaze.

"I was with Logan last night. Until late. That's why I'm tired today."

"And?"

"And, we had a good time together. But nothing's going to come from it."

Colt frowned. "You're not giving me all the juicy details about your sex romp with him last night."

"No."

"Which can mean only one thing."

She yawned, then took another drink of her water. "Oh, really? And what's that?"

"You like this guy."

She shrugged. "He's all right, in a doesn't-have-much-to-say, chip-on-his-shoulder kind of way."

"Oh, please. You've had the hots for him since you first met him. Then you spend the entire day—and night—with him, and you refuse to spill details when it's obvious you had sex with him? That means you like him. Just like when I first hooked up with Tony. Remember that?"

"I do remember. You never even told me you two were together."

Colt wagged a finger at her. "Exactly. And now you and Logan are the same way."

"The same what way?"

"You're not talking about him."

"So? I told you there's not much in the way of details. It was just sex, Colt. How does that mean I like him?"

"Because if he was just a fuck buddy you didn't respect, you'd be giving me blow-by-blow—pun intended, by the way—details right now. And you're not. Which means—"

"Nothing," she finished for him. "It means I'm tired, Colt."

Undeterred, he leaned back in the booth. "Oooh, and you're bitchy, too. Trying to get rid of me?"

She knew he wouldn't be insulted. "Trying to."

He got up and pressed a kiss to the top of her head. "Take a nap. Then call me later after you finish your final scene. We'll have dinner."

She watched him walk to the door. "Colt?"

He turned to her. "Yeah?"

"I love you."

He grinned. "I know you do, honey. Love you back."

After he left, she rolled the bottle of water around in her hands, pondering her strange mood. Normally, sex exhilarated and relaxed her. Instead, she was more tense now than before she'd spent the night with Logan.

Probably because they'd stayed up all night, followed by a very long day filled with scenes and retakes.

Speaking of which, she looked at her phone, realizing she was due on set in ten minutes. With a resigned sigh, she finished her water and headed to makeup, where her sweatfest was repaired.

Theo was cranky today, too, which hadn't helped her mood. His insistence on perfection, doing take after take, was wearing on her.

In this scene, she and one of the other actresses, Philippa Sanchez, were strategizing their moves. As prisoners of the aliens, they had been separated from Colt and some of the other humans. She and Philippa were to be bartered and sold as slaves. It was a dialogue-intense scene, one in which she and Philippa, their characters previously at odds on Earth, learned to work together.

Des thought the first take worked beautifully. Theo hated it and wanted another. Then another. Des could tell from the looks Philippa shot her way that she agreed Theo was out of his ever-loving mind.

At the end of the third take, Des signaled for the prop guy to release her, then got up from the ground where she and Philippa had been shackled together and walked over to Theo.

"What isn't working for you in this scene, Theo?"

He didn't even bother looking at her. "I've given you direction, so you should know. Your dialogue is stiff."

Taking a deep breath, she said, "I don't agree. I think the first take worked beautifully. Our dialogue flowed naturally and the transition from enemies to friends was seamless."

He shot her a look. "That's why I'm the director and you're not. I see things you don't. Now get back into position so we can shoot it again."

Irritation pricked every one of her nerve endings. She spun around and went back to the set, flopped on the floor and got back into position.

"He's an ass," Philippa whispered to her.

Des gave her a smile. "Understatement."

"I don't know what bug crawled up his ass today, but I hope it worms its way out soon, or we'll be here the rest of the day."

Des nodded. "At least I'm not alone in my assessment. I thought the first take rocked."

"So did I. The rest of these takes are just a colossal waste of time."

Three more takes later, Theo pronounced the scene "Good enough."

Whatever. Des was toast. All she wanted was a hot shower, something to eat, and a nap.

"Des," Theo said, as everyone scattered, no doubt wanting to get as far away from him as possible. "Can I speak to you?"

What she wouldn't give to say no to him. But the last thing she wanted to do was give him more fodder to be a dick for tomorrow's scenes. "Sure."

"There were photos of you online today at the gossip sites."

Oh, there was a revelation. When weren't there photos of her? "Of?"

"You in town. With the ranch owner."

"Okay. And?"

"And you didn't come back to your trailer last night."

"What are you, my father?"

"I'm just concerned about you. I know you had that bad breakup with James. I don't want you to rebound with some redneck hillbilly out here and get yourself in trouble." He laid his hand on her arm.

She took a step back. "I'm an adult, Theo, and perfectly capable of making smart decisions."

He gave her a direct look. "Are you?"

So many things she wanted to say to him. None of them appropriate. Then again, he was being so inappropriate right now. "Look, Theo. You're my director. Other than that, we have no involvement in each other's personal lives. So stay out of mine."

She walked away, determined to shut off this day—and Theo—from her mind. She went into her trailer, closed—and locked—the door, stripped off her clothes, and headed straight for the shower. Washing off the day always felt so cleansing, always renewed her.

After climbing out, she dried off and put on shorts and a tank top, then fixed a peanut butter and jelly sandwich.

Even the thought of ordering dinner exhausted her. It had been a grueling day and she felt beat up. She grabbed her phone and looked at it.

No messages.

Not that she expected Logan to call her. Or text her. Why would he? He likely had as busy a day today as she had, and was probably as tired as she was. He probably wasn't even thinking about her.

She squelched the disappointment and tossed her phone on the counter, went into the living room and turned on the TV, surfing channels as she ate. She settled on an older romantic comedy, finished her sandwich, and curled up against the cushions.

With the air-conditioning set on low, it grew cooler in the trailer. She grabbed the blanket off the back of the sofa and covered herself, then lay down to finish watching the movie.

She was asleep before Richard Gere and Julia Roberts made it to the opera.

# *Chapter 9*

"SO YOU HAVEN'T seen her?"

Martha had asked him that question at least fifteen times a day over the past three days.

"No, Martha. I haven't seen her."

"But you've spoken to her. You've called her. Or done that texting thing."

"No, Martha. I haven't spoken, called, or texted Des." It was like a goddamned inquisition over dinner. Maybe cold sandwiches would be better, judging from Martha's steely gaze.

"But you spent the whole day with her."

And it was a good thing Martha didn't know he'd spent the night with her. He scooped vegetables onto his plate and dug into his barbecued chicken, deciding that not saying a word was the preferable option. Maybe if he could get his meal finished, he could get out of there without answering any more questions.

But if there was one thing he knew about Martha, it was that she never let a topic die.

"You should call her, Logan."

Logan took a long swallow of his iced tea. "Okay. I'll call her."

Not that he planned to, but if it got Martha off his back, he'd lie.

And it did, because she didn't say another word the rest of the meal. Which meant all they talked about were ranch things. And he didn't end up with indigestion.

After dinner he went outside to work on one of the tractors. It was still hot, and would be long after sundown. If late June was this hot, August was going to be brutal this year.

When he finished, it was dusk. Not that it was any damn cooler, but at least the sun had stopped beating on his back. He went into the barn to wash his hands. He dug his phone out of the pocket of his jeans and stared at it, mentally cursing for allowing Martha to put thoughts into his head that had no business being there.

What would he even say if he texted Des? She was likely busy, maybe even still shooting. Did they even film after sundown? He had no idea about what kind of light was needed.

After their night together, he figured he'd gotten whatever attraction he'd felt for her out of his system. It had been one hot night, too, and it wasn't the weather he was thinking about now. Being with Des had been . . . amazing. She was a wildcat in bed—and in the kitchen, in the shower, and on the floor. She was his match in every way, at least sexually.

But he wasn't looking for a relationship. He'd never be looking for a relationship, and thinking about her every day since that night they'd spent together wasn't going to do him any damn good. She was an actress, and that meant her life was all corners of the world. A woman like her would never be happy settling in on a ranch.

His father had made the mistake of ending up with the

wrong woman. It had cost his dad a lifetime of happiness, and it had cost his children a loving mother.

Logan never intended to make that mistake.

But Des had approached him with a no-nonsense attitude, open-eyed about what was between them. She knew that her time on the ranch was limited and that whatever they had would be temporary. He'd be crazy to walk away from whatever fun they could have together while she was here.

He pulled up her number that she'd put into his phone that night and typed the words.

Been thinking about you.

And then he stared at the screen, wondering if he'd made a mistake.

A few minutes later, he got his answer.

Is that right? I've been thinking about you, too. What are you up to tonight?

With a smile, he typed a response.

Worked on the tractor after dinner.

She responded right away.

Sounds thrilling. Are you finished now?

Yeah. Want to come up here? I can pick you up.

I do want to see you. I'll drive over. Be right there.

He let go of the breath he'd been holding, which was ridiculous. It was no big deal, right? Except his heart was hammering in his chest like this was his first goddamn date.

Dumbass. He needed to get over it. He went up to the house to take a quick shower. By the time he got dressed, a black SUV was pulling up in front of the house. He stepped outside as Des was walking up the steps.

She wore a dress and sandals and didn't say a word, just slid her hand around his neck.

"You smell good," she said.

"Just got out of the shower." He wrapped an arm around her and tugged her against him, instantly hardening at the feel of her body.

"Is that right? Too bad, because I intend to get you dirty."

His lips met hers and he kissed her, realizing how much trouble he could get into with this woman. He ached for her, his body instantly reacting to the feel of her, to her scent, to the way she wound around his senses whenever she was near. She felt good, and she tasted even better. And as he carried her up the steps and into his house, he pushed the door shut and locked it, not wanting anything or anyone to interrupt his time with her.

He pushed her against the door and explored every inch of her with his hands, lifting her dress to touch her skin. She was so soft, and his hands were calloused.

"I'm sorry," he said as he kissed along the side of her neck.

"For what?"

"My hands are rough."

She pulled back and reached for the top of her dress. There must have been a button there because it fell forward, revealing her breasts.

No bra. He liked that.

She grasped his hands and put them on her breasts. "I like your hands. I like the way they feel on me. Touch me, Logan."

He didn't need more encouragement than that. He circled his palms over her erect nipples, then zeroed in on the buds, grasping them between his fingers to pull and pluck at them, watching the way she laid her head back against the door and met his gaze with a full-on heated one of her own. When he kissed her again, this time there was a fierce hunger that couldn't be denied.

He picked her up, and she wrapped her legs around him as he headed for the stairs. But she moved against him, the urgency he felt as she rocked against him, the way she grabbed onto the banister, stopping him partway up, meant they weren't going to make it to the bedroom.

Using a swift turn, he sat on the stairs, placing her on his lap.

Des was breathless as she spoke. "Condoms are in your bedroom, though, right?"

He dug one out of the pocket of his jeans.

"I wasn't sure where we were going to end up, so I thought this might come in handy."

"Good thinking." She smiled at him and stood, taking the condom from his hands before shattering his world by lifting her dress.

She hadn't worn panties, either.

If possible, he got even harder as he stared up at how beautiful she looked.

He cupped her legs, looking up at her as she grabbed the handrail on the stairs.

"Logan," she whispered.

"Kneel down on my chest," he said.

He felt her legs tremble as she did, and then he tasted her. Hot, sweet, as wild as the wind across the plains. His hands swept over her butt and her hips while he held her there, giving her everything she needed, watching her breasts rise and fall as she breathed in and out.

He'd never seen anything more beautiful, or made love to a woman like this, who gave herself to him so freely. And when she came, it was with an unabandoned cry of pleasure, trembling against him with her orgasm.

She looked down at him, smiling as she slid down his body, rolling over his erection.

"Now," she said, her cheeks flushed. "Where were we?"

She tore open the condom wrapper, then unzipped his jeans and placed it over him. He clenched his jaw as he watched the way she rolled the condom on him.

"You're deliberately taking your time," he said.

She lifted her gaze to him and smiled. "I am, aren't I?"

But when she settled over him, and he got to watch the way their bodies connected, he hissed out a breath and grasped her hips, lifting her off of him and sliding her back down.

And then, she laid her palms over his chest and took control, riding him with sure, deliberate movements meant to pleasure them both.

He lay back on the stairs and watched her rock back and forth, the way she bit down on her lip when he thrust deeply into her. She dug her nails into him, which only heightened the sensations for him. He felt everything about Des, from the way she tightened inside to the way her nipples peaked when she was close to orgasm. Her lips parted and she fell forward to take his mouth in a hard kiss, her tongue sliding inside to tangle with his.

He met the challenge with one of his own, sliding his fingers into her hair and holding her there as he felt the rise of his own need. He was enveloped in a maelstrom of a storm, and he rode with it, letting it take him over, taking Des with him. She whimpered against his lips as she came, and this time, he let go, too.

It was intense, a little bit overwhelming, and damned good. He groaned with his release, shuddering against her.

And when they both came down, she lay against his shoulder, the wood stairs biting against his back.

He didn't care. He held on to her, stroking her skin.

Des finally sat up and smiled at him.

"You're not much for words, are you, Logan?"

"Hey, you're the one who came over here and attacked me. I would have been fine with a conversation."

She laughed. "Sure. You just wanted to talk."

"Okay. Maybe not."

They headed upstairs to the bathroom to clean up. Des got redressed.

"Where are you going?" he asked.

"Back to my trailer."

He pulled her against him and kissed her, a long, thorough kiss that got him hard again. "I don't think so. We still haven't had that deep, intense conversation you want to have."

She untied the strings at the top of her dress and let it fall, then came toward him. "Okay, Logan. Get to talking."

He stepped backward toward the bed, leading Des with him. "I might have forgotten what I was going to say."

She pushed him onto the bed and he rolled her onto her side, tugging her against him. But she smiled as she laid her palm on his chest. "That's okay. I don't feel much like talking tonight."

And that's why he liked her. No relationship talk. No What Does This Mean Now That We've Had Sex? conversation. Just the two of them enjoying each other. No thinking about tomorrow.

Which worked just about perfectly for him. And, apparently, for Des, too.

He bent his head and kissed her, with no thought at all about that whole tomorrow thing.

# Chapter 10

DES HADN'T EXPECTED to ever see Logan sitting in the makeup trailer of her movie set.

She'd challenged him and baited him about it, of course, mainly because he'd criticized her weaponry moves. She'd had to fight back, right? And she figured he'd never agree to get into costume, and especially not makeup. Most men would laugh and say they would, then never follow through. She should have known Logan wasn't most men.

While they were lying in bed two nights ago, he'd asked her when she wanted him to fulfill his obligation to act as an extra in her movie. Shocked, she'd told him today, and he'd said he'd make arrangements for him and Martha to be here.

Bright and early this morning, they'd shown up on set and had been directed right away to makeup. When she'd heard he was there, she wandered over to find him being fitted for a giant alien head, his face already being painted a hideous shade of purple on one side and green on the other, horns sticking out from his brows.

Des stayed mostly out of the way as she sipped her coffee and leaned against a nearby desk. "You look attractive," she said.

He looked at her out of the corner of his eye. "I think this is a new look for me. It makes me look mean. I think I'll get a lot of respect from the hands."

She laughed. "I think you'll scare the cattle."

"Maybe they'll respect me more, too."

She laughed. "Maybe. I'm going to go check on Martha."

Martha was in the trailer next door. Des could hear her talking as she walked in.

The makeup team was laughing as Martha told them stories about the ranch.

"Hey, Des." Eddie, one of the makeup guys, nodded to her.

"Hi, Eddie. How's it going?"

"Great. Martha's going to be hideous."

Martha laughed. "Thank you, Eddie. That might be the nicest compliment I've had in ages. Good morning, Des."

"Morning, Martha. Are you having fun?" She regarded Martha in the mirror. She had hair sticking up everywhere, black and white and purple to match the alien race, and her face makeup was moving along nicely.

"I'm having the time of my life. I can't wait for the hideous teeth of the Quazena people."

"They are pretty hideous. I hope you have a wonderful day on set, and you don't find it too tiring."

"Are you kidding? This is a lifelong dream."

Des patted her arm. "Great. Have fun, and I'll see you on set."

Des had to get her own makeup and hair done, so she was busy for a while. She didn't see Logan and Martha again until they were setting up for the scene. It was a crowd scene in a courtyard. The Quazena people were gathered for Des and Colt's trial. It was a loud and raucous scene, and the extras who were brought on were supposed to gesture in grunts and monosyllabic tones, which would be dubbed in later in Quazenic language tones—whatever those were going to be. The lead actors who were playing aliens had been trained to speak in the Quazena language, but the extras would mainly be panned over, so getting the language perfect wasn't an issue for them.

The assistant director came out and explained the scene to the extras, then Des and Colt and the other actors came out and got into position. Theo then called for action, and the high council of Quazena called out and asked the people to pass judgment for the invasion. Colt looked over at Des, and she gave him a look that told them they were going to be judged for crimes they hadn't committed. When the crowd rallied behind the council, shaking fists, some of the assigned actors throwing things at Des and Colt, she looked over at Colt, who tried to fight his bindings. She shook her head at him.

And then Des began to speak in Quazena, at least the first few words, something that shocked the council. She switched to English so the movie viewers would know what she was saying, but it would be understood she was speaking in the alien language.

"You judge us, but you don't even know who we are. My father brokered for peace for your nation. You knew him. You fought alongside him. He died trying to free your people." Des brought forth the tears needed for this emotional scene as the crowd and the council quieted to hear her speak. "He told me many stories of how peaceful the Quazena were, how they only wanted this war to end."

She looked out over the crowd, spotted both Martha and Logan standing near the front, their expressions giving nothing away.

"And now all you want is war. Where has your compassion gone, your quest for peace?"

"It died along with our mates and our children, when your people tore it away with your weapons."

"That's not true!" Colt tore against his chains. "Tell them that's not true."

She shook her head. "They won't believe us." She lifted her head to the council. "Someone is lying to you, trying to make you believe that it was the humans who betrayed you. We are your allies. My father was your friend."

The leader stood and came over to her, lifted her chin with one of his claws. "We have no friends." He took a step back and looked out over the crowd.

"They die."

The crowd exploded with cheers.

"And . . .cut," Theo said, loud enough to be heard over the roar of the crowd. "Thank you, everyone. That's a wrap for this scene."

Everyone clapped. Des and Colt were released from their chains and Colt hugged her. So did Richard, the actor playing the alien king.

"Incredible scene, Des. You killed it," Richard said.

"Thanks, Richard. So did you."

She wandered down the stairs and through the crowd of extras to find Logan and Martha standing together.

"Oh, honey. You were magnificent. I had to stop myself from crying, since I had to be against you in that scene."

"Thanks, Martha. I'm so glad you liked it."

"Martha's right. You pretty much nailed it up there. I kind of felt some sympathy for you."

She laughed. "Well, thanks. That's high praise coming from you."

"Do you have more today?" Logan asked.

"Yes. One more scene after this one. You're welcome to stay around and watch."

"No, thanks. I have work to do. I need to get this junk off of me and get back to work."

"Wait," Martha said. "First we need photos."

Logan rolled his eyes.

"Martha's right. You do look pretty incredible." Logan

had on green and purple makeup, a steel breastplate, and leather pants. Despite the hideous makeup, the pants were sexy as all get-out on him, and the breastplate made him look like a fierce warrior. She'd like to get him naked except for the pants. Unfortunately, she had a call coming up soon, and she couldn't think of a legitimate reason to get him away from Martha.

Too bad. Maybe she'd steal the leather pants from the costume department and see if he'd wear them for her again.

"Did you bring your camera, Martha?"

"I did." She pulled it out of her leather apron and handed it over to Des.

Des snapped a couple pictures of Martha and Logan together, and then the two of them separately.

"How about one with you in it, too, Des?" Martha asked.

"Sure." Des grabbed her assistant, and Jessica took some pictures of her with Martha and Logan.

"This is so amazing. Thank you. We'll go turn our costumes in now," Martha said.

"Okay, if you head back to makeup, they'll help chisel off some of the major stuff, then you can shower off the rest."

Martha wandered off.

"Did you have fun?" she asked Logan.

"Actually, I did. More fun than I thought I would. Thanks for making me do this."

"You're welcome. Now go get that stuff off your face and hands before I laugh."

He did laugh. "Okay, I'll see you later."

He wandered off, and she turned and watched him, admiring the tight fit of the leather across his very fine ass.

AFTER TURNING IN his costume, it took a while to get the horns off Logan's eyebrows, and the people in makeup were nice enough to use whatever cream they had on hand to remove the majority of the stuff from his face. He got to use their bathroom to wash the rest off his face and hands.

Martha was busy watching some of the alien actors practice a battle scene, so he decided to wander around for a bit and let her enjoy. Ranch work could wait for a little while longer. He'd hate to drag Martha away from all this.

He looked for Des on a few of the sets, but didn't see her. Maybe she was taking a break, so he headed to her trailer to see if he could grab a few minutes with her before he had to head back to the ranch.

He walked up the steps and was about to knock, but heard the sound of voices. Not wanting to interrupt if she had someone in there, he was about to walk away, but then stopped.

"And I told you, Theo, I'm not interested. Now get the hell out of my trailer."

"I can make this bad for you, Des. I can make sure you'll never work again."

Logan frowned. Was this jackass serious?

He heard Des laugh. "And with one well-placed phone call to the media, there'll be a front-page story about how you're constantly hitting on your leading ladies, and then your wife will know what a cheating bastard you really are. Don't ever threaten me, Theo, and don't ever hit on me again. Because I have way more ammunition than you do, and plenty of other actresses who are more than willing to come forward and testify to what a scumbag you are."

Logan wanted to kick this sonofabitch's ass. He started to knock on the door, but it was swung open wide by Theo, who shot a glare at Logan, then shoved past him and down the steps. Des was right there at the door, her eyes widening when she saw him.

Logan turned to go after Theo, but Des grabbed his arm. "Don't."

"He needs to be taught a lesson about how to treat women."

"I took care of it, Logan. He won't be bothering me again."

"Are you sure?"

"Yes."

He stared after the now-long-gone director, anger still boiling inside of him. "I don't like that guy."

She laughed. "Neither do I. But trust me, I can handle him."

He shifted his gaze to Des. "I trust you, and you did handle him."

But Theo was still an asshole, and he needed to be reminded about the right way to treat a woman. Logan would make sure of that. Maybe not today, but he was going to have a serious conversation with Des's director at some point.

*Chapter 11*

ON THE DAY before the Fourth of July, Des finished up her scenes by noon. She'd been avoiding Theo, much to his irritation, but she didn't care. She hit her marks, did what she was told, and anything beyond that he could kiss her ass.

Colt had the same scenes as she did today, so he finished up early, too.

"We should head over to the ranch today," Des suggested as they walked off the set and headed back to their trailers.

"Yeah? And why is that? So you can ogle the hot rancher?"

Des smiled. "I was thinking maybe Martha could use some help with preparations for tomorrow."

Martha had invited the entire cast and crew over to the ranch for tomorrow's big party. Since the Fourth landed in the middle of the week and Theo was being a dick about the tight shooting schedule, no one was getting more than a couple of days off. Some people had family flying in today, and Martha said there'd be plenty of food for families, too.

Des could only imagine the chaos.

"She probably could." He stopped at his trailer. "I'll take a shower, then meet you at yours and we'll head up to the ranch."

Des smiled. "Awesome."

Des hurried down the path to her trailer, took a quick shower, and decided on shorts and a T-shirt with a pair of tennis shoes. After being in makeup for the past two days, she didn't want to put any on, figuring Logan would be busy working today, anyway. Besides, he likely wouldn't care if she wore makeup or not, which was one of the reasons she liked him.

One of the many reasons she liked him.

Warning bells clanged in her head and her stomach tightened at the thought of Logan.

They'd only had two nights together, and it wasn't like he communicated with her regularly—or at all—when they were apart. She knew the score with him and what their relationship was—and wasn't. But still, she liked spending time with him. He was honest with her, never gave her any bullshit, and that was refreshing.

She finished drying her hair just as Colt showed up at her trailer.

"Ready?" he asked.

She gave him the once-over. He wore jeans, a tight T-shirt, and boots, his hair combed back and his skin tanned from being in the sun, which showcased his gorgeous steely blue eyes. "Is Tony flying in tomorrow?"

"Tonight. Along with Sarah and Callie."

"It'll be great to see them all. And Tony's going to die when he sees you dressed like that. You might not ever leave the trailer."

"Wouldn't that leave the gossips talking."

She looped her arm in his. "Well, we'll have to see about finding time for the two of you to be alone. I know how much you miss him."

"I do, Des. But you know how it is and has to be—for now."

She laid her head on his shoulder. "I want you to be able to live an honest life, Colt. And a happy one."

She heard Colt's sigh, knew how very unhappy he was with living the lie. But she also knew how important his career was and how afraid he was to risk it all by coming out.

Though she still didn't feel it was that much of a risk. His millions of female fans adored him and would love him no matter what. She was certain of it.

Then again, this was a monumental decision—both a career and a life decision, and not hers to make, so she'd just butt out.

They climbed into one of the available SUVs and drove over to the ranch. On the way over, she spotted several men on horseback leading cattle from one of the pastures. It was easy to pinpoint which of them was Logan.

"Colt, slow down," she said.

She rolled down the window and gaped as Logan and several of the other hands maneuvered the cattle across the rise. There had to be a couple hundred head of cattle, and five hands working them, expertly keeping them from straying. Logan was closest to her, easily maneuvering his horse as he moved the cattle in the direction he wanted them to go.

They disappeared over the rise in a cloud of dust, heading toward the ranch.

"You've got it so bad for him," Colt said.

She turned to him. "Shut up. I do not. I just find the whole cattle operation fascinating."

He put the car back in gear with a grin. "It wasn't the cattle you were looking at."

No, it hadn't been. But she'd be damned if she'd admit that to Colt.

They pulled up in front of the house. A couple of the dogs were hanging out nearby, so Des stopped to pet them.

"Hi, kids. How's it going today?"

She lingered for a few minutes to play with the dogs, then they went to the front door and rang the bell. Martha came to the door, surprise lighting her face when she saw them.

"Des. Colt. What are you two doing here?"

"We thought you could use some help with prepping stuff for tomorrow," Des said as Martha let them in.

"Oh, that's so sweet of both of you. But don't you have to work today?"

"Finished up for the day," Colt said, laying a kiss on her cheek.

Martha blushed and led them into the kitchen.

There was a lot going on in there. Several pies had already been baked, and Martha had food cooking on all the burners at the stove. Plus, there was something in the oven, and she was prepping fruit at the counter.

"I'd like to say I have it all under control, but it's crazy here."

"That's why we're here to help," Des said. "We'd be bored in our trailers, and this looks like a lot more fun."

She and Colt went to the sink to wash their hands, then dove in, and, with Martha's instructions, got to work. Colt peeled bags and bags of potatoes, and Des sliced enough fruit to feed the entire town of Hope. They went from one task to another.

"Just how many people are coming tomorrow, Martha?" Colt asked as he dropped the ten pounds of potatoes he'd sliced into a giant pot of boiling water.

"I'd say we usually end up with about a hundred people. Plus your movie crew. And you said you had some friends showing up, too?"

"Just a few, I promise," Des said. "But if it's too much—"

She waved her hand. "It's no problem. Trust me, I'm not the only one doing the food. I'm just making a few side dishes. Everyone from town and the neighboring ranches also bring food. And we provide all the meat."

"That's very generous, considering it's quite a lot of people." Des couldn't imagine feeding that many.

"Well, we're a big ranch, and we like to give back to our community. It's like we're one big family. We have a huge area out to the side yard where we set up picnic tables for people to eat at. Logan and the crew will finish work early today and they'll start cleaning up the area and set up the tables."

Just as she said that, the back door swung open and a very dusty Logan stepped in.

Des's heart skipped a beat. If she thought he'd looked sexy right after a shower the other night, seeing him covered in trail dust from head to toe did something to her libido.

His gaze zeroed in on her. "I didn't know we had company."

"We popped over to help Martha," Colt said with a grin.

Logan nodded. "Nice to see both of you. Thanks for helping out."

"It's our pleasure."

"Are you hungry?" Martha asked.

"Yeah."

"Get washed up and I'll fix you something to eat. Then you and the guys can get started on the picnic area."

"Okay."

Des loved to watch the interplay between Logan and Martha. It was obvious the two of them had developed a mother-and-son type of relationship because he followed her commands so easily. And he treated her with respect, as if she were a parent, not a ranch employee. It made Des happy to know he had that type of parental love in his life, especially in light of what had happened with his mother.

"Have you two had lunch yet?" Martha asked.

"No. We came over as soon as we finished shooting for the day."

"Well, you should have said something. No one goes

hungry around here, but you two have voices, you know. If you're hungry, you should speak up."

They'd been given a talking to, hadn't they? "Yes, ma'am."

"Now go wash your hands and you can eat with Logan and the crew."

Des and Colt shuttled off to the bathroom behind Logan. "Guess she told you," Colt said.

Des nudged Colt with her shoulder. "Shut up. She told you, too."

Logan stood at the sink and shook his head.

"What?" Des said, hip-checking him to get him to move.

"Nothing."

She grabbed for the towel to dry her hands. "Oh, I think there's something on your mind. What is it?"

"No, really. Nothing. I'll see you in the kitchen."

He walked away without saying a word. Des stared after him. "I do not understand that man at all."

"He likes you. And he doesn't want to."

Des shook her head. "That doesn't even make sense."

"Honey, men often don't make sense. Don't even try to figure us out."

She put her arm around Colt's waist. "But that's why I have you. You have the supersecret code to men."

Colt snorted. "I'm sworn to secrecy, and to the man code."

"You're so full of shit." Des rolled her eyes and walked back into the kitchen.

"I made turkey sandwiches," Martha said. "And there's iced tea and fruit salad and some chips. Nudge all those cowboys out of the way and help yourself."

Six sets of eyes looked up from the table at her and Colt. Used to being stared at, Des was undeterred. She found a spot at the table and took a seat, then introduced herself. So did Colt.

"So you're making the movie?" one of the guys asked. She thought his name was Ayers.

"Yes."

"That must be interesting."

"It is. Any of you or your family are welcome to come watch us film. Just let me know and I'll get you passes."

"That's awful nice of you," Ben said. "I know Martha enjoyed her visit that day. And she couldn't stop talking about her day as an extra. I loved the photo of her in her alien makeup."

Des laughed. "I think she and Logan both had fun that day."

Logan cleared his throat. "The men can't afford to take days off to go watch you make movies."

Wow. He was in a mood. "We also do filming later in the day, after you all finish work. And maybe their families would like to come watch."

Logan shrugged.

"June—that's my daughter," one of the guys said to Colt and Des, "she's a big movie fan. And she really likes Colt's movies. I know she and her mama would love to come."

"That's sweet," Colt said. "Like Des said, we're happy to provide passes. You just let us know, or let Martha know and we'll arrange it through her."

"You bet I will," Martha said, then gave Logan a stern look.

Logan ate his sandwich and didn't make eye contact with anyone. Or add any more to the conversation.

But at least Logan didn't say no this time.

Des figured he must have PMS—penis malfunction syndrome. Because he was acting like a dick.

After lunch, Logan told Martha he was going to clean the picnic area, then pull the tables from storage and start cleaning them up.

"Can I help you with that?" Colt asked.

Logan gave him a look. "Aren't you here to help in the kitchen?"

Ignoring the insult, Colt said, "I think Des has that handled. But if you don't need my help, I'm happy to stay here and assist Martha."

Des shot Logan a scathing look. Logan shrugged. "Sure. You can come with me."

"Great." Colt winked at her.

"This is your way of escaping potato peeling," she whispered as Colt walked by.

"No idea what you're talking about."

Logan had about as much use for Colt as he did a whiny city boy, which he figured Colt was. But if Colt wanted to follow him around, he'd put him to work. He assigned some of the crew to the task of hosing down the cemented area where they were going to organize the picnic tables, while he and Colt headed back to the barns where the picnic tables were housed.

They brought out twelve tables, not an easy feat, because the barn where the tables were stored was about fifty yards away. He figured city boy would give up after dragging the second table.

Colt surprised him. Drenched in sweat, he helped Logan pull all twelve tables, then helped him wash them down without complaint. Then again, he did have some muscle, so maybe all that time at the gym helped with his endurance.

"You always this quiet?" Colt finally asked him as they scrubbed the tops of the tables.

"Usually."

"Or is it just me you don't like?"

"I don't feel one way or the other about you."

Colt smiled and kept his head down on the task at the hand. "Good to know."

Wiping the sweat from his brow, Logan used the hose to wash away the last of the grime and dust from the tables.

Colt took a step back to get out of the way, then they used towels to dry them off.

"This will do until tomorrow morning. Martha will put tablecloths on them then."

He saw Des making her way toward them with a couple of beers in her hand.

"I thought you two looked a little sweaty and might want to take a break and have a beer."

"Sounds good to me," Colt said. "Thanks, honey."

Logan was too thirsty to say anything other than "Thanks."

"You're welcome."

"How's it going inside?" Colt asked.

"Great. We've got just about all the side dishes wrapped up. How about out here?"

Colt looked to Logan, who'd taken a couple of deep swallows of beer to cool down his parched throat. "Fine."

"That's descriptive," Des said. "Anything else need to be done out here?"

"Not today. We'll drag out the fireworks and finish decorating in the morning."

"Okay. I'll finish up with Martha here, then I guess we'll head out." She paused, looked at Logan, and when he didn't say anything, she shrugged and headed back to the house.

"What is it with the two of you?" Colt asked.

"That's none of your business."

"Obviously, but she likes you. And sometimes it seems as if you like her back. Other times you don't give her the time of day and you act like a dick to her."

"Again. None of your business."

"It is my business when it affects Des's feelings."

Logan leaned against one of the picnic tables and took another drink of his beer. "Why's that? Because you have a thing for her?"

Colt laughed. "You're way off base there, Logan."

"Am I? Or do you have feelings for her, and she just sees you as a friend? You must really hate that, seeing her with other guys when you're the one who wants to be with her."

Logan waited to see the rise in Colt's anger. But all he got was another laugh. "You don't know me. Or, for that matter, Des. Maybe you should spend time getting to know more about her. She's loyal and faithful, especially to the people she cares about. But if you screw with her, she'll cut you out of her life completely like you never existed."

"And you think that matters to me."

Colt laid his empty beer on the table. "I don't know if it does or not. I hope it does, because *she* matters to me, but not in the way you think."

Colt walked toward the house, leaving Logan standing there contemplating what Colt had just said. Whatever the hell Colt had said.

He ran his fingers through his sweat-soaked hair, trying to figure out what was wrong with his attitude today. Maybe it was walking in the house and finding Des leaning against Colt, laughing with him, seeing the ease the two of them had together.

He didn't believe there was nothing going on between them. There had to be something, and Logan didn't like being in the middle of that.

Then again, he and Des had made no promises to each other. They weren't exclusive. If she wanted to screw ten other guys, she could, couldn't she?

Though the thought of it stabbed him in the gut, and he didn't like feeling that way, didn't like the hold she already had on him.

But was that hold in his mind? She'd never put a claim on him, never asked him for any kind of guarantees. She'd never asked for . . . anything.

And why was that? Most women, if he was with them more than a couple of times, started hinting about relationships and promises and wanting to take things a step further.

Not Des. She'd just showed up and they'd been having fun and then she disappeared just as fast.

Maybe, just maybe, Colt might be right, and he should find out a little bit more about the woman who kept him lying awake at night.

AFTER SAYING GOOD-BYE to Martha, Colt and Des climbed into the SUV to head back to the set.

It had been an exhausting day, but Des had had a good time. She wished she could have spent more time with Logan, but she knew he'd been busy. He had a ranch to run, plus getting things ready for tomorrow had kept him doubly occupied.

"How was your time with Logan?" she asked as Colt drove along the gravel road leading them back to the set.

"Oh . . . fine," Colt said, his expression revealing nothing.

Sometimes it was a pain in the ass to be friends with actors. They could mask their emotions so easily if they wanted to.

"Colt. Really. Did something happen?"

"Oh, you could say something happened."

But he didn't say anything, and she refused to press him like an emotionally needy woman. Because she wasn't. Emotional or needy, that was, especially as it related to Logan.

They returned to the set and headed back to their trailers. Des stopped at Colt's.

"Are you going to talk to me?"

Colt turned to her and grinned. "He really does like you, Des. A lot."

Her heart drummed up a fast rhythm. "How can you tell?"

"Because he thinks there's something going on between you and me, and he's really pissed about it."

"He does? He is? Why? Did he say something to you?" She hated even asking these questions, but she couldn't help herself.

"He did, and yes, he is, and yes, he most definitely said something to me. I thought for a minute there he was going to knock me on my ass."

She climbed up the stairs so she could be eye level with Colt. "You aren't serious."

"I'm deadly serious. I could feel the testosterone radiating off him. If I didn't already have the love of my life, I would have been swooning. Hell, I *was* swooning. On your behalf, of course."

She laughed. "Stop it. What did he say exactly?"

"First he asked if the two of us had something going on, then he intimated that I was pining away for you because you saw me as just a friend."

She crossed her arms. "He did not say that to you."

"Yeah, he did."

She leaned against the railing and contemplated for a few seconds, before looking at Colt. "What a dick."

Colt laughed. "Nah, just guy talk."

"Yeah, guy talk about me. He thinks I'd use you that way? Seriously, what a douchebag. What kind of a bitch does he think I am?"

Colt held up his hands. "Whoa. Calm down, Des. I think he meant to insult me, not you."

"I don't care. I'm insulted. I would never hurt you that way."

"Honey, if I was straight and we were friends and I had the hots for you, but you didn't feel the same way, the conversation Logan and I had today would have been an honest one. Because you don't feel that way about me, do you?"

"Well, no. But I would be honest with you and tell you that. I'd never string you along or make you my sidekick. Jesus, what do you men think we women do?"

"Be honest. Some women do that to guys."

She blew out a frustrated breath. "I guess."

"So don't be too hard on Logan. He doesn't know the truth about me."

"And he won't be hearing it from me, so don't worry."

He gave her a short kiss. "I know that. Listen, I'm going to go make a phone call. All this talk about romance and relationships has made me miss my guy. And I want to find out when his plane lands."

"When do Tony and the others fly in?"

"Late tonight."

"Are you going to the airport to pick them up?"

"No, I've arranged for a car service. Less likely for the paps to pick up on them arriving, or to connect Tony and me together."

"Good idea. You have fun with your reunion. Give Tony my love, and say hi to Sarah and Callie for me."

"Thanks, honey. I'll see you in the morning?"

"Yes." She kissed his cheek and moved on to her own trailer, where she spent the next hour pacing. It was still early in the evening, and she didn't feel like reading or watching TV. What she felt like doing was giving Logan a piece of her mind. Which she wouldn't do, of course. Not tonight, anyway.

He had a lot of nerve giving Colt a hard time. If he wanted to know something, why didn't he come to her and ask her?

She already knew the answer to that. Because he was the most stubborn, uncommunicative man she'd ever met. And he made assumptions. Lots of assumptions based on—absolutely nothing.

Maybe if he actually had a conversation with her, he'd know she was just friends with Colt and had been forever. No, wait. She'd already told him that. Apparently he didn't believe her, which meant he'd indirectly called her a liar.

She dragged her fingers through her hair while simultaneously wearing out the rug in the trailer.

This was getting her nowhere. She needed an outlet for her frustration, and she wasn't going to find it here. She changed into her running clothes, put on her tennis shoes, then stretched before heading out of the trailer to take a run. Maybe a few miles in this oppressive heat would burn out some of her irritation.

She breathed in and out, even though it was like breathing fire, digging her feet in and pushing off as she got a head of speed going. She couldn't run like she normally would if it wasn't so hot, but she cleared her head and ran along the dirt path, concentrating on enjoying the scenery.

She often ran along the hills in L.A., though out there she couldn't be alone. Not like here, where all she could see were hills and valleys and ponds. The landscape of trees was breathtaking, too, and she even glimpsed cattle as she came up over the rise on her third mile.

And that's when she saw Logan's truck, parked at the far end of the road. He was out there leaning against his truck drinking a beer and watching the sun go down.

Her first thought was to turn around and head back to the set. She'd gotten most of the mad out of her system on her run, and the last thing she wanted was to get riled up again. But she wasn't a coward, either, so she slowed to a walk to catch her breath and stopped at his truck.

"A little late for you to be out, isn't it?" he asked.

Still breathing a bit heavily, she said, "Last time I looked, I was an adult and capable of making my own decisions. And, as far as I know, I'm not on a curfew."

"You seem a little mad."

"Do I?"

"Yeah."

He went around to the door and grabbed a bottle of water, unscrewed the top and handed it to her.

"Thanks." She nearly inhaled half the contents of the bottle, which helped.

"You want to talk about it?"

"You went after Colt and questioned my relationship with him."

"He told you about that, huh?"

"Yes, he did."

"I'm not very reasonable when it comes to you, Des. And I don't understand it myself, so I don't think I can give you a good explanation for why I talked to him the way I did. But I'm sorry, and I'll apologize to Colt tomorrow."

Well, shit. Logan's apology instantly burst her giant bubble of anger. And his explanation made it seem as if he felt something for her.

"Thanks. And what do you mean you're not reasonable when it comes to me?"

He pushed off the truck and came toward her, swiping her sweat-soaked hair from her eyes. "Don't ask me to define it when it confuses the hell out of me. You confuse the hell out of me. You make me feel things."

She lifted her gaze to his, saw that confusion on his gorgeous face. It was almost as if he was angry with her. But within that anger, she also saw passion rise up, as it always did when they were together.

"Are you sure you're not confusing sex with some other feeling?"

He wrapped an arm around her waist and tugged her close. "I like having sex with you. There's no doubt about that."

"But when it comes down to having an actual relationship with a woman, my guess is that's where you bow out?"

She gave him credit for not backing away. "Yeah. That's where I bow out."

"Why? What scares you about that?"

"Nothing scares me."

Now she pulled away. "Bullshit. Be honest with yourself, at least, Logan. It's your parents' relationship, the way your mom reacted to living on the ranch that makes you hesitate with women, isn't it?"

"So now you're the expert on me, Des?"

"No. But it doesn't take an expert to figure out that's why you don't do anything permanent with women. I can't really blame you, either. Who'd want to take the risk of repeating the past?"

She saw him visibly relax. But she wasn't going to let him off the hook so easily.

"But you have to realize that not every woman you meet is going to be like your mom, right?"

"I know that. Doesn't mean I'm ready to settle down yet. Or that I'll ever be ready to take that chance." He turned and looked out over the valley. "It's a tough life out here. It's a lot to ask of a woman who isn't born into it, who doesn't have a natural love of the land."

She walked over to stand next to him. "You want some-one to love this as much as you do."

"Yes."

"Understandable. And I guess you haven't found that woman yet."

"I don't think that woman exists. No one will be able to understand what it's like to work the land as if you're part of it, to live and die according to the whims of nature and the cattle market." He glanced over at her. "Would you understand that? Could you feel a part of that?"

"Today? No. But a woman who loves you could learn to love the land and your work the same way you do."

He shook his head. "My father thought that when he married my mom. He was wrong, and it made him mis-erable."

Both his father's and his mother's choices had made Logan miserable, and the one thing Des understood was suffering the consequences of someone else's choices. She wrapped her hands around his arm, always surprised and excited by the strength she felt there.

"Logan, you can't damn yourself and your future because of your father's choices or your mother's sins. You have to allow yourself to fall in love, to find someone you care about and ask them to become a part of your life out here. It's an amazing life and one that's worth sharing. You have to start making your own choices instead of living with the consequences of someone else's."

"What would you know about that?"

She leaned against the truck. "I hated that my father was army, that whenever I'd get settled in one spot and make friends or get my bedroom decorated just perfectly, my dad would get new orders and we'd have to pull up stakes and move again. We were like nomads, and I never once in my life felt settled.

"My mom always accepted this, and of course she had married into the army, so she knew that was what life was going to be like. But I hated it, and I vowed that some day I'd have a permanent house in one location and lots of friends and I'd never move again."

Logan laughed. "And then you became an actress, and now you travel all over the country and the world. So what does that mean?"

Her lips lifted. "That life very rarely turns out like you expect it to. I had planned to get married, raise a bunch of kids, and settle in one place. I was never going to move them around like I was moved constantly when I was a kid. But that didn't happen for me. I told you the acting bug bit when I was in high school. I never in a million years thought I'd become a success. I did move out to Hollywood when I turned eighteen, figuring I'd give it a try for a year or two, just to see what would happen."

"And now you're a success and making money and you could buy a house anywhere you want to, yet you still live in a condo in L.A. Why?"

Wasn't that the million-dollar question? "Because I still don't feel . . . settled. I still feel like that nomad, like I haven't yet found that place I can call home yet."

"So you're saying you're not happy?"

"I am happy. I have the career I've always dreamed of

and I love the travel, which isn't at all like all the moving around I did as a kid."

He crossed his arms and gave her a look. "Because you're the one calling the shots now?"

"I guess so. There's a lot to be said for being in charge of creating your own destiny, Logan."

"In other words, you're not going to marry some dude in the military."

She gave him a horrified look. "God, no. Any more than you're going to marry some citified chick who's going to give you three children, then abandon them."

His jaw went tight and she laid her hand on his arm. "Your dad didn't make a mistake, Logan, he just fell in love. But you learned from the mistakes your mother made. Give yourself some credit and know when the time comes, you'll choose the right woman, the one who'll love this land as much as you do, and who'll be here for your kids."

Logan looked at Des, this citified chick she was just talking about. He wondered if she realized how much she had just been describing herself. A worldly young woman whose life was just starting out, who still had dreams yet to fulfill.

A woman like her would never be satisfied with a life on a ranch.

Not that he was thinking of marrying her or anything. He could never see her as a ranch wife, could never imagine a Hollywood actress as a wife and mother, working the land side by side with him.

But he liked talking to her, and there weren't a lot of women he could open up to like he had with Des. She understood him, and after tonight, he understood her a lot better, too.

So after she was finished shooting her movie she'd go her way, and he'd go his.

And maybe, just maybe, he'd find that one woman who'd love his ranch and want to have his children and settle down on his ranch. Because he was thirty-four and it was getting damn time to start creating his future.

A future that didn't include a hot and sexy actress with black silky hair and ever-changing eye color. Because she'd be off creating her own happiness—somewhere else.

He didn't know how he felt about that.

"So, now it's dark and I didn't bring a flashlight. Care to give me a ride back?" she asked.

Pushing aside the unsettling thoughts tightening his insides, he said, "Sure. Climb on in."

He drove her to the set and parked in the lot, then got out.

"You don't have to walk me to my trailer, Logan. It's not that far from the lot here."

He came up beside her. "It's dark out, and yeah, I do have to walk you."

They passed a trailer where there was a lot of heavy laughter and loud music.

"Colt's trailer," she said. "Some of our friends are in from L.A. They'll be at the picnic tomorrow at the ranch, provided you don't mind."

"Don't mind at all. I'm surprised you're not there partying with them."

She looked straight ahead. "I wasn't in much of a partying mood tonight."

He cupped the back of her neck. "Because I made you angry."

"Partly. Some of it was on me."

He felt the tension in the muscles of her neck, and when she got to her trailer, he said, "Ask me to come in."

She turned to face him. "Logan, would you like to come in?"

He liked that there was no game-playing with Des. She wore her emotions—and her desire—right on the surface, never hiding anything from him. When she was mad, he knew it. When she wanted him—he knew that, too. "Yes."

She opened the door and he followed her inside, closing

it and locking them in. Not that he'd know who had a key, but just in case her friends decided to come looking for her, he wanted them to know they weren't going to have access to her tonight. "No party for you tonight."

Her lips kicked into a sexy half smile. "I don't know about that. Party for two, maybe."

He drew her against him and swept his hand into her hair, pulling out her ponytail, letting the raven strands fall over her shoulders.

She palmed his chest. "Wait. I'm all sweaty from my run and need a shower."

"I've worked all day and I'm all sweaty, too. You don't need to smell like a spring shower for me to want you, Des. Unless you want me to head back to the ranch and take a quick shower."

She leaned into him and licked his neck. "I like you a little salty. And you smell like a man who works for a living."

He shuddered as she ran her tongue across his throat, then tugged at his T-shirt, lifting it out of his jeans.

He jerked the shirt up and over his head, tossing it to the floor.

"We could shower together," she suggested.

"I like the sound of that."

She took him by the hand and led him to her bathroom.

"It's not the biggest shower," she said as she turned on the water. "Which means it'll be a tight squeeze."

Logan sucked in a breath. "I can deal with things that are tight."

The corner of her mouth quirked up. "Is that right? You'll have to show me." She grabbed a condom, brought the packet with her and stepped in.

It was an okay shower—not huge, but not a tiny box like he'd expected. It would do, and as long as he was in there with Des, he didn't care. He was content enough to watch her dip her head back and let the water run over her. And when she stepped out of the way, he did the same.

"Turn around," he said.

She did, and he grabbed the bottle of body wash, poured some into his hand, and lathered it up.

He liked having the freedom of touching her, of exploring her skin. He lifted her arms and watched as the soap trailed down in slow rivers. He drew her hair over her shoulder to expose her back, then massaged the soap in, using his thumbs to dig in where her muscles were taut with tension, rewarded with her moans of pleasure.

His cock tightened at the sounds she made. He turned her toward the water so she could rinse, then he came around to her front and lathered his hands.

She lifted her gaze to him and kept it trained on his face while he rubbed soap over the front of her shoulders, her collarbone, and over her breasts. Naturally, he lingered at her breasts, the soap slick as he cupped the globes in his hands.

Her chest rose and fell with her quickened breaths as he rubbed his thumbs over her pebbled nipples, then, dropped to his knees so he could wash her legs.

"I could get used to this," she said. "I like your hands on me."

"Rinse," he said.

She took a step back under the water, rinsing the soap off, then stepped forward. Logan slid his hands up her calves, water running over his hands as he snaked his fingers over the backs of her knees.

Des giggled, obviously ticklish there. He filed that information away for another time as he directed her legs apart, then raised himself up to put his mouth on her center.

She gasped when he touched her with his tongue to taste her. Here, she was hot, moist, and primed for him.

"Logan." Even with the rush of water in the shower, he heard the way she said his name. He always liked hearing his name fall from her lips, especially when she was tight with passion. Like now, when she arched against him, silently asking for more of what he was giving her.

He lashed his tongue against her soft flesh, holding tight to her buttocks as he laved her clit and took her over the edge, listening to her passionate moans as she bucked against him with her orgasm.

She was shaking as he stood. He took her mouth in a kiss that left him rock hard and hungering with a need to possess her.

"Now it's my turn to wash you." She grabbed the soap and lathered her hands. He loved how small her hands were, and he had no objection to the slide of her fingers over his skin, the way she dug her nails across his shoulders, then pressed her thumbs in, lightly massaging his muscles.

She washed his back, swirling her palms over his flesh as she moved ever lower. He let out a groan when she reached around, caressing his cock with her soapy hands, lingering there to stroke him.

"Now, rinse," she said.

He stepped into the water and rinsed off, then turned around.

When Des dropped to her knees, he held on to the side of the shower, water pouring down his back and over his shoulders. She took him in her hands and stroked him, teasing him as her lips hovered close and she tilted her head back to give him a look that burned him and made it hard for him to take a breath.

She took him between her lips and flicked her tongue over the soft head, and he let out a groan. His gaze fixed on her full lips, the way she pressed them over his cock and brought his shaft inside her sweet, hot mouth.

He had nothing to grab on to but the glass shower doors for support, and hoped like hell he didn't wrench the damn door clear off the track as Des took him deep and nearly shattered him right then.

She had a sweet tongue and a devilish mind because she held him and teased him and destroyed him with her mouth. And when he was near the brink, when he could feel everything within him ready to explode, he whispered her name.

"Des."

She held tight to him, refusing to yield even as he exploded. He shook with the force of his orgasm, his gaze never leaving her face as he watched her take what he gave until he had nothing left. It was the most intimate act, and it had left him weak and nearly brought him to his knees. He was blinded by the sheer force of the pleasure she'd given him, and nearly wrecked by it. He reached for her, pulling her up to kiss her, tunneling his fingers into her hair to hold tight to her, because he was so far out of balance right now he needed her as a lifeline.

And when he found that balance again, he pushed her under the water so he could wet her hair, then reached for her shampoo and washed her hair, enjoying rubbing his fingers into her scalp.

"Mmm, that feels good," she said. "I don't think I want you to stop. Do you think you could rub my head for about an hour?"

"I could rub a lot of parts of you for a very long time."

"God, Logan. The things you do to me."

He rinsed her hair, then she applied conditioner and rinsed that out. He washed his hair, then he turned off the water, which by now was getting cool. Not that he minded since his body was plenty heated up by their shower play.

Des opened the cabinet near the shower and handed him a towel. He dried off, watching Des as she towel-dried her hair, then ran a comb through it.

"That's enough," he said, taking her hand and pulling her into the bedroom.

He flung himself onto the bed, bringing Des down on top of him, already hungry for more of her.

"What? You're not exhausted from that bout in the shower?"

He cupped her butt. "Not even close."

She wriggled against him. "You have a lot of stamina, Logan."

He gave her a grin and rolled her under him. "You have no idea, Des."

# *Chapter 12*

---

DES MET UP with Colt, Tony, and the others early in the day. Colt had made breakfast and given her a call so she could come over and join them. And as Logan had slipped out of bed in the middle of the night, telling her he had to be up before dawn to see to some things on the ranch, she was alone.

Unfortunately. But she understood he had work to do, so she'd kissed him good-bye and told him they'd be over sometime mid-morning to help out.

It was great to see Tony, Sarah, and Callie again.

"I heard you all partying last night."

"As much partying as we could do, given the location," Tony said. "But it's enough to just be here with Colt."

Colt put his arm around Tony as Des leaned back against the counter and surveyed them all while sipping her coffee.

Sarah and Callie were their closest friends in L.A. and also knew about Colt and Tony, often hanging out with them in groups. Sarah, a striking, tall brunette with a killer figure, was a makeup artist, and Callie, the cutest petite blond who wore her hair pixie short and had amazing piercings, was a hairstylist. And then there was Tony, drop-dead, movie-star gorgeous with black hair and deep dark brown eyes, such a beautiful contrast to Colt's blond surfer-boy looks. Tony really should have been in front of the camera, but made his living as a cinematographer. Having them all in the business meant they had a lot in common. And they all knew how treacherous the media and gossip sites were, so they held Tony and Colt's secret close.

"Were you in L.A.?" Des asked Tony.

He shook his head. "No. I just finished a shoot in London." He yawned. "This jet lag is killing me."

"You can sleep on the plane," Colt said. "Because I'm going to spend every minute with you that I can."

"No problem there. I've missed you."

Colt squeezed his hand. "Ditto."

"You two are disgustingly sweet together," Sarah said. "Why can't I find a guy as great as either one of you?"

"They're gay or taken," Callie said. "Or they all live somewhere other than L.A., because they sure as hell don't live where we do. And the awesome ones aren't in the movie business, because most of the men we deal with are pricks."

Des laughed. "Amen to that."

"Hey, we're men," Colt said.

"Yeah, and you're gay. And taken. So I've made my point," Callie said.

Tony laughed. "Sorry, honey. You and Sarah—and Des—are amazing women. Someday you'll find amazing men."

"Unlike James," Colt said with a wrinkle of his nose.

"Ugh. James was an ass," Callie said. "I can't believe he cheated on you, Des."

"And with Kristina Parker? Please." Sarah shook her head. "I can't believe any man would dip his pen in her inkwell."

Des snorted. "Well, he's getting what he deserves. She's

a media-hounding shrew, and she'll drive him crazy. Honestly, I wasn't all that broken up over it."

Callie studied her. "You weren't, were you? Why is that?"

Des shrugged. "I guess I just wasn't that into him."

Sarah laughed. "His loss. I think you're amazing."

"So does the owner of the ranch here."

Des shot Colt a look. "Shut up, Colt."

"Ooh," Tony said. "Is there a hot romance brewing between you and a cowboy?"

"No." Des didn't want anyone to know what was going on between her and Logan. Besides, it was just sex. And she wanted to keep it quiet. Sarah and Callie would make a big deal about getting to know Logan.

"Come on, Des," Callie said. "Spill."

"Nothing to spill. He's been nice and accommodating to everyone on the crew. Actually, mostly it's his house manager, Martha. She's a motherly type. You're all going to love her. Plus, she's a big fan."

"And you're deflecting the topic away from the sexy rancher," Sarah said, eyeing her suspiciously. "Why is that?"

"She has the hots for him. And the feeling is mutual. It's very obvious," Colt said. "You'll all see it today."

Des wanted to throw her shoe at Colt. "It is not obvious. I told you, it's mainly Martha. And you all had better be on your best behavior around her. She's been very sweet to us."

"Best behavior today," Tony said. "We won't let you down."

"But we're going to be watching you, Des," Callie said, using two fingers to point toward her own eyes, then back at Des. "Watching you and the rancher."


LOGAN WAS GLAD he'd gotten up before dawn to get some work done this morning, because it was ten a.m. and already hellishly hot. It was going to be a long day, made even worse by all the people who would soon be piling in.

But this was one of Martha's favorite days, short of Christmas Day, and he'd make sure it was a fun day for her.

He and the crew had covered all the tables with the brightly colored tablecloths Martha had provided, and then they'd gone to the shed and dragged out the fireworks he'd bought earlier in the week. There were kegs of beer spread throughout the yard and pitchers of iced tea in the house. As far as he knew, everything was finished except for the food, which was already in preparation. Meat had been cooking since early this morning and would be ready in plenty of time.

People were already starting to arrive, though some of those were Martha's friends from church who liked to come early and help her set up. He waved to them as he hollered for one of the hands to show people where to park.

Though most everyone who came every year already knew. Before long, rows of cars had started to pull down the long gravel driveway. He had Caleb and Jared, a couple of his cousins, at the entrance to the ranch to make sure it was people from town and neighboring ranches actually driving through the gates. Those Hollywood photographers weren't welcome today—or any day, for that matter.

Logan hoped the paparazzi would want to take a day off and enjoy the holiday. But from the reports he was getting from Caleb, they were lined up along the gates taking pictures of people driving in.

Whatever. They could take all the photos they wanted— at the gate. That was as far as they were getting.

He'd gone into the house to grab an iced tea, then got waylaid by several instructions from Martha, who needed him to carry a few things outside. By the time he found his glass of tea again, an hour had passed and the ice had melted. Plus, he was sweaty, so he went upstairs to wash off the sweat and change his shirt.

He made his way back downstairs and heard Des's

voice, his lips curving as he remembered the way she'd cried out as he thrust into her last night.

Since getting a hard-on with a house full of people would be a bad idea, he cleared his mind of thoughts of a naked Des, blew out a breath, and found her and Colt in the kitchen with Martha, some of Martha's friends, and a few people he didn't know.

Des looked gorgeous today, wearing two tank tops, very short-shorts, and tennis shoes. Her hair was pulled back in a ponytail, and she wore a couple of long necklaces. He wanted to drag her up to his bedroom and have his way with her for about six damn hours.

Or longer.

"Oh, there you are, Logan," Martha said, giving him a warm smile. "I was wondering if you were hiding from me so I wouldn't give you something else to do."

"You know I wouldn't do that. What do you need?"

Martha looped her arm in his. He could tell she was happy and relaxed, instead of jittery or nervous. This was Martha's day to shine. "I don't need anything, but Colt and Desiree brought some friends along. Would you two like to introduce them to Logan?"

Des eyed him warily. He had no idea what that was about, but she was a woman, and as such, he knew they were subject to moods.

"Logan," Colt said, "these are our friends from L.A. This is Tony, Callie, and Sarah."

Logan shook all their hands. "Nice to meet all of you. Welcome to the ranch."

"It's an amazing ranch, Logan," Callie said. "Just driving over here from the set was an incredible view."

"Des tells us you have like . . . forty thousand acres or so?" Sarah asked.

"Somewhere around that, yeah."

"You must love living on so much land," Tony said.

"It's all I know, since I grew up here. But yeah, it's my way of life, so I love what I do."

"I can imagine," Tony said. "Beef cattle? Angus?"

"Yeah. You know cattle?"

"I was raised on a farm in North Dakota, so yeah. I sure miss the openness of the land. Would you mind a short tour? If you're too busy, I'd understand."

Logan accepted the glass of iced tea Martha handed him. "I've got some time for that. Let's head outside."

"Oh, my God. Look at all these dogs," Sarah said.

Des smiled as Sarah dropped and petted all the ranch dogs. She had to join in, too, and so did everyone else.

"The dogs are really popular," Logan said to Tony.

"We love animals. Most of us live in tiny condos or apartments and don't have dogs or cats. So it's nice to have a big spread like this—and lots of animals to love on. I miss being around them."

"I couldn't imagine not having animals around. I guess because I grew up with them," Logan said.

After everyone was finished with the dogs, they moved on down the road, though the dogs followed.

Des watched as Logan bonded with Tony, unable to help the smile that broke out on her face as she listened to him talk cattle-ranch operations. The rest of them followed behind, Des admiring the way Logan's jeans fit his most spectacular butt, the way his scuffed boots looked as he walked like he was such a part of the land. His T-shirt stretched tight across his muscled back, making her itch to run her hands over his naked skin.

"Oh. My. God," Callie said as they meandered along several feet behind Logan and Tony. "You did not tell me Logan was so friggin' hot."

Des's lips curved. "I didn't know I was supposed to."

"Please tell me you have zero interest in him and I can hit on him immediately," Callie said.

"Screw that," Sarah said. "I'll fight you for him, Callie."

Des had no idea how to respond to that. "I guess you're welcome to try."

"I think what Des is trying to tell you is that you can

try, but she's wearing him down almost nightly by screwing his brains out."

Des shot Colt a look, laughing as she answered him. "That is not at all what I'm trying to say. And besides, it's not every night."

"Aha!" Callie said. "I knew it. Damn you, girl. He is smokin'."

Her gaze tracked to Logan, who leaned against the fence talking to Tony. "He is, isn't he?"

And for as long as she remained on this movie shoot, he was hers.

At least she'd try to make sure it stayed that way. She supposed today would be a good opportunity to check the temperature of Hope, see if any other woman had put a claim on him. If not, great. If so . . .

Huh. She had no idea what she'd do about that, because they'd never once discussed their relationship, they didn't really have a relationship, had never even gone out on a date, which meant she couldn't really call Logan hers.

That kind of sucked. But that was the nature of her job and the types of relationships she built when she traveled so much. She couldn't very well expect Logan to enter into an exclusive relationship with her when in less than two months she'd be gone. That would be a ridiculous request. He was free to see whomever he wanted to. And so was she.

The problem was, she only wanted to see him. At least right now. And while she was only seeing him, she'd be damned if she wanted him to see anyone else.

So how the hell was she supposed to broach the subject with him? It wasn't like he enjoyed deep, meaningful conversations. Especially about relationships.

Maybe she should just let things between them go unsaid. Though Des wasn't much for letting things go unsaid. It went against her nature. If she had something on her mind, she usually blurted it out. Things that went unsaid had a tendency to fester and get ugly later. Her mother was always the quiet, keep-your-feelings-to-yourself kind of person. Which is why she'd allowed her father to move her twelve times in thirty years.

That wasn't going to happen to Des. If she wanted something, she was damn well going to ask for it, just like if she didn't want something, she'd say that, too.

So after Callie, Sarah, and Colt headed over to join Logan and Tony, Des wandered over, too, trying to keep it light between them, until Tony started talking to the others about the cattle and ranch operations. Des drew Logan aside.

"I have a question to ask you, and I expect you to be honest."

"Okay."

"Are you seeing anyone else?"

He frowned. "Huh?"

"You know. Some other woman."

"No. Why would you think that?"

"I didn't think that. I was just . . . wondering."

"The answer is no."

"Okay. Would you mind not seeing anyone else while I'm here?"

His lips curved. "You mean like today?"

She smacked him on the arm. "No. I mean like while I'm here on your ranch."

"So if you're not on the ranch I can see someone?"

She pinned him with a look. "Logan, I'm trying to be serious here."

"Sorry. Des, I don't have relationships with women. Hell, I've seen you more than I've ever seen any other woman."

Her body tingled. "Great. Then let's keep doing that."

"Fine."

"Okay, then."

He pulled her against him and wrapped his arms around her. "Just so you know, this whole temporary exclusivity thing goes both ways."

She palmed his chest. "I'm not interested in seeing anyone but you."

"Good. Then let's keep it that way. While you're on this ranch."

Then he surprised the hell out of her by planting one very hot, very deep kiss on her, right in front of her friends.

"Holy shit," she heard Callie say.

When he released her, she met his gaze, saw the fire in his eyes, and nearly melted into the ground right there.

"Deal?" he asked.

"Yes. Deal."

He took her by the hand and they waded into the crowd of people. She felt his stamp of possession on her, and as her friends came up beside her, Callie gave her a very smug, very knowing look. She cast a smile at her friends, just daring them to make a smart-ass comment.

None of them did, whether because of the way she'd glared at them or because they were all too afraid of Logan's reaction, she didn't know. Frankly, she didn't care. She felt sixteen again, like a boy had just asked her to go out with him. She knew it was silly, and yes, it was temporary, but today, she felt really damn good. So what was wrong with that?

As she gazed up at Logan and he gave her a look of pure hungry desire, she decided there wasn't a single thing wrong with how she felt at the moment.

Sometimes even temporary flings could be fun.

# Chapter 13

LOGAN HAD NO idea what had transpired earlier in the day with Des, but she'd asked him about seeing other people, and maybe it was the challenging look in her eyes, or because she'd been with her friends, but something possessive took hold of him at that moment and he'd decided that while she was filming her movie, she was his.

Hell of a thing, considering he was a man who didn't have relationships, who rarely invited women to spend the night at his house. Yet, here he was at the annual Fourth of July picnic, with nearly half the town of Hope in attendance, and he had his hand firmly grasped in Des's for everyone to see.

Not that he cared much what anyone thought. He never had.

But then his brother and Emma came up to them. Of course, the first thing Luke's gaze zeroed in on was Logan holding Des's hand. And damned if he was going to shake loose of her. He'd made a commitment—well, sort of—and he wasn't going to back down, no matter how much of a smirk his brother was giving him right now.

Emma hugged Des. "I'm so glad you came today," Emma said.

"I wouldn't miss it. All the food, and I've heard the fireworks show is legendary."

"Oh, it definitely is. Come on, there are some friends here I want you to meet." Emma tugged Des by the hand. "Logan, I'm going to drag her away from you for a while, if you don't mind."

Logan nodded. "I don't mind."

He watched Des walk away, and soon she was lost in the crowd.

"Beer?" he asked Luke.

"You know it."

They headed over to the keg and Luke poured them both a cupful of beer. "Let's go grab a seat somewhere."

They found an unoccupied picnic table, though it took a while to get there, since they both had to stop and greet several people, including Carter Richards, one of Luke's best friends, who grabbed a beer and joined them.

They spent some time talking about work, about the ranch, and Carter's auto shop businesses as well as the movie crew that were milling about meeting all the people from town.

"How's the shoot going?" Carter asked him.

"Fine, I guess. I've been over there a couple of times to watch them shoot. Looks like it's going good."

"He's dating the actress who's starring in the movie, though," Luke said.

Logan shot his brother a look. Luke grinned back at him.

"No, shit," Carter said. "Desiree Jenkins? She's a beauty."

"Yeah." Logan took a sip of beer.

"So how serious is it?" Carter asked.

"It's not." And Logan wasn't going to get into a conversation about Des with either his brother or Carter.

"I'm taking you don't want to talk about this." Carter smiled and took a long swallow of his beer.

"I don't," Logan said.

"Yeah, but it's so much fun to probe," Luke said, obviously unwilling to let the subject drop. "I saw you and Des holding hands earlier."

"What are you, twelve?" Logan asked. "Mind your own business."

"Ooh, they were holding hands," Carter said. "It must be serious. I don't think I've ever seen you out and about with a woman before, Logan."

"Maybe that's because I keep my personal business to myself."

"Mind if I join in?"

Logan hadn't seen his friend Sebastian Palmer in a while. Bash ran the No Hope At All bar in town.

"Bash. Thought you'd have the bar open today," Logan said.

Bash swung his legs over and took a seat at the picnic table. "Why would I do that, when I knew everyone in town would be here? Besides, Martha makes great food, and I can drink beer instead of serving it up."

Logan grinned. "Glad to see you."

"So what you're telling me is that all the drunks will be on the ranch today," Luke said.

Bash nodded. "Pretty much." He turned to Logan. "Nice fan club gathered at the gates. How's the movie business?"

Logan shrugged. "Hell if I know. I just rent the land."

"And he's dating the leading lady," Carter added.

Bash gave him a look. "No, shit. That didn't take long. I never knew you had such smooth moves."

"We're not dating." Christ, all he'd done was hold her hand. And this was just with the guys—his friends, who were gossiping about it like the Sunday after-church ladies.

"So you're not with her?" Bash looked confused.

"Not in a relationship sense, no."

Luke laughed and slapped him on the back. "Poor, Logan. You don't even know how to define your relationship with Des. Does she know this?"

"Know what?"

They all stood as Des came over to the table. "Your boyfriend/not boyfriend has no idea how to explain what the two of you have going on," Luke said.

Logan panicked, just knowing that they were all going to tell Des how he'd colossally fucked this up. And then she was going to be pissed, and this easygoing thing between them was going to be over.

Des quirked a smile and slid into a spot next to Logan. "Oh, that's easy. We're having smoking hot sex as often as we can get our hands on each other."

Leave it to Des to shut everyone up.

Luke cleared his throat and Carter laughed.

"I like this woman," Bash said, grinning at Logan, then stood and leaned over the table, his hand outstretched toward Des. "I'm Bash."

She shook his hand. "Nice to meet you, Bash."

Carter introduced himself, too, and Logan exhaled. "Have fun with the girls?"

"I did. And my friends seem to have disappeared."

"They'll be fine. I saw Colt leading them down the path a ways toward the corral. I think he's showing them the horses."

"Okay."

Luke brought Des a beer. "Thanks," she said. "So, you've all been gossiping about Logan and me? I expected that from all the women, not a bunch of guys."

Bash laughed. "We weren't exactly gossiping. We just asked a simple question that Logan had a problem answering."

"I see." She looked over at him. "The sex answer usually shuts everyone up."

Logan nodded. "I'll be sure to use that answer with the ladies from church."

Des laughed. "Okay, maybe not them. But everyone else would be fine."

"You really don't care much about gossip, do you?" Logan asked.

She took a sip of beer. "Not really. So much is written about me in the gossip columns, anyway. Most of it untrue. Why would I care if you say something and it gets out? It's true, isn't it?"

She was so refreshingly honest, she kept him off balance. "I guess it is."

Des turned to Carter and Bash. "So tell me about yourselves. I know Luke's the cop. What do you both do?"

"I own some auto repair and body shops in Hope and in Tulsa," Carter said.

"I could have used you when I backed my Honda into a fence post," Des said with a wry grin.

"Recently?" he asked.

She laughed. "No. Back when I was a teenager. I try to avoid being an idiot these days. And I've since learned how to use a rearview mirror."

Carter nodded. "I don't think many of us escaped the teen driving years unscathed."

"I did," Logan said.

"So did I. That's because we learned to drive as soon as our legs were long enough to reach the pedals," Luke said.

Logan nodded. "Yeah, living on a ranch has its advantages. We were maneuvering tractors around before any of the rest of you got your permits."

"Braggarts," Bash said. "Some of us didn't get early driving lessons and had to learn the hard way."

"So you're saying you had your share of car issues?" Des asked.

Logan let out a snort. "How do you think he earned the nickname Bash?"

"Oh." Des looked at him. "That bad, huh?"

"Hey," Bash said. "My name is a shortened version of Sebastian."

"And because you drove too fast and got into three fender benders in the first six months after you got your driver's license," Logan added.

"Really," Des said.

Bash shrugged. "Those weren't all my fault."

"Yes, they were," Luke said. "You were a road menace."

"But you all still got in the car with me."

"You got your license first," Carter said. "We had no choice."

Des laughed. "And what do you do for a living, Bash?"

"I own a bar."

"In Hope?"

"Yeah."

"How fun." She turned to Logan. "We should go there some night."

"If you'd like."

"Do you have music?" she asked Bash.

"Yeah. And pool tables, and TVs. A little of everything."

"Awesome. We'll definitely come by."

"I'll hold you to that."

Logan finally stood. "I'm going to take Des for a walk, see if we can find her friends and introduce her to a few people."

"In other words, you don't want us grilling her anymore," Luke said.

"Yeah, that's pretty much it."

Des waved. "See you later, guys."

He didn't even think, just slid his hand in hers.

"You sure about this?" she asked, looking down where their hands were linked. "People might talk about us, or God forbid, ask you more questions you're too uncomfortable to answer."

"Okay, so I didn't handle that well. After our talk, I

wasn't prepared yet to deal with the onslaught of those assholes hitting me with questions about our relationship."

She laughed. "It's not a problem, you know. I can maintain a respectable distance."

"I don't want you at a distance. I want you next to me."

"Where you can keep an eye on me?"

He stopped, turned to her. "No. Where I can touch you and look at you and drag you into a corner somewhere and kiss you."

"I like the sound of that."

She'd thought he was joking, but as they got near the side of the house, he pulled her down the walk, toward the back of the house. No one was back there, and he cupped the side of her neck and put his lips over hers, kissing her deeply, thoroughly, until she was dizzy. She raised up on her toes and wrapped her arms around him, drawing him closer.

And when he pulled away, she saw the heat of desire in his heavy-lidded eyes.

She blew out a breath. "Wow."

"Yeah. Too bad there are hundreds of people here, because right now I'd like to drag you up to my bedroom and—"

"Oh, Logan, how are you?"

He quickly put Des in front of him as a woman appeared in the backyard. "Mrs. Springfield. Thanks for coming today. This is Desiree Jenkins. Desiree, this is Bonita Springfield. She and her husband, Ralph, own a farm nearby."

Des felt the hard evidence of Logan's erection against her backside. She smiled. "Very nice to meet you, Mrs. Springfield."

"Oh, call me Bonnie. I was looking for Martha. Have you seen her?"

"No, ma'am. I haven't. You might check inside."

"I'll do that. Nice to meet you, Desiree."

"You, too, Bonnie."

Mrs. Springfield went inside, and Des exhaled, then

turned around to face Logan. "That's what you get for dragging girls behind the house to steal kisses."

"It was worth it."

He was right about that. He took her hand and they made their way toward the front of the house again.

"So tell me about your visit with Emma."

"She introduced me to her friends, Jane and Chelsea. They're awesome. They want to plan a girls' night out sometime while I'm here."

He rolled his eyes. "That sounds . . . interesting."

"I'm seriously contemplating it. I don't have a lot of girlfriends."

"What about . . . what were their names again? Callie and Sarah?"

"They're mainly friends of Tony and Colt."

"I see."

"Yeah. So, anyway. They talked about going into Tulsa and having a spa day followed by a night on the town."

"And you'd like to do that."

"I'd like to do that. Like I said, I don't have a lot of friends, and Emma seems really nice."

"She is really nice."

"In Hollywood, most of the women I know are actresses. So, of course, all we talk about is being a working actress, and what role we're auditioning for, and blah blah blah. It'd be nice to be with women who aren't actresses or in the industry."

"They'll probably ask you about your work, though."

"I don't mind, because we'd be able to talk about their work, too. Which isn't acting."

"I can see your point."

"I'm sure you like talking with your friends about things other than cattle ranching, right?"

"True enough."

"Or do you even go out with your friends?"

"Not really."

She paused, turned to him. "Why not?"

He shrugged. "I don't know. Days are long on the ranch, and then I go to bed."

She shook her head. "Logan, you've got to get out more. Life is short, and meant to be lived. You have to get out and party. Get laid."

He raised his brows and gave her a direct look. "I am getting laid."

"Yes. And I'm sure I'm not the only woman you've been with in years, so obviously you get out some."

"Okay, I get out some."

"Or do women come knocking at your door just to get a piece of you?"

He didn't say anything.

"You have got to be kidding me. Your prowess is that well known?"

"I don't even know how to respond to that."

As Des looked around while they resumed walking, she noticed they got looks from a lot of women, something she hadn't paid attention to before. So maybe Logan was a popular guy. A single rancher—owner of a very big ranch, as a matter of fact. A guy who didn't spend a lot of time hanging out at bars and doing a ton of womanizing. That would make him quite the catch in a small town like Hope. She'd just bet women were clamoring for a piece of him. Mysterious men were always attractive, and a quiet, incredibly handsome and sexy-yet-keep-to-himself kind of guy like Logan would be very attractive.

"So . . . what do you do, exactly? Go down a list of available women and just call one up when you need some action?"

"No."

"Then tell me how it works. They call you up and you decide if you're in the mood to get laid? Oh, scratch that. You're a man. You're always in the mood to get laid, right?"

He frowned. "I'm not having this conversation with you."

. She laughed and slipped her arm through his. "I'm seriously curious, Logan. What it must be like to be in such demand. Do they line up at the gates at the end of the workday and you walk up there and choose the one you want?"

"Now that's just ridiculous. They take a number. First come, first served."

She tilted her head back and laughed. "I'll bet there's a long line, too."

He crooked her a devilishly sexy smile. "Darlin', you have no idea."

Judging from the lingering looks cast in their direction from many of the women at the party, she could imagine there was a line of women waiting to get to Logan. Not that she could blame them. She counted herself lucky he chose to be with her at the moment.

Not that she'd given him much choice, since she'd cornered him and thrown herself at him. Then again, he could have said no and pushed her away, right?

She couldn't resist her smug smile. Today, at least, he belonged to her, and she intended to enjoy every second with him.

They ate amazing barbecue, and she stuffed herself on Martha's potato salad, ate copious amounts of fruit salad, then made a mess of her face eating corn on the cob. Logan helped her out by wiping corn pieces from the side of her mouth with his napkin. They'd found Colt, Tony, Callie, and Sarah and had grabbed a long table along with Emma, Luke, Bash, and Carter, and after introductions had been made, they'd all bonded and had traded stories of life in a small town versus life in Hollywood.

Callie definitely had her eyes on Bash. Not that she could blame her. What red-blooded single woman wouldn't? Bash was gorgeous and had obviously come to the party without a date. Colt made it a point to sit near Sarah and not next to Tony, though Des knew where his heart wanted to be, so she cast him a sympathetic gaze. Colt just shrugged and smiled at her.

As the day wore on, Des was amazed by the number of people who'd shown up.

"Do you always get this many people?" she asked Logan.

He nodded. "It's a big deal. And the fireworks are pretty cool. But I think we have more than the usual crowd, likely due to you and Colt being here."

She'd met and talked to a lot of people today, yet not once had she ever felt rushed or crowded. People stopped and shook her hand, and she'd taken a few pictures, but most of the folks had been extremely courteous. Not at all what she was used to from other places.

"People here are nice. Usually I'm bombarded by crowds. Everyone here has been so polite."

"You're here to enjoy yourself and relax. This is your day off. No one wants to be rude and trample on that. If they see you have a spare minute, they'll want to say hello and maybe get a picture with you, but no one's going to intrude."

Des took a deep breath and let it out. She could get used to a lifestyle like this, where she was treated just like everyone else. And no paparazzi in sight. It was idyllic and peaceful, and she couldn't recall having a better day. Even Theo hadn't bothered her today. He'd come to the barbecue, but he'd stuck to hanging out with his crew or talking to the people of the town. He'd steered clear of her.

Which meant today couldn't get any better.

Or maybe it could, since she hadn't yet had any significant alone time with Logan, and she was definitely looking forward to that.

There was still a lot of fun stuff left in the day.

"Excuse me," Logan said, getting up. "I'll be back in a few minutes."

He went over to the table where Luke was sitting, then whispered something in Luke's ear. Luke motioned to Bash and Carter. Suddenly, they'd all gotten up and disappeared into the crowd.

Emma and Jane came over to sit with her. "Any idea what that's about?"

Des shrugged. "No idea."

"It's too early for fireworks."

"Maybe they're off to have a shot of tequila," Callie said. "And if so, how rude of them not to share."

Emma laughed. "There's plenty of hard liquor in the house. You're welcome to it."

"In this heat, I think I'll stick to tea today. But later tonight when it gets dark, that tequila might sound really good."

About a half hour later, they reappeared. And with them, Theo, who shot off in the opposite direction.

Des stood. "What happened?"

Logan gently pushed on her shoulder to sit her back down, then pulled up a seat next to her. "Nothing. The guys and I just had a . . . discussion with your director."

Colt frowned. "What's going on with Theo?"

Des sighed. "He came to my trailer several days ago and hit on me."

"He did not," Colt said.

"Yeah. And when I turned him down, he threatened me and said he'd make sure I never worked again."

"That perverted sonofabitch," Sarah said, shaking her head. "He's such a snake."

"I took care of it," Des said. "I threatened to go to the press and get some of my actress friends to do the same, and blow the lid off his cheating ways."

Callie laughed. "Good for you, honey. Someone should. His wife is a real sweetheart and doesn't deserve to be treated like that."

"What did you do, Logan?" Colt asked.

Logan didn't answer.

But Luke did. "We took him into the barn and had a . . . discussion with him about the appropriate way to treat a lady."

"And what could happen to him if he ever makes a threat against Des again," Bash added.

"There's a right way and a wrong way to treat a woman, especially on my ranch," Logan said. "I don't care what kind of papers I signed allowing the movie to be filmed. You threaten someone on my property, and I'm going to do something about it."

"I didn't see any bruises on his face," Colt said.

"Oh, I think Logan got his point across. Within the limits of the law." Luke grinned.

Tony sprouted a wide grin. "He's not used to someone calling him out. He was probably so scared he pissed himself."

Colt snorted. "I would love to have been there for it. He'll probably surround himself with his bodyguards the rest of his stay here on the ranch."

"As long as he leaves me alone, I don't care what he does," Des said. "He's an arrogant ass."

"But a very good director, unfortunately," Colt added.

Des sighed. "So true. But I don't think I ever want to work with him again."

"He won't be bothering you," Logan said.

Des's heart swelled. She couldn't believe he'd done this for her. She turned to him. "Thank you."

His lips curved. "You're welcome."

*Chapter 14*

TYPICALLY ON THE Fourth of July, Logan wandered among the crowd, stopped and talked to everyone, but spent the day as an observer. He had no complaints about that. This was his day to relax, eat good food, drink some beer, and maybe end the night with a beautiful woman who had caught his eye.

Right now his eye was on a certain raven-haired beauty laughing with a group of her friends and his, with different people from town winding their way through to stop and visit. Des had easily integrated herself with the people of Hope. And it wasn't because they were starstruck, either. Okay, maybe some of the folks in the town might be, but not his brother or his best friend, and not Emma or Jane or Chelsea. They lived way too much in the real world that had real-life problems to fawn over celebrities, especially any who were arrogant and full of themselves. So it said a lot about Des—and her friends—that they had been so easily accepted into their circle.

Logan liked the people Des associated herself with.

Colt, of course, was an actor, but the other people weren't. She didn't need to be seen with people who only graced the covers of magazines. She was comfortable with people from all walks of life, and as she sat having an intense conversation with Chelsea, a high school math teacher, Samantha Reasor, who owned the local flower shop in town, as well as Megan Lee, who ran the bakery and coffee shop, it looked like they had all become the best of friends already. One of them would say something and the rest of them would nod, then the other would speak, and they all would laugh. But the one thing Logan noticed was that Des wasn't the one doing all the talking. She was mainly listening while the others talked, unlike a lot of Hollywood types who liked to talk about themselves.

The one thing he'd discovered about Des was that she asked a lot of questions, wanted to find out about people, and she was a great listener. She wasn't at all the Hollywood type person he'd expected.

And he still didn't know what the hell he was doing with her, or why she was interested in him, when a young stud like Colt was there to share the movie with her, and Colt's trailer was only twenty feet or so from hers. She and Colt spent a lot of time with each other and had known each other for years. He certainly was good-looking. And young.

Logan shrugged and stopped trying to figure it out. Maybe it was just like she said, and she and Colt were just friends.

"Enjoying the view?" Bash asked, handing him a cup of beer.

Logan took it and nodded. "Yeah."

They walked together, finding seats on the porch. "She's pretty amazing, Logan. She's fun to be around and has a great sense of humor. She's also young, beautiful, and loaded with talent. A real rising star."

He took a long swallow of beer. "Yeah."

"So what the hell is she doing with you?"

"No idea."

Bash laughed. "That's what I've always liked about you. No ego. Maybe she's the lucky one, being with you."

"I don't think so."

"Come on. She gets to spend time on the ranch, and who wouldn't enjoy that? You know she's bombarded all the time with media and people who want a piece of her. With you, she can just be herself. You offer her something no one else can. You don't ask anything of her, and she's free to walk away, knowing you'll never put strings on her."

Logan had never thought of it that way. "I guess that's true."

"Because if anyone is a no-strings-attached kind of guy, Logan, it's definitely you, right?"

Everyone knew him so well. Including his best friend. "Yeah, that's me all right." He tracked Des through the crowd, his gaze settling on her. She looked so pretty today—hell, just like every day. She was smiling with a group of people, some she knew, some he knew she didn't. She gave equal attention to everyone, listening to them talking, answering questions, and putting her arm around Emilia Gray, one of the ladies from church who had to be well in her eighties. Emilia's husband, Dale, whispered in Des's ear and she laughed.

Something tightened within Logan whenever she laughed.

"Or maybe that's changed?" Bash asked.

He pulled his attention away from Des and onto Bash. "What are you talking about?"

"I always wondered if you'd stay single, if there'd be no one in your life who'd make you crave settling down and raising a family."

"You of all people know how I feel about that."

"Yeah, I do. But I also see the way you're looking at Des, and I'm wondering what makes her different from the rest."

"She's no different from anyone else."

Bash's lips curved in that knowing, smart-ass way that always irritated Logan. "Isn't she?"

"No."

"You know, Logan, one of the things I've always liked about you—actually, the reason we've always been friends—is because you're a no-bullshit kind of guy. You don't lie to me, and you've never lied to yourself. You've always been straight with me about everything, including how you feel." Bash inclined his head toward Des. "So what's up with her?"

Logan zeroed his attention in on Des. The way the breeze blew through her hair, and how she didn't fuss with it. The way she paid attention to Emilia and Dale as if they were the most important people at the picnic. The way her lips curved, and how he remembered the taste of her. "I don't know. I guess maybe she is different. Sexy, ballsy as hell, really honest with her feelings and her outlook. I like her. She's actually a very nice person."

"You've been with nice women before."

"That's true."

"So, again, why is she different, because I've never seen you so riveted to another woman the way you are with Des. And I know it's not the Hollywood thing."

"No. It's not the Hollywood thing."

"It's just her, isn't it?" Bash asked.

"I guess so." He looked at Bash. "But you and I both know she's not going to stay here. She's not going to make a life here. And that's not the kind of woman I'm looking for."

"Okay. So what happens if you fall in love with her and she heads back to Hollywood?"

"Not gonna happen. I don't fall in love."

Bash snorted. "Do you know how many times I've heard that same song and dance from the people I serve beers to? 'She doesn't love me. I don't love her. I don't need a woman in my life. I like being alone.' It's all bullshit, Logan. Everybody needs someone."

Logan shot a direct look at Bash. "Do *you*? Because it seems to me you don't have someone standing beside you."

Bash shrugged. "I've been down that road, and have the scorched earth of a broken marriage and the battle scars to show for it. But at least I tried. You haven't even given it a shot."

He'd never let anyone talk to him the way Bash did. But he and Bash had been friends since they were six years old, and Bash knew everything about him, about what he went through with his mother, and after his dad died. His friend knew about his reluctance to repeat the mistakes of the past, and had never judged him for it.

Until now. "You know how I feel, Bash."

"I do. I just don't want you to die alone."

Logan laughed. "Come on, man. I'm hardly alone. I have a whole family on the ranch."

"That's not the same thing as having someone in your bed at night and a house full of kids to pass on your legacy to. And you know what the hell I'm talking about, so don't shine me on with your bullshit about being happy with the way things are. Believe me, if anyone knows about the kind of crap a woman can rain down on you, it's me. I'm more aware than anyone you know, including your brother, who had his own past nightmares with a bad marriage. But even Luke got past it, despite the hell of your mother, and found himself a good woman. So maybe you can stop using her as an excuse and move forward with your life."

Logan dropped his chin and leveled a look at Bash. "You know, I didn't expect a lecture today."

"No, I imagine you didn't. But I've been thinking about you a lot lately. You have a lot to offer a woman."

"Not a woman like Des."

"Maybe not. And maybe if you see something you want, you should go after it and figure out how to make it work, no matter how hard it's going to be. Nothing worth having is easy."

"Now you sound like my dad."

Bash laughed. "I always liked your dad, so I'll take that as a compliment."

"I think you're spending too much time at the bar dispensing advice. It's all going to your head and you've got a know-it-all complex going."

"You think? How am I doing? Pretty good, huh?"

"You're an asshole."

Bash nudged his shoulder against Logan's. "Yeah, love you, too, buddy."

DES HAD A wonderful day, and from the looks of things, so had her friends. Callie had her eye on the gorgeous Bash, who seemed to have no problem spending time with the beautiful Callie, even though she was only going to be in town for the day. The two of them disappeared for a while, and when they came back, Callie's cheeks were pink and her hair was mussed up. Des grinned, making a mental note to ask Callie about that later.

"Having fun?" she asked Colt as they sat down and reconnected over some delicious coconut cream pie.

Colt nodded. "It's a great day. Hot as hell, tons of people around, and my friends are here. What more could I ask for?"

"Oh, I think you could ask for more."

Colt's gaze gravitated over to the fences, where Sarah and Tony were engaged in deep conversation. "Yeah, well, if wishes were horses . . ."

"You could have everything you wanted, Colt. All you have to do is want it badly enough."

"I want it, honey. More than you could know."

Des's gaze moved over the crowd and settled on Logan, surrounded by a group of guys. Some were the ranch hands, some were his friends, and there were a few more she hadn't met yet. He seemed relaxed, even laughed a few times.

Several times during the day she'd looked up to find him watching her. She had to admit she didn't mind that at all.

As if they had some kind of psychic bond, Logan averted his attention from the group of guys he was talking with, searching the crowd until his gaze settled on hers. His lips curved, and she felt the intensity of his look all the way down to her toes.

"Speaking of having something you want . . ." Colt said.

She sighed and clasped her hands together as she turned to face her friend. "I know. He really gets to me in ways I can't explain."

"You don't have to explain anything. I understand chemistry."

"I think it may be more than just chemistry and sexual attraction, Colt."

"Are you developing feelings for Logan?"

"I'm trying not to. You know as well as I do that the two of us are worlds apart."

Colt shrugged. "That doesn't mean anything if you two are right together."

"I just can't see it working. He's not looking for anything permanent, and I'm—"

"What? Restless? Unhappy?"

"How did you know?"

Colt slid his hand in hers. "Because I'm your best friend. I've known for a long time that career alone hasn't been satisfying you. You've wanted something more."

"Have I? Even I didn't know that until recently. I love what I do, Colt."

"So do I." He looked over at Tony. "But at some point, we realize there has to be more to life than just working all the time."

Had Des reached that point? She'd been working for seven years, hardly an eternity by anyone's standards. But she'd done it mostly alone. She'd had on-and-off relationships, but nothing serious with anyone, certainly nothing that would make her question her needs and desires and what she wanted in the future.

Until now.

And what did that even mean, that she was looking at Logan differently from any other man she'd ever known?

It meant nothing, because as she'd told Colt, there could be no future with someone like him.

Mainly because she knew he'd never want a relationship with her, or with anyone else.

They were having fun with each other, not looking to tie each other up with anything permanent, and it was best she just leave it that way.

When it started to get dark, she wound her way back to Logan.

"Having a good time?" he asked.

"I'm having a great day. Thank you for letting us come here."

"Wouldn't have it any other way. I'm glad you and your friends could spend the day with us."

"You have a good family and amazing friends. I've never been so relaxed."

He smiled. "Wait 'til you see the fireworks."

"I'm looking forward to those."

Colt and Tony and the others joined her, and Logan set them up with chairs near the fireworks area.

"Guard your eardrums," Logan said with a wide grin. "I'll be back later."

He disappeared with Ben, Luke, and a few of the crew and started setting up what looked like an armament of fireworks. The crowd gathered close, everyone grabbing a seat. Living in a city, Des had gone to some fireworks shows, but had never been able to set them off herself.

She wriggled in her chair and looked over at Colt, who had finally gotten the chance to sit next to Tony. The two of them might not be able to hold hands, but at least they could share this together, and for that Des was glad.

When the first firework went off, Des's eyes widened as the burst lit up the sky, the sound exploding like thunder. The crowd made sounds of approval, and so did she, as another followed right on its tail. Logan and his men kept the beautiful streamers coming one after another, from trailing sparklers to loud explosions of bright balls of color. For nearly a half hour, Des was treated to one of the best fireworks shows she'd ever seen, especially this close.

She had no idea what they'd spent on this spectacle, but it must have been a lot. Logan definitely knew how to entertain the town. At the end, everyone stood and applauded, then began to say their good-byes.

Emma found her and hugged her. "I'm going to call you next week to set up our girls' day."

"I'm looking forward to it."

Des helped Martha with the cleanup, as did Colt and their friends, so they had everything put away in no time at all, while Logan and his crew took care of clearing the fireworks debris outside.

"Thank you for all the wonderful food today, Martha," Des said as she slid the last of the plastic ware into the dishwasher.

Martha hugged her. "You were such a big help. And you were supposed to be a guest."

Des laughed. "I enjoyed helping out. You had quite the crowd today."

"And lots of helping hands, so it was no trouble at all. It isn't often we have this big a gathering. We always have so much fun with it. Did you like the fireworks?"

"They were spectacular. Like wow spectacular."

Martha hung up the dish towel and leaned against the counter. "Logan and Luke have always loved fireworks. So did their father. He was always such a big kid about it. When the boys were younger, the Fourth of July was a small affair. The missus hated fireworks, disliked all the noise. But when the boys got older, Mr. McCormack started getting bigger fireworks. Each year the show would expand a little, mostly, I think, to irritate her."

Des laughed.

"And then we started inviting some of the neighbors, because Mr. McCormack liked having people over."

"Well, who wouldn't? Isn't that the best part of a holiday?"

Martha crossed her arms. "Mrs. McCormack didn't enjoy that at all. She wanted to go on vacation in the summer, to somewhere tropical like the Caribbean or to Hawaii. Honestly. Like a working rancher had time to take summer vacations."

"That hardly seems likely, does it, given the amount of work to do around here?"

"True. Anyway, everyone else loved the Fourth of July get-togethers on the ranch—other than Mrs. M., of course. And every year more people came as word spread. Mr. M. and the boys all had a great time, and the fireworks got bigger and bigger until it became a huge extravaganza, like what you saw tonight."

"It sounds like great fun, and an opportunity for all the people in town to sit back, relax, and reconnect."

"Exactly."

Though Des didn't understand how Logan's mother didn't love the idea of joining in with her community. But . . . whatever. Judging from what Logan had told her about his mother, she probably wasn't a big people or community person, so it was no surprise to hear she hadn't been on board for this kind of party.

Des was, though. She'd had a blast and was sorry to see it end.

Martha yawned. "That's my cue to go find my husband. I'm exhausted."

They headed outside. Colt was leaning against their SUV, obviously having brought it up from the back of the property where all the vehicles had been parked. He, Logan, and Ben were all talking.

"Ready to go, Ben?" Martha asked.

Ben nodded, shook Colt's hand and said good night to Des. They climbed into their truck and headed down the road.

"You coming with us, Des?"

She looked at Logan.

"I'll make sure she gets back to the set," he said.

A shiver ran up her spine. She was looking forward to the rest of the night.

# Chapter 15

COLT NODDED AND smiled at Des. "See you in the morning."

"Okay. Have a good night."

She hoped Colt wrangled some fun alone time with Tony before he had to fly back tomorrow.

After they left, Logan looked at her. "Care for something to drink?"

"I've had way too much iced tea today. How about a beer?"

"Sounds good."

They went inside, and Logan shut the front door. She noticed he didn't bother to lock it, which made her shake her head. Life out here was so different from what she was used to in L.A.

Logan pulled a couple of beers from the fridge, then left the room. She followed him up the stairs, smiling as he led her into his bedroom, then out on the deck. He popped the top on one of the beers and handed it to her as she took a seat in one of the Adirondack chairs.

"Since it's such a clear night, I thought you might want to look at the stars."

She settled back and took a sip of beer. "Thank you."

She tilted her head back and looked out over the night. Just as she'd imagined the first time he'd brought her out here, the sky was breathtaking—nothing but black except for all the stars. So many stars, in fact, they took her breath away.

"I can't believe you don't enjoy this view every single night, Logan. It's awe-inspiring."

"It is nice."

She dragged her gaze away from the spectacle and looked at him. "Nice? It's amazing. Do you know what I see when I walk out onto my balcony at night?"

"No. What do you see?"

"Other condo buildings. And a Dumpster. No stars."

"You could buy your own place, couldn't you? One with a view?"

"I could. But I don't want to make a permanent home in L.A."

He took a couple swallows of beer and stared out over the land. "Where do you want to live?"

"I don't know. I've just never felt settled enough to consider setting down roots anywhere."

"A product of your upbringing?"

She laughed. "Maybe. And because I travel so much for work, the condo I live in has always suited me. Until recently."

"What changed recently?"

"Me, I guess. I've been . . . restless. Unhappy."

He laid his beer down on the table next to him, and turned his chair to face her. "Tell me why you're unhappy."

"I don't know. Maybe that's the wrong word. Whenever I think it, I'm almost ashamed. What the hell do I have to feel unhappy about? I have this amazing career that I'm so lucky to have. Do you know how many women would kill to be where I am? So many actresses fight and struggle to get work. And I've been working steadily since I was nineteen."

"Maybe that's why you're unhappy. Maybe you need a break."

She laughed. "Working actresses don't take breaks. You take a break, you're forgotten."

"I think that's bullshit. If you're good at what you do—and from what I hear and the little I've seen, you're definitely good—then you can afford to take some time off. When was the last time you had a vacation?"

"I don't know. I have breaks in between movies."

"What do you do on these breaks?"

"Clean my condo. Go catch up on movies I haven't seen. Reconnect with my friends. Visit my parents. Read scripts for new projects."

"That's not a vacation."

She gave him a look. "Isn't that a little like the pot calling the kettle black? When do you take vacations?"

"I'm not unhappy."

"But are you fulfilled? Do you have everything you want, Logan?"

He didn't answer for a few seconds, then said, "I'm satisfied."

"Now you're avoiding. I think you're just like me. Satisfied means you're okay, but you feel like there are holes in your happiness." She stood and walked to the edge of the deck and stared out over the vast expanse of land. "For a while I was content with that. Now I'm not. I don't want there to be holes anymore."

He got up and stepped behind her, wrapping his arms around her. "Only you can do what it takes to make yourself happy, Des. No one else can be responsible for that."

She took a deep breath, sliding her hands along his muscled forearms. "I know."

"So what do you need?"

She leaned her head back against his shoulder. "Right

now? Just this. To be with you here tonight with a million stars overhead and no one else around."

"And tomorrow?"

She turned and laid her hands on his chest. "Screw tomorrow. I don't want to think about tomorrow when today was so perfect, and tonight I'm here with you."

He threaded his fingers into her hair and kissed her, and every other thought left her mind except his hands on her and the way his mouth moved over hers. Logan had a way of making her forget everything that wasn't important. And what could be more important than the seductive slide of his hands down her back, his tongue tangling with hers, or the sounds he made as he backed her against the wall of the deck?

She found it hard to breathe as he slid his hand under her shirt and palmed her stomach. Logan's touch was always magical, zipping through her nerve endings and making her feel as if she'd never experienced these kinds of sensations before.

And when he lifted her tank tops over her head, she went for his shirt, too.

He took a step back and drew his shirt off.

It was dark, very little moon tonight, but she used her sense of touch to slide her hands over his chiseled abdomen and up over his chest. Her heart beat a staccato rhythm as he slipped his arm around her and undid her bra, then drew it down her arms and cast it on the pile of clothes on the chair.

She met his gaze, wishing it were light outside so she could see his eyes, but she felt his heartbeat pounding away like hers, and when he brushed his fingers over her nipple, she gasped, her body going haywire as he rubbed back and forth, shocks of pleasure shooting straight to her core.

But there was more to come because he shifted her, and then his mouth was at her breast. Her world spun as he flicked his tongue over the bud, then pulled it fully into his mouth to suck.

"Logan." She grasped his hair and held on, feeling dizzy, sizzling with the need to make these sensations go on forever. He worked her other nipple, then kissed the underside of her breast, dropped to his knees and tugged her shorts and panties down. She stepped out of them.

"Have I ever told you how beautiful you are, Des?"

She looked down at him. "No, I don't think so."

"Well, you are. Every part of you, from your cute, pink painted toes to your long legs and your amazing eyes. And right here, too." He put his mouth on her and swiped his tongue across her sex.

She trembled, letting out a moan as he brought her to new heights of pleasure. Des focused on the stars as Logan focused his mouth on the center of her universe, until she tightened her fingers in his hair, unable to hold back her moans of pleasure. And when she let go, she released with a loud cry. Logan held on to her as her knees buckled, the strength of her orgasm making her tremble.

He was right there seconds later, his face even with hers, pulling her against him, his erection brushing her hip as he kissed her with a force of passion that rocked her and brought her right back to that feverish desire she'd felt only moments ago.

She fumbled with the button of his jeans, and he helped her. He broke the kiss only long enough to free himself, grab a condom, and put it on, and then he'd backed her against the wall, spread her legs, and slid inside her.

She loved the passion, the need he seemed to feel to be with her. It was the same hunger that fueled her, and when he thrust inside her, she kissed him, flicking her tongue against his, mindless with the passion that never seemed to lose its fuel whenever she was with him.

He took her bottom lip between his teeth and tugged, flaming her fire to incendiary levels. She whimpered as he drove deeper, rubbing against that sensitive spot that tingled and tightened within her while she was grasping his cock, claiming him as hers.

He pulled back, searching her face. "Des."

The strain in his voice as he moved against her reflected what she felt. The tension, the need that occupied every nerve ending in her body, that stretched her taut on a rack of need, making her body tighten as he pulled back, then slid within her again, hitting every one of her pleasure spots until the stars she saw weren't in the sky but within.

She held tight to his shoulders as she fought for balance, as she hovered right on the brink until he rolled against her. When she released, he was right there with her, catapulting both of them over the edge. He grasped her chin and held her, kissing her with a passion that only served to batter her senses with an onslaught of pleasure that brought tears to her eyes.

She was shaking as she floated back down to earth, her limbs hardly able to hold themselves upright. Fortunately, Logan had a firm hold on her as they disentangled and they made their way back into the house.

"Shower?" he asked.

"Yes." He turned on the shower and they climbed inside. Logan gently washed her, and she had the pleasure of running her hands over his body. They dried off and Logan stepped out onto the deck to grab their clothes and bring them inside.

"Would you like to stay tonight?" he asked.

She nodded.

"What time do you have to be back tomorrow?"

"We don't film tomorrow. We have two days off."

His lips curved. "I could put you to work tomorrow here."

She crawled onto the bed and lay on her side, her head propped up in her hand. "Think you could make a rancher out of me?"

"I don't know. You do have boots, right?"

"Indeed, I do."

He got in bed and lay down beside her, lazily stroking her hip. "Then tomorrow, let's see what you've got."

She grinned. "You're on, McCormack."

# Chapter 16

DES FROWNED AS she was poked in the butt.

"What?"

"Let's go. Time to get up."

She blinked and looked outside "It's still dark."

"Yup. Come on. You want to work cattle today, we have to get an early start."

She rolled over onto her back and grabbed her phone from the bedside table. "Jesus, Logan. It's not even five a.m."

"Welcome to cattle ranching, Des. Changing your mind?"

In the foggy part of her sleep-addled brain, she recognized the challenge she heard in his voice. She slid out of bed and yawned. "Nope."

"You'll need jeans. I'll drive you to your trailer so you can grab a change of clothes."

"Great. Coffee first, though."

"Already have it brewed."

"You're like some kind of vampire." She grabbed her

clothes and, in a daze, climbed into them. True to his word, Logan had coffee made downstairs.

Martha was already there, too, and something that smelled an awful lot like food came from the stove.

"Morning, Des," Martha said, looking not at all shocked to see her there.

"Good morning, Martha."

"There's bacon and egg sandwiches for breakfast this morning. Logan tells me you're going to stay on the ranch and work with him today."

"I'm going to attempt it. We'll see how it goes."

Martha handed her a brown paper bag. "You'll do just fine. Grab yourself some coffee in one of those cups with a lid. You two can eat in the truck while you go get yourself some different clothes. I'll see you for lunch."

"Thanks, Martha." Des filled her cup, slid on the lid, and took the bag from Martha. She headed out the front door, where Logan already had the truck ready. She climbed in and put the bag between them.

"Martha didn't say anything about me being there."

"Why would she? She likes you. Hand me one of those sandwiches. You should eat, too."

"Who can eat this early?"

"You will. We're going to burn a lot of fuel, so force yourself even if you're not hungry."

She opened the bag, the smell of bacon wafting out, which immediately woke her stomach. While Logan drove over the ruts in the road, Des unwrapped the other sandwich and took a bite.

"Yum."

Logan nodded while busily chewing.

"I'll dash in and change clothes. I won't take long."

Logan put the truck in park and turned in off. "I'll walk in with you."

She should be used to his manners by now, but they still surprised her. "Okay."

It only took her a minute to change into her jeans, a T-shirt, and her boots. She braided her hair and then she was ready. She finished her sandwich and her coffee in the truck on the way back to the ranch.

"What are we doing today?" she asked Logan as they made their way to the pasture.

"Moving and sorting cattle."

"Which means what, exactly?"

"We sort them according to size before we work them. Then when we return them to the pastures for grazing, they're all of equal size. It makes a difference when we load them up for sale later on in the year."

"Okay."

"Do you know how to ride a horse?"

"Sort of."

"That means no. We'll go slow. You'll get the hang of it."

She laughed. "I love your confidence in my abilities."

When they entered the barn, Logan chose a horse for her.

"This is Athena. She's a sweet mare and perfect for you."

The gray-and-black dappled mare had a thick black mane over her crest, and stood very still while Logan saddled her.

Des ran her hands over her and spoke to her in quiet tones. Logan led her out to the fence where his own horse, who Des learned was named Frosty, waited for them.

"She's beautiful, Logan."

Logan patted Athena. "Yeah, she is. She doesn't get to ride as much anymore, so she'll enjoy working today."

"Is she older?"

"Older than some of our working horses. She's enjoying her retirement, but she's still got some miles left in her, don't you Athena?"

Des admired the way Logan spoke to the horses. There was a warm respect in his voice, as if he knew the work the horses did was just as valuable as the humans'.

"Seriously," he asked. "Have you ever ridden at all?"

"I have. But it's been a few years."

"At least you've been up on a horse before. Slide your foot in the stirrup and I'll help you up."

She got her foot in the stirrup, and Logan gave her a leg up. Athena was tall, and a stout horse, but Des felt comfortable on her, and the horse wasn't skittish at all. Des knew the rein commands, so she followed Logan over to where his men were waiting.

"We're going to head north a couple miles. Then we'll gather up the cattle and drive them down here so we can sort them."

"Sounds fine. Obviously, I'm going to attempt to not get in the way, and hope someone will yell at me and tell me what to do."

Logan motioned to one of the younger hands, who rode up to them. He couldn't have been more than eighteen or nineteen, though he rode with confidence, just like Logan.

"This is Vic, one of my cousins. He's home from college for the summer and getting a little work in on the ranch. Vic, this is Des. She's an actress working the movie on the ranch. You might know who she is."

"Hey, Vic. Nice to meet you."

Vic blushed a hard shade of crimson, but tipped his hat. "Ma'am."

"Vic's going to be bringing up the rear. She's a little rusty on riding, so stick close to her and let her know what needs to be done."

Des turned to Logan. "I assume you'll be leader of the pack?"

Logan's lips curved. "I'll be back and forth. Ben will run lead. So I'll be back here to check on you."

"I'm sure Vic and I will do just fine. Won't we, Vic?" She smiled at him, and his blush deepened.

"Yes, ma'am."

"Call me Des, okay?"

"Yes, ma'am."

Des quirked a smile. Vic was awfully adorable, with

his tall, lean body and oh, God, those dimples. He probably had a lot of girlfriends at school.

"I'll see you later?" Logan asked.

Des nodded. "Yes. I'm looking forward to this, so you just do your thing."

"Take good care of my girl, Vic."

"Will do," Vic said.

Logan turned his horse and galloped away. He and Frosty moved as one, and Des had to admit he looked damned sexy riding.

"This way, ma'am."

"Vic. If you're going to call me ma'am all day, we're going to have a problem. Call me Des."

Vic gave her a crooked smile. "Okay. Des."

Oh, yeah. Definite lady-killer material. What was it with these McCormack men? It had to be in their genes.

She followed Vic as they set up behind the cattle. She figured they'd sit and wait until Ben, Logan, and the others got them moving, but Vic took off right away, inching the cattle in the direction he wanted them to go, which in turn got the ones ahead of them moving.

"Stay on their left," Vic told her. "Our job is to keep them in formation. Cattle like to wander, so holler if you see any stragglers, and I'll take care of them."

"Will do." The entire herd started their trek south. For the first part of the trip, everything seemed to be going fine. It might have been several years since Des had ridden, but Athena was a joy to ride. She took direction well and wasn't spooked by any of the noises of the men's whistles or shouts or the constant mooing of the cattle. Obviously, this horse was well versed in what to do. Des stayed abreast of the cattle at the tail end, keeping her gaze peeled for any that might look like they were about to bolt.

When one did, straying off as they passed one of the ponds, she hollered over to Vic, who came around from his side in a hurry and herded the wayward heifer back toward the herd.

Crisis averted, and back to smooth sailing.

It took a while to traverse the two miles back to the ranch because a large herd of cattle didn't move as fast as horses. Once they returned, they directed all the cattle into a large holding pen, and she followed Vic to the barn where Logan was waiting for them.

"How'd she do?" Logan asked Vic as he held his hand out for her.

"She did good. She was alert and noticed one of the heifers trying to make a dash for the lake. She's a good hand."

Logan helped her off the horse. "Good for you. I knew you'd catch on quick."

It had been hot as blazes out there and sweat dripped down her back. Grateful for the hat Logan had given her, she took it off and swiped the sweat from her brow. "Thanks."

"Let's go take a break. We'll have lunch and something cold to drink before we start on sorting the cattle."

She was glad he'd insisted she eat breakfast because between the heat and how much leg work it took just to manage her horse, she was already exhausted and had burned off all those calories from her sandwich.

Just the thought of heading inside to Logan's cool, air-conditioned house made her want to cry with joy.

She followed along beside him, hurrying to keep up.

The air-conditioning hit her as soon as they stepped inside. "I think I'll go wash up a bit first."

"I'll do the same. You can take my room if you'd like."

She nodded. "If I'm not back downstairs in fifteen minutes, it means I've passed out, facefirst on your bed."

He smiled and tipped her chin with his fingers, then brushed her lips with his. "Don't fall asleep. We haven't even started on the hard work yet."

"That's not tempting me to stay awake, Logan." She turned and headed up to Logan's room, staring longingly at his bed before moving into the bathroom to wash her hands and splash cold water on her face.

She stared at herself in the mirror, horrified by her beet red face, the splotches of dirt kicked up on her arms and neck by the horses and cattle, and her hair . . . well, there was no help for her hair. Between the sweat and the cowboy hat, her hair was flat and stuck to her head, and she couldn't understand why in the world Logan had wanted to kiss her.

Ugh. Her appearance gave new meaning to the phrase "rode hard, put up wet," which she had never appreciated until she looked at herself in the mirror.

And the hard work hadn't started yet? She was never going to make it, and she mentally praised every single female working rancher, because they were way tougher than she was. It wasn't like she was some sissy, either. She was a runner. Hell, she'd run a half marathon. She worked out regularly, had learned several forms of martial arts.

But this? This was a real workout.

Doing what she could to smooth out her hair, she went back downstairs and found Logan and Ben in the kitchen with the rest of the guys.

"There you are," Martha said. "Logan said you might be taking a nap."

She poured herself a glass of iced tea and nearly downed it in two gulps. "No, I was just washing up."

"You lost that bet," Ben said to Logan as Des slid into one of the chairs at the oversized table.

"What bet is that?" Des asked.

"That you wouldn't make it past this morning."

Des turned to look at Logan. "You bet against me?"

"Yeah. Sorry. But this heat wave is an asskicker, and I've seen your trailer."

She frowned. "What about my trailer?"

"It's a luxury item. It has a whirlpool tub."

"*Your* bathroom has a whirlpool tub, too," she shot back to Logan.

A chorus of *oohs* and *ahhs* broke out. Des ignored them.

"Yeah, but I've never used it," Logan said. "I'll bet you've used the one in your trailer."

Irritation prickled her skin. She knew he was baiting her, teasing her. And normally, she could handle it. But right now she was tired and hot and just damned pissed off. "Bring it on. I can take whatever you can dish out."

"Be careful what you wish for. You might get it."

That brought about more whistles and laughs from the guys.

"Okay, boys, knock it off," Martha said, bringing Des a sandwich. "And, Logan, I'm ashamed of you. Des is our guest. You're supposed to be showing her a good time."

"She asked to work the ranch today. I'm showing her how it's done. She can quit anytime she wants."

Oh. So that's what this was about. He was testing her to see if she'd walk away.

Like his mother did.

Not a chance.

She shrugged and picked up her sandwich. "I'm not a quitter. Never have been."

"We'll see how you feel about that by the end of the day."

LOGAN KNEW HE was being an asshole, but there was something inside of him that demanded he test Des to her limits. He didn't know what had come over him. Normally, he would have gone easy on a guest. They'd had plenty of people want to try their hand at ranching, and he and Ben and the hands always gave them easy tasks.

It had to be near a hundred degrees out there today. When they'd stopped for lunch, Des's face was as red as a tomato, and she'd looked like she might pass out. She'd handled the morning just fine, and if he'd been a nice guy, he'd have told her to sit the rest of the day out.

But she'd been so goddamned determined, and she'd

never once complained. So why not see if she had the grit she claimed, right?

So now, as she stood in the lane while they sorted cattle, he'd once again let Vic work with her.

Not a peep out of her as she ran to open one gate and close another so the cattle would head into the correct pens.

She learned fast, too.

The task took several hours, with no shade and in the baking afternoon sun. Des wore a long-sleeve shirt, jeans, boots, and a hat. He knew what it was like to work in those temperatures, but he had been born and bred to this, had been working cattle since he was a little kid.

Des wasn't used to it, and typically they'd give their guests a sample of the work process, then give them a break.

Logan hadn't given her a break. He was treating her like any of his other hands, making her put in a full day's work.

What kind of a dickhead did that make him?

A first-class one. And he didn't understand what the hell was the matter with him.

"You gonna cut that filly loose before she drops, son?"

Logan looked up at Ben, and lifted his chin. "She's doin' fine."

"She ain't fine, and you know it. You have a fight with her or somethin'?"

"No."

"Then what the hell is your problem? Even with your momma on her meanest day, your daddy would have never treated her the way you're treatin' Des. So you go cut that girl loose, Logan, or I'm gonna do it for you."

It was unheard of to be lectured by Ben. It hadn't happened since he was in his teens. And he was ashamed it was happening now.

"You're right. I'll go take care of it."

"You do that. The boys and I will handle things here. We're almost done anyway."

Logan walked around the outside of the pens and made his way to the rear where Des and Vic were working. He slid under the chute, signaled for one of the other hands to take Des's place, and headed toward her.

She looked a wreck. Her boots were filthy and covered in cow shit. As a matter of fact, so was she. But she never even glanced his way, just worked with machine-like precision alongside Vic.

She'd make a fine hand. He admired her work ethic.

Logan whistled and everyone came to a stop, including Des.

"Brian's going to take over for you, Des" he said, motioning to Brian, who stepped into the chute.

Des narrowed her gaze. "Why? I've got this covered."

"I know. You did a great job today. Most seasoned hands wouldn't be able to handle the kind of day you did. But that's enough. You proved your point." He led her out of the chute and back toward the house.

"I had no point to prove," she said, staying in step beside him. "I think that was you."

He stopped and turned to her. "No, I didn't."

"Didn't you?" She took off her work gloves and handed them to him, then pulled her phone out of her back pocket and hit a button. "Hey, it's Des. Can you come get me? I'm over at the McCormack ranch."

She waited, her gaze staying firmly on Logan. "Great. I'll see you soon." She tucked her phone back into her jeans.

"Des."

She held up her hand. "Look, Logan. I get that you don't trust many women. But I thought we were past that, that things between you and me were different. I guess I was wrong."

She headed over to the barn so he followed. She stopped at the sink, shrugged out of her long-sleeve shirt, leaving her wearing only her tank top. She turned on the water and grabbed the soap, then started scrubbing her hands and arms. And the whole time, she ignored his presence.

"I don't know what you're talking about," he said.

This time, she wouldn't look at him. "Don't you? Betting against me? Trying to test me to see if I'd crumble and run?"

She'd read him perfectly. "I can explain that."

She turned off the water and grabbed a paper towel to dry her hands. "I don't need you to explain anything. I get it, I really do. But I can't do anything about how you feel." She grabbed her shirt and headed outside.

There was a black SUV waiting by the house. Des walked over to it.

"Des, we need to talk," Logan said.

She laid her hand on the door handle, then lifted her gaze to his. "Oh, I think you said enough today, Logan."

"Let me take you back to the set. We can have dinner, talk things over."

"No. I'm tired, I'm hot, and I smell like cow shit. Furthermore, I'm pissed as hell at you for daring to compare me to—" She shook her head. "Never mind. All I want to do is soak in my nice whirlpool tub—because you know us rich actresses do things like that—and then I'm going to bed."

She opened the door, slid in, and shut it. He heard the click of the door locks, the sound ringing with a firm finality that made his stomach clench.

He watched her drive away, feeling every inch the asshole he'd been today.

And knowing it might be a long damn time before he saw Des again.

# Chapter 17

"AND . . . CUT."

Des exhaled, too tired from the heat to even complain about three takes for the scene. She just lifted her gaze to Colt, who looked as exhausted as she was. Fortunately, it was an early-morning scene, and the only one for today.

Thank. God.

It was Saturday, and they had spent all week filming the penultimate battle scene that would occur at the end of the film, something she thought Theo was going to save until last. But he explained he wanted to get a look at it earlier, just in case there were any needed changes that would have to be made.

Which meant special explosive effects and fire, which meant they had to get in touch with Logan and the local fire department to bring in water trucks because it was as dry as a tinderbox on the land. They also had their own water crews to douse the fires with water trucks as well. Everything had been planned out well in advance, and the scene would be played out with stunt people, except the close-up shots and dialogue between her and Colt prior to the explosions.

They went ahead and did the explosions and stunt work earlier in the week. Des stood by and watched as they filmed those on another part of the set. It was amazing to watch, and Theo had been satisfied with the way it had turned out. Fortunately, the land around the set had remained fire-free.

She had seen Logan and his crew out there with their water trucks, ready to intercede should a fire get out of control. He appeared to be searching for her in the crowd, but she'd stayed out of sight.

"Why aren't you going over to say hello to Logan?" Colt had asked her.

They were filming that scene at dusk, when the winds had died down and the heat wasn't so oppressive. She and Colt both wanted to watch, so they were leaning against one of the buildings just out of sight of the set.

She shrugged. "I'm taking a cooling-off period from Logan."

"Which means you had a fight with him."

"I didn't say that."

"You didn't have to. What happened between the two of you?"

"Nothing."

"Des."

"I don't want to talk about it, Colt."

Fortunately, he didn't press her, and they stood side by side and watched the scene unfold. The stunt people were magnificent, as were the pyrotechnics crew. After it was over and it was clear there were no fires, Logan and his people left and Des exhaled.

She hadn't seen him in a week. She'd been busy with her scenes, on call almost all day every day. Besides, she was still mad at him.

He had called her, though. And texted her.

She hadn't answered either. What was the point? Logan

wasn't going to be the kind of man to ever trust a woman. He had issues, and she'd long ago given up chasing after men with issues.

So when Emma called asking if Des was up for their spa day in the city, Des hesitated. Maybe it was time to distance herself from everyone in Hope.

But then she had second thoughts. She liked Emma and her friends. Why the hell should she back away from making new friends just because of Logan?

So she accepted. Emma told her they'd come to the ranch and pick her up, then squeeze her into the car so the media would never know she was in it.

She loved the idea of sneaking off the ranch, though she doubted Emma and her friends would be able to pull it off. Emma told Des she didn't know her friends and what they were capable of.

She went to her trailer and took a shower, then put on a sundress and slipped on her sandals. As soon as she finished drying her hair, her phone rang. It was security, telling her she had visitors.

"I'll be right there," she said.

She headed up to the main entrance to the set, where Emma, Jane, and Chelsea stood waiting for her.

"You look pretty. Are you ready for your adventure today?" Emma asked.

"Definitely."

"Great," Chelsea said. "Get in the far back of the SUV and lie down."

Des laughed. "Is this like a kidnapping?"

"Sort of. We're going to hide you from the paparazzi. They'll never know we're leaving with you."

"I find that hard to believe. They'll likely follow."

"Oh, we're going to decoy them by making a few stops first. If the paparazzi find anything exciting about the gas station and Walmart, then they need a life."

Des often thought the paps needed a life, but she was willing to go along with it. She climbed into the third-row seats and lay down. The windows were darkly tinted, so she'd be hard to see.

"Aww, you put a pillow back here," she said as she stretched out.

Jane leaned over the backseat to look at her. "We can't have you uncomfortable. You're not uncomfortable, are you?"

"Are you kidding? After the week I've had, I might take a nap back here."

"Go ahead," Chelsea said as she pulled away. "We'll wake you when we're close to the spa."

Des laughed, especially as Emma gave her a blow-by-blow of the goings-on when they reached the entrance to the ranch gates.

"Paparazzi are hovering close, trying to get a peek in the windows. Quit waving at them, Jane, you're only encouraging them."

"I'm trying to throw them off by being friendly," Jane said.

"Are they following?" Des asked.

"A few of them are," Chelsea said. "Bastards."

Des wasn't surprised at all.

"Don't worry. We have this covered," Emma said.

By the time they got into town, after a stop midway at a gas station, where the paparazzi had hovered yet again, and Jane had rolled down her window to smile and wave at them, exclaiming in a deadpan fashion that for some reason they weren't at all interested in taking *her* picture, they were off.

They pulled into the parking lot of the Walmart shopping center in Hope. Chelsea left the motor running and Emma and Jane hopped out.

"Be back in a few," Jane said, then shut the door.

"There's only one car left," Chelsea told her.

Des sighed. "Some of them are extremely persistent."

"I think they're all assholes. I'm sure their parents are so proud of their chosen professions as stalkers."

That, at least, made Des laugh.

Chelsea did a fine job of looking bored and scrolling through her phone.

"And, he's gone," Chelsea said. "Nothing exciting ever happens in a Walmart parking lot."

Chelsea pushed a button, waited a second, then said, "He's gone. Y'all can come out now."

Within a few minutes, Jane and Emma came back out. Jane was carrying a bag.

Chelsea gave her a look. "I didn't expect you to actually shop, Jane."

"Hey, I needed a few things."

They took off and hit the highway, Emma watching in her mirror.

"You can sit up now, Des. There's no one following us."

"I don't know," Des said, finally sitting up. "I was enjoying the luxury back there."

"It is a great SUV, isn't it?" Chelsea asked. "Will just bought it for him and Jane. I was excited to drive today. Jane was too nervous to be the getaway driver."

"I was not. Okay, maybe I was. I'm not good at this kind of thing."

Emma laughed. "This kind of thing. As if trying to lose the paparazzi is something we do all the time."

"Shut up, Emma," Jane said.

It was going to be a great day. Des could feel it.

And by the time they arrived at the spa—a place Chelsea swore was swanky, totally discreet, and sworn to secrecy—Des was more than ready for a day of fun.

Chelsea parked in the back of the place and made a call. The back door opened and a very beautiful woman with dark brown hair and blue eyes opened the door to let them in.

"You must be Desiree Jenkins. I'm Francine Willows, owner of Absolute Beauty. Welcome."

"Thank you, Francine."

"When Chelsea called me and told me she and her

friends—and you—wanted a special spa day, I took the liberty of closing the place to our outside clients today. The fewer people who know you're here, the less likely those pesky media types will descend upon you."

"You're amazing. I can't tell you how much I appreciate it."

"It's my pleasure. Of course we're going to take a million pictures of you here today, and after you're gone, we'll post them on our website and use them for promotion. With your permission, of course. And I promise we'll do your hair and makeup and make you look stunning in those photos."

Des laughed. "Be my guest."

They started out by undressing and heading to the hot mud room. Despite the heat outside, the temperature in the mud room was set very cool, and the hot mud felt awesome on her skin. She could certainly use the treatment since she was all dried out from filming in the heat. She sipped on some lemon water while she baked. After, she rinsed and Des chose a sea-salt scrub that felt absolutely delicious.

Then it was time for a massage, a forty-five-minute experience that was so luxurious and relaxing that Des fell asleep. Her masseuse gently woke her, and she showered off and was taken to the salon for a manicure and pedicure that perked her up, especially since all the girls sat next to her and had the same treatment. It was fun listening to Emma talk about her and Luke's wedding plans.

"When's your wedding date?" she asked Emma.

"In October. It takes a lot to plan a wedding, and with everything else going on, Luke and I wanted to just be with each other first. Plus, Jane and Will are getting married in September."

Des shifted her gaze to Jane and smiled. "You are? Congratulations."

"Thank you. We waited a while, too, but I'm tired of waiting. The kids and I want Will living in the house with us. It'll be a very small affair, just immediate family and friends. I've already been through this once. And that marriage didn't end so well."

"But this one really counts," Chelsea said.

Jane was beaming. "Yes, it does. And then as soon as ours is over, Emma and Luke are next."

Emma laughed. "We had talked about how our weddings are a month apart, but it's just so perfect."

"And mine isn't going to be a big deal. Just a small event, really. While Emma and Luke's is going to be big."

"Well, I wouldn't say big . . ."

"She says that now. But she's in definite bride-panic-planning mode." Chelsea grinned.

"Okay. Maybe I am. Thank God for these women, or I'd definitely be in a panic."

"Who's in your wedding party, Emma?" Des asked.

"Jane and Chelsea, of course. And my sister, Molly, will be my maid of honor."

"Yeah, providing you can get her back here for the ceremony," Chelsea said.

Des frowned. "Does she live out of the country?"

"No. She lives out of state. But she never comes home. It's a long, complicated story. Molly left home right after high school and hasn't been back to Hope in years. She . . . doesn't like it here, for some reason."

"Oh. Well, that might be difficult, then. But surely she'll be here for you . . . for your wedding."

Emma sighed. "I hope so. I'm counting on her."

"Have you talked to her about it?" Des hated to pry, but she found the idea of her sister not wanting to come home for the wedding so fascinating.

"I have. She says she'll be here, that nothing would stop her from standing next to me when I marry Luke."

"She'll come, Emma," Jane said. "She promised."

"I agree," Chelsea said. "Don't worry. Molly won't let you down."

"I know. I'm not worried. Luke and I flew out to Baton

Rouge last month where she's currently living. She told us both she was on board and excited. We went over wedding plans, and even long distance, she's been such a big help with all the planning."

Jane leaned across the stations and grasped Emma's hand. "But it's not the same as having your sister here with you while you plan the biggest day of your life, is it?"

Des saw the tears glimmer in Emma's eyes. "No, it's not. But as long as she's here on the day of my wedding, it'll be the best wedding gift ever."

"If she loves you like she says she does, if she promised you," Des said. "Then she'll be there for you when you need her the most."

Emma smiled and nodded. "I believe that. I have to believe that. My wedding just won't be the same without my little sister standing there beside me."

Des wished she had closer ties to her brother and sister. It sucked not having the draw to family other people did. Other than Colt, she had never bonded with anyone. Colt was close with Sarah and Callie, but they were on the periphery of her life. She wanted girlfriends like Emma, Jane, and Chelsea.

Maybe it was time to put down roots and settle down somewhere, start making some friends.

"You should come to the wedding, Des," Emma said.

Des's eyes widened. "What?"

"Seriously. We'd love to have you come."

"Oh, that would be so much fun," Chelsea said. "You're part of our pack now. You have to come."

"Say you will, Des," Emma said. "I mean, of course, depending on your schedule."

Des wanted to cry. Right there in the salon with one of the nail technicians smiling up at her as she painted her toenails, Des wanted to cry.

"You really want me to come to your wedding?"

"Of course I do. You can even bring a date."

"Yeah, like Logan," Chelsea said with a wink. "He'll

be the best man, so you know he's definitely going to be there."

"Oh, well. Logan. Uh. I don't think he'd want to bring me to the wedding."

"After the way the two of you were together at the party on the Fourth? Why not?" Emma looked confused.

"I sense a story brewing," Jane said. "Is something up with you and Logan? Or should we all just mind our own business?"

She'd told Colt, one of her best friends for years, to mind his. She hadn't wanted to talk about it.

"Let's have dinner somewhere and we'll talk."

"Are you sure you want to get out there in public?" Chelsea asked.

She didn't, but she wasn't going to gossip in the salon. Especially about Logan.

"I have an idea," Emma said. "We'll call in an order and have dinner at my place. We'll send Luke over to your place, Jane. He can hang with Will and the kids."

"Sounds like a great idea."

After they finished hair and makeup, Francine took photos of them all together, then a few of Des by herself, and with Francine. Des paid for all of them, much to Emma's dismay.

"Hey, we invited you. This was our invite and we were going to pay."

"But this was such a treat for me today. It's my pleasure to take care of the bill."

"Well, thank you," Jane said. "But we're buying dinner."

Des grinned. "You're on."

After thanking Francine and her staff, they headed over to Emma's place. As they came inside, the dogs bounded over. Des bent and petted Annie and Daisy.

"How was spa day?" Luke asked.

"Great," Jane said, laying her purse on the counter. "We were pampered from our toes to our hair."

"I can tell. You all look beautiful," he said, though his gaze settled only on Emma

Emma grabbed Luke by the shirt and gave him quite the hot kiss.

Des had to admit it made her a little jealous to see the fire and passion between them, the easy way they were with each other.

Chelsea fluffed her hair. "Thanks."

"Oh, I bought a few bottles of wine. And some tequila and mix, in case you want to make some margaritas."

"No wonder you're going to marry this guy," Des said. "He thinks of everything."

Emma slanted a very hot look toward Luke. "Indeed he does. And thank you, babe."

"You're welcome."

"Okay, you two. Enough of the mushy stuff. Out the door with you, Luke," Chelsea said, giving him a playful shove. "You have fun with Will and the kids."

"I intend to." He turned to Emma. "And I'm taking the dogs with me, if you don't mind. Will suggested Archie might enjoy Daisy and Annie playing with him."

"That sounds like a great idea. They both love Archie."

Luke nodded. "Okay, then. Here are the rules: Have a great time, but no dancing on the table naked unless there's video for me to watch later, Em."

She laughed, then squeezed his hand. "Thanks for doing this."

"No problem." He brushed his lips across hers, gave her a lingering look that melted Des's feet to the floor, then disappeared.

"Wow," Jane said. "Are you sure you don't want us to leave and Luke can stay?"

Emma grinned. "Oh, I'll be thanking him for his cooperation later."

"I'll just bet you will," Chelsea said. "In the meantime, let's do something about getting dinner ordered."

They decided on Italian food, and Jane ran to pick it up

while Chelsea opened the bottles of wine, and Emma cleared her paperwork off the table. By the time Jane came back with the food, the wine had been poured and the table had been set.

Des realized she was hungry. Apparently so were the rest of them. They dove into the food, a delicious combination of spaghetti and meatballs, lasagna, and a magnificent salad.

They drank wine and talked. Mainly, Des listened while the rest of them talked.

"And then I had a surgery yesterday that was exhausting. I'm getting my share of orthopedic surgical experience. In fact, one of my mentors from college in South Carolina is doing a class on new techniques in veterinary orthopedic surgery in September. I'm going to attend it."

"Oh, Emma, that's great," Jane said. "Is that the Dr. Moore you're always talking about?"

Emma nodded. "I had him for four classes in vet school, and I don't know that I would have made it through without him." Emma turned to Des. "Some of those instructors were assholes that couldn't care less whether you passed or failed. Dr. Moore saved my life, always encouraged me to push through, no matter how hard it was."

Des nodded. "I've had a few mentors through the years, too. Directors and casting agents can be brutal. Sometimes all it takes are a few kind words. In my business, you don't always get a part, especially one you want badly. My agent especially has been my lifesaver. I couldn't imagine having made it in this business without her."

"It's good to have people on your side," Jane said. "I couldn't survive a week of school without Chelsea."

"Aww," Chelsea said, taking Jane's hand and squeezing it. "The feeling is mutual, honey."

"I admire both of you so much," Des said. "Being an army brat, I moved around a lot, and I had my share of amazing teachers, and quite a few that sucked."

Chelsea laughed. "Believe me, Jane and I have seen

plenty of both. This summer, I'm one of those teachers who suck."

"You are not," Jane said. "You took on summer school this year so I could be with my kids."

Chelsea sighed. "It's like the kids are zombies in there. Try to teach math in the summer to a group of high school students who don't want to be there in the first place. You might as well kill me now. What was I thinking?"

"You were thinking that someone has to help these kids get to the next level," Emma said. "And maybe they don't want to be there, but you'll encourage them to do whatever it takes to pass."

Chelsea smiled at Emma. "You're so sweet and naïve, Em. These kids don't give a shit about math. They're going to do the barest minimum to get through my class. Which means a C minus. They'd much rather be at the lake. Not that I blame them. *I'd* much rather be at the lake, too."

Des laughed. "Summer school is rough. And it's probably not that the kids don't want to learn. It's like you said. They're frustrated. All their friends are out having summer fun, and they're stuck in the classroom."

"You speak from experience?" Chelsea cocked a brow.

Des took a sip of her wine and nodded. "Unfortunately, yes. I had to do a summer of math, too. It was hideous. No offense to either you or Jane."

"None taken," Jane said.

"Here, either." Chelsea shook her head. "By the end of the school year in late May, I'm toast. And then summer school starts up. Every year I say I'm not going to do it. Some years I don't, but this year for some reason I said I would."

"Because there was no one else to do it and seven students signed up," Jane said.

"That's true. It was either me or Jane. And Jane has kids, and I don't. So I said yes."

"There are only two weeks left, Chelsea."

She lifted her glass and stared at the golden liquid. "Maybe I'll start bringing wine."

"For you or the kids?" Des asked.

Chelsea laughed. "I'll get back to you on that one. In the meantime, why don't you tell us about Logan?"

Des grabbed the bottle and refilled her glass. "Oh, yeah. That." She was kind of hoping they could continue to talk about everyone else instead of her. She loved learning more about them.

"The day after the Fourth I spent the day working on the ranch with Logan."

"Really," Jane said. "That sounds like fun. Hard work, probably."

"It was hard. But it was also enlightening. And fun. And hot," she finished with a laugh.

"I can imagine. It's one of our typical Oklahoma summers," Chelsea said.

Des explained everything she'd done that day, from the time Logan got her up before dawn, until they were finished for the day.

"Holy crap, Des," Chelsea said. "I'm surprised you didn't throw in the towel by lunch."

She shrugged. "It was okay, and I thought I was doing well. But Logan didn't go easy on me. I mean, he treated me like he would any of the other hands that work for him."

Jane leaned back in her chair and swirled the wine around in her glass. "He was testing you."

"I guess so. I didn't figure it out right away, but I believe he was."

"He's scared, Des. And he obviously cares about you, otherwise he wouldn't have pushed you so hard."

"It's because of his and Luke's mother," Des said.

"He shared that with you?" Chelsea asked.

Des nodded. "He did. And I understand it, but I'll be damned if I have to pay for her sins."

Emma laid her hand on Des's arm. "You shouldn't have

to. What Luke and Logan's mother did was reprehensible. It scarred both of them, made them wary of getting close to anyone, especially women. But there's no way you should have to pay the price for her abandoning her children. Logan's just going to have to wake up and realize all women aren't like her."

"It's not like we were headed down that road anyway."

"Maybe Logan thinks you are. Maybe he's in love with you and he's confused."

Des slanted a look of disbelief at Jane. "Logan is not in love with me. I don't think he's capable of loving anyone."

"I disagree," Emma said. "I also agree with Jane. I think he was testing you, working your ass off at the ranch that day to see if you'd bolt. God knows, from what Luke tells me, his mother hated ranch life and never wanted to take part in any of the activities there."

"Exactly," Chelsea added. "And here you are, someone who's the polar opposite of him in terms of lifestyle and career. If he didn't care about you, he'd never have tested you. He would have given you the standard McCormack Day at the Ranch experience."

Des lifted a brow. "There's a McCormack Day at the Ranch experience?"

Emma laughed. "Yes. I think anyone who wants to"— she used air quotes with her fingers—" 'experience life on a working cattle ranch,' as they call it, they give them a pretty darned easy day. Nothing like what you told us you went through."

"I survived it, and the worst part about it was, I had fun."

"Until Logan made it not fun," Jane said.

"Exactly."

Emma refilled all their glasses. "So the question now is, what are you going to do about that?"

"I don't know. I need some advice."

"Don't ask me," Chelsea said, taking a swallow of wine.

"Men are a mystery to me. One totally screwed-up mystery. You'd be better off asking Jane and Emma. Obviously they have them figured out."

Jane laughed. "We do not. We've just learned how to live with their idiosyncrasies."

"True that," Emma said. "Never in my wildest imaginings did I think I'd ever settle down this soon. Or ever. And Luke? He's a mass of contradictions and complications. But oh, he's so sexy. And so sweet. He bought us wine tonight, you know."

Des smiled as Emma began to slur her words. Friends were great. Drunk friends were even better. "I don't know that you need to understand them, but you can still offer me some advice on what you think I should do about Logan."

"Or *to* Logan," Chelsea said, weaving a bit in her chair. Then she laughed.

And so did Jane.

And then Emma laughed, too.

Des cracked a smile. "You all are not helping."

Jane set her glass down on the table. "Okay, you're right. We are not helping. But honestly, Des, what do you want to do? Are you mad enough at him that you think he's not worth it, or do you have genuine feelings for him?"

That was the big question, wasn't it?

"I have feelings for him, things I've never felt for another man before. But I don't really know how he feels. And God knows I have no idea what he really wants."

"It seems to me that you've never had any qualms about telling him how you feel or what you want. Isn't that right?" Chelsea asked.

"True."

"So why the hesitation now? Unless you're afraid you won't like the answer."

Des sighed. "You're right about that. I've never been afraid of any man, ever. I've always been very honest with my feelings, my wants, and my needs. Until Logan. He makes me crazy. And conflicted."

"Because you've fallen in love with him," Emma offered.

"I don't know that I'm ready to admit that yet. It's all wrong between us."

Emma waved her hand back and forth. "Trust me, there are no spectacles." Emma frowned. "No, wait, that's not the right word." She laughed. "Obstacles. There's the word I was looking for. There's no obstacles that can't be overcome between two people who truly want to be together."

Jane raised her glass. "I'll drink to that."

And they did. More than once.

# *Chapter 18*

---

LOGAN WAS SITTING on the deck outside his bedroom when he saw Luke's truck driving past the house. It was late. He pulled out his phone to see it was past midnight. He headed downstairs and waited about twenty minutes.

Luke pulled up to the house and got out, then headed up to the porch where Logan had pulled up a seat.

"Raiding my cattle?" Logan asked.

Luke's lips curved. "Making a delivery."

Logan cocked a brow.

"Dropping your drunk girlfriend off."

"Drunk, huh?"

"Girls' night. I had to drive her, Chelsea, and Jane home."

Logan nodded. "Bet that was fun."

"You have no idea. The three of them babbled all the way to Jane's house about nail polish colors. Then after I dropped Jane off, Des and Chelsea played some movie-trivia game. After Chelsea's drop-off, Des talked to me nonstop the whole way here."

"About nail polish?"

"Even worse. About you."

"Huh." Logan looked out over the dirt road toward the barn. "Care to elaborate?"

"Not particularly."

"Okay." He'd really hate to beat the shit out of his little brother, but if it came to that, he would.

The two of them sat in silence for a few minutes.

"You gonna tell me or not?" Logan finally asked.

"About?"

"Des."

"What about Des?"

"Goddammit, Luke."

Luke let out a short laugh. "I'm going to preface this by telling you she was pretty toasted, so she'll probably be embarrassed tomorrow by all the babbling she was doing about you."

That made him feel a little better, especially considering she hadn't given him the time of day in the past week. "What did she say?"

"She's confused." Luke turned to face him. "What the hell did you do to upset her?"

"I was a dickhead."

"That's not unusual for you."

"Funny. She stayed the day after the Fourth of July to work at the ranch. I was hard on her."

Luke folded his arms. "So you didn't give her the typical McCormack Day at the Ranch treatment."

"No. I mean I treated her like shit, pushed her hard all day long."

Luke didn't say anything for a few minutes. "To see if she'd run like hell? Like Mom?"

Funny how everyone had spotted it right off. Except him. "I didn't even notice I was doing it. Ben did, though. And now you."

"You've never done that with any other woman."

"No."

"So why Des?"

"Hell if I know."

"Don't you? She means something to you."

Logan stood and went to the porch railing to look out over the land before turning to face his brother. "How could she mean something to me? You know who she is, what she does for a living."

"So? Why would that even matter if you care about her?"

"You went through it with Becca. Dad went through it with Mom. City girls don't belong on the ranch."

"That's bullshit, Logan, and you know it. If she's the right woman and she loves you, it won't matter what she does for a living. Becca wasn't the right choice for me. It wouldn't have mattered where she and I lived. She hated the life I chose. And Mom should have never married Dad. She knew ahead of time what her life was going to be like. Dad showed her what a life on the ranch was going to be, yet she chose it, and then she was miserable, and made everyone around her miserable, too."

Logan shook his head. "What Des and I have together is something . . . fun, you know? It just got out of hand that day, and I need to apologize to her for being so hard on her. We need to get back to having fun together."

"Yeah, because God forbid you should actually fall in love with someone, make a commitment and ask someone to share your life. You might actually be happy."

Logan narrowed his gaze at Luke. "Hey, screw you. I know what I'm doing."

"Do you? Because it seems to me you don't have a fucking clue."

Luke pushed up to stand, then headed toward the stairs. He stopped beside Logan and laid his hand on Logan's shoulder.

"Think about what's important to you, Logan, what you

want for your future. Think about what's going to happen when that movie's done, the trailers leave, and Des is gone. Are you going to be okay with that?"

Logan's stomach tightened at the thought of her being gone, of not seeing her ever again.

"I'll be just fine when she leaves."

Luke squeezed his shoulder. "Sure you will. Hey, I'm going to head home to my gorgeous, drunk, and probably passed-out fiancée. I'll talk to you later, okay?"

"Yeah, okay. Thanks for bringing Des back."

"No problem." Luke headed down the stairs and got into his truck, then rolled down the window. "Hey, Logan?"

Logan walked down the steps and stopped at Luke's truck. "Yeah."

"You do realize you just thanked me for bringing your girl back, right? For someone who claims not to care, you sure seem to care."

Shit. "Night, Luke."

Luke's lips curved. "Night, Logan."

# *Chapter 19*

DES WOKE WITH a blistering headache and a mouth that tasted like she'd ingested the entirety of the hot, dry dirt on the ranch.

Bleh. She slid out of bed and headed into the kitchen for the largest glass she could find, then consumed two full glasses of water.

That helped. Next, she made a cup of coffee and poured some juice.

Now semi-awake, she downed two acetaminophen and swore she'd never drink wine again.

After taking a shower and finding craft services so she could consume some carbs, she felt nearly human again.

"Hey." A set of arms wrapped around her. She smiled as Colt kissed her cheek.

She turned around. "Hey, yourself."

"You look like crap."

She laughed. "Thanks. I feel like crap."

"I thought a spa day was supposed to make you look

and feel rejuvenated, not like you just crawled through the desert."

"Ha ha. The spa day was fun. It was the three-bottles-of-wine night that did me in."

"Ah. Yeah, damn that wine. Come to my trailer and tell me all about it. We don't have call for another hour."

"Thank God for that. I'm going to need some cucumbers on my eyes." As they passed the craft services table, she snatched a pastry. "And another croissant."

"I have one of those gel eye packs in my fridge," Colt said as he led her into his trailer. "It'll do wonders for the dark circles and bags under your eyes. And the splitting headache you no doubt have."

Leave it to Colt to be brutally honest about her appearance. But that's why she loved him.

"Thanks." She slid onto his sofa and picked off a piece of the croissant, letting its buttery deliciousness melt in her mouth. While she ate, she filled him in on her day and night with the girls.

"Should I be jealous I'm being replaced with new girl-friends?" he teased, putting a glass of lemon water in front of her.

"Thanks. And no. You know I'll always love you best." She made a kissy face at him.

"Of course you will. Girls will never tell you when you look hideous."

She tore off another piece of croissant. "So true."

"Or that you should stop eating that oh-my-god-it's-too-many-calories-and-your-butt-is-going-to-get-huge croissant."

She stuck her tongue out at him. "That's probably fact, but this morning, I don't even care. This damn thing tastes like it's saving me from the fiery pit of hell."

Colt grabbed his cup of coffee and sat next to her. "That bad a hangover, huh?"

"Yes. That bad."

"Poor baby."

"I know. We were talking and drinking, talking and drinking, and the next thing you know, Emma's fiancé Luke is bringing me back here, and I'm spilling my guts to him about how I'm crazy about his brother. I talked his ear off about Logan the whole drive from Emma's house to here. Like thirty-five minutes of me blathering on non-stop about how his brother doesn't understand me. Ugh. I was a hideous basket case. Poor Luke. I don't think I'll ever be able to face him again."

Colt laughed. "That's awesome, Des."

"It was not awesome. I was very much a girl last night."

"A girl who's crazy about Logan. I'm sure Luke understood."

She was disgusted with herself for behaving like that, and for telling Logan's brother, of all people, how she felt. What was wrong with her?

"Enough about me. Tell me what you did yesterday."

Colt looked down at his coffee, then up at her. "I had a long Skype session with Tony."

"Oh, that's sweet. I'm so glad."

"He just heard that he's going to be the cinematographer on *Shapes in the Darkness*."

Des laid her croissant down. "Is he? The paranormal you're starring in with Alexis Green?"

"Yeah."

"That's awesome. Think of all the time the two of you will be able to spend together while you're filming."

He nodded, then stared down at his coffee again. Des frowned. "Colt? Is something wrong?"

"No. Nothing's wrong. Actually, for the first time in a very long time, everything is starting to feel right." He lifted his gaze to hers. "I'm going to come out, Des. I decided yesterday."

Her eyes widened. "You did? Did you talk about it with Tony?"

"Yes. After he told me about the movie, I decided enough was enough. I don't care what my management team says. I want to be with Tony—really be with him. We're going to be on a movie set together, and I don't want to sneak around on set or pretend we don't care about each other."

She grasped his hand. "I'm so glad."

"I'm terrified, Des."

She leaned into him and put her arms around him. "Don't be scared, Colt. People will still love you as much as they do now."

"You know that's not true. I'll lose some fans once they find out I'm gay."

She took a deep breath and let it out. "You're right. You will. Some people won't be able to see past the homosexuality to recognize that you're still the same person, that you're still the same outstanding actor you've always been, that the love scenes and chemistry you've shared with all the actresses you've worked with over the years has been just that—acting—just as it would be with any heterosexual actor who does a love scene with some actress, then goes home to his wife or his girlfriend. It's unfortunate that who someone loves has to be the world's business, but to some people, it matters."

She laid her head on his shoulder. "But to the people who love you, the people close to you in your personal life, and all your fans who adore you that really count—it won't matter at all who you love, Colt. They won't care who you go home to at night, because they love your movies."

She heard his shaky sigh.

"God, I hope so, Des. I really hope so. My entire career depends on this."

She grasped his jaw and turned his face toward hers. "I love you. I always have and I always will. And you know whenever and however you choose to do this, I will be there for you, standing beside you, supporting you."

"Thank you. I don't know what I'd have done without you in my life all these years."

She saw the tears shimmering in his eyes, and she pulled him close and hugged him tight.

Colt had always been there for her when she needed him. Now was her chance to be there for him.

"Have you thought about how you're going to do it?"

"I don't know yet. I haven't told my management team yet. They're not going to be happy."

She shrugged. "The bottom line is, they can advise you, but it's your career and you get to make the decisions. Then they'll have to deal with the fallout. If there is any."

"Oh, there'll be fallout. You know there'll be at least some. If not a lot."

"Don't borrow trouble when there might not be any. This is all going to work out for you. For Tony. Then all this hiding and skulking around in the shadows will be over, and you can live your life out and proud. Tony can finally move into that sweet little house of yours, and the two of you can make a life together, like you've always dreamed about."

Colt smiled. "I like the sound of that."

"Hang on to that, and think about being free."

He laid his head against hers. "Honey, it's the only thing I'm thinking about."

DES PONDERED COLT'S dilemma after she finished her scenes for the day. He was so brave coming out, knowing what was at stake.

And if he could suck it up and not be afraid, so could she.

It was time for her to visit Logan. After they filmed their scenes for the day, she showered and changed into a pair of white capris, a dark blue spaghetti-strap tank with a flowing sleeveless silk button-down top over it, then slid into her sandals. She grabbed one of the SUVs and took a ride over to the ranch. She stopped at the house first. Martha was there.

"Des, I'm so glad to see you." Martha enveloped her in a hug. "I was just finishing up for the day and waiting for Ben so we could head home. Are you looking for Logan?"

"Yes."

"He went to the cabin to go fishing. I packed him up his dinner, so he might be out there awhile. Ben and I have a meeting to attend in town tonight, so we're heading out early. Do you know where the cabin and pond are?"

Remembering that night they spent together at the cabin, she nodded. "I do. Thanks, Martha. I'll go find him."

She drove the few miles to the cabin, practicing in her head what she was going to say to him when she found him.

She had no idea, only that this distance between them was uncomfortable. She only had a little time left before they wrapped their location shoot, and the one thing she did know was that she wanted to spend that time with Logan. It was ridiculous to be mad at him.

She parked next to his truck and got out, but didn't see him outside near the pond, so she went up to the cabin and knocked. No answer.

Huh. She went around to the back of the cabin, then walked down the flagstone path toward the pond. She finally saw him at the far end of the pond, sitting under a tall tree close to the water. The tree's branches bent low, offering a large spot of shade from the blistering afternoon heat. He had a line in the water and he was leaning against the trunk of the tree, his cowboy hat tipped low across the top of his face. He didn't wave to her, so for all she knew, he might be asleep.

Not wanting to wake him, she slowed her steps as she crept closer. His legs were outstretched, his ankles crossed. He still wore his boots, dirt caked across the bottoms of his jeans. His dark blue T-shirt was stretched tight across his impossibly chiseled shoulders and chest. She wanted to pull out her phone and snap a picture of him in that pose. How could a man leaning against a tree, who looked to be asleep, be so damn sexy?

She was only about five feet away when he said, "What brings you here, Des?"

She nearly jumped out of her sandals. "Dammit, Logan. I thought you were asleep."

"Not asleep. And be quiet. You'll scare the fish away."

She sat next to him on the ground and stared out over the pond. "Catch anything yet?"

"No."

"How long have you been here?"

"About an hour."

"Don't you usually fish before dawn?"

"I'm usually up and working cattle before dawn. But yeah, that's the optimal time. Doesn't mean you can't catch fish now. This is a cool, shady spot with a lot of trees. And I have good bait."

The trunk of the tree was thick enough that there was room for her to lean against it.

"Your white pants are going to get dirty," he said.

"I don't care." She pulled her knees up to her chest and wrapped her arms around them, then stared out over the water. It was such a beautiful location, the entire pond rimmed by low hanging branches from all the trees that peppered the area. Logan was right, she had definitely cooled off, now that she was in the canopy of shade here. It was quiet, the only sound the rustle of a slight wind through the tall treetops.

She wanted to talk, but then again, Logan wasn't saying anything either, so she stayed quiet and watched his line in the water. It wasn't moving. The surface of the water barely moved, and as she managed glances at Logan from the corner of her eye, she noticed his eyes were open and he was staring intently at his fishing line, as if he was willing a fish to jump on it.

"Nothing's happening," she finally said.

"Give it time. Fishing takes patience."

"Now you sound like my dad."

"Your dad's right. You have to wait them out. One will come along eventually."

"I don't know how you can sit here for so long and do . . . nothing."

"I'm not doing nothing. I'm thinking."

She shifted her gaze from the line in the water to him. "About?"

"A lot of things."

They had taken twenty steps backward in their relationship. This was like day one all over again, and she didn't have the patience to start over again. "Okay, I can see you don't want to be bothered by me. I'll take off and leave you alone to your thinking." She pushed off to stand.

"Don't leave."

She paused.

"Wait right here." He handed her his fishing pole. "Hold this. I'll be right back."

When he got up and started walking away, she said. "What if a fish bites?"

"Pull it in," he said, then disappeared.

She stared at the pole and the line sunk into the water. "Pull it in. Whatever." She hadn't fished since she was eight years old. Could she even remember what to do with a fish if she caught one? Was it like riding a bike—one of those things you never forgot how to do?

She kept her gaze trained on the line, while alternately searching for Logan's return.

When she saw him approach with another fishing pole and a cooler in his hands, she rolled her eyes.

"Want me to bait it for you?" he asked as he sat down next to her and handed her a pole. He stuck his in the ground.

"I didn't realize I was going to be fishing."

"It's good for you. It'll relax you."

"Do I need relaxing?"

"Yeah."

She could think of several other ways to relax, none of

them involving fishing or a pole—at least not a fishing pole—but she kept her comments to herself. "Fine. Where's the bait?"

He pulled a smaller cooler out from the side of the tree and handed it over to her.

She opened it up, wrinkling her nose at the smell of the fish bait. "Lovely."

"You're a tough girl. You can take it. You need me to do any of this for you?"

"No, I've got it."

She got her hook on the line, then selected a piece of the bait and hooked it on before casting her line in the water. Logan was right about one thing, though—she was already regretting the white pants. At least she had on dark tops.

She settled in against the tree again and studied her line, while Logan opened the other cooler.

"Beer, pop, or water?" he asked.

"Water is fine for me right now."

He pulled out a bottled water and unscrewed the top, then handed it over to her. He popped the top of a can of beer for himself.

"Thanks." She took several long swallows, put the lid back on, then set it to the side.

She sat there and stared at the line, her gaze wandering over the water.

"I'm sorry about that day after the Fourth," he said.

She glanced over at him. "It's okay."

"It's not okay. I acted like an ass and I pushed you harder than I should have." He turned his head and met her gaze. "I'm going to ask for your forgiveness, but I don't deserve it."

The wall around her heart fell. "You have it. I understand that what we have—whatever has been going on between us—is confusing."

"That doesn't ever give me the right to treat a woman—to treat you—the way I treated you that day. And it won't happen again. You're a guest on this ranch and I care about you. I just don't know what to do with all these feelings I have for you. It's kind of mixed up in my head."

She admired his honesty, something she rarely got from a man. "I understand. It's complicated."

His lips curved. "Yeah."

"We don't have to do anything about what's between us, Logan, other than enjoy each other while I'm here."

He nodded. "I know. And I think I felt some pressure that there had to be more than that."

Which meant he didn't want more than that. Okay, now that she knew where she stood with him, she could make her remaining days here work. "We can just have fun, like we did at the beginning. And when it's over, it's over."

"Right."

Now that that was all settled, she felt just *so* much better.

Or not at all.

But then her line twitched. At first she thought she imagined it, but it pulled again.

"I think I've got a bite," she said.

"I saw that. Just hang on to it for a second until he latches on, then start reeling him in."

Excited now, she pushed to a standing position. Logan did, too, just as she felt a hard tug on her line. "I think this might be a big one."

He came up behind her and helped her hold on to the pole. "Okay, start reeling him in."

She unlocked her reel and started pulling in the fish, gently, so he wouldn't break the line. With Logan's help, they pulled the catfish out of the water and Logan grabbed hold of him.

"Fairly decent-sized one, too." Logan removed the hook and held him up in front of her. "Want to take a picture?"

She laughed. "No. I'm good."

He tossed the fish back in the water.

"Not keeping him?"

"Nah. I might catch him again, though."

She shook her head. "All that effort for nothing. And I was already anticipating fish for dinner."

"You haven't eaten?"

"No. Have you?"

"There's a sandwich in the cooler here, but I haven't eaten it yet."

"I see."

He grabbed the poles. "Come on. We'll go back to the house and we can eat something there."

"Martha said she and Ben had to leave early tonight."

"I can cook."

"You. You cook."

"Martha isn't always around to fix food for me. I can make my way around the kitchen. Not like her, of course, but I manage."

"Okay, chef. Let's see what you've got."

She followed him back to the house, parking alongside his truck.

"Go on inside and help yourself to something to drink," he said. "I'm going to put the fishing poles and bait away, and clean out the cooler. I'll be right in."

"Okay." She went inside and headed into the downstairs bathroom to wash the fishy smell off her hands. She also shrugged out of her silky top since she still wore her tank and bra underneath. After slipping off her sandals, she made her way into the kitchen and took inventory of the contents of the fridge.

There were vegetables, but she just knew Logan wasn't a salad-for-dinner kind of guy. Having seen the calories they burned off during an average day, especially a hot summer day, she pulled two steaks out of the freezer and placed them in the microwave to defrost, then grabbed some broccoli and cauliflower, along with tomatoes, peppers, and lettuce to make a salad. She mixed together a quick marinade for the steaks, and after they defrosted, slid the steaks in the marinade and got to work slicing the vegetables.

"What are you doing?" Logan asked as he came into the kitchen.

"Fixing dinner. Well, sort of. You're going to cook the steaks I'm marinating, while I make the side dishes." She leaned against the counter, waving the knife back and forth. "I assume you like vegetables."

"I do."

"Great. Then you'll have to trust me."

"I said I'd fix dinner."

"And you're going to. You're going to be out in the heat doing the grilling, while I stay inside where it's cool making the sides. It's a big win for me."

He gave her a dubious look. "I didn't invite you here to the house so you could cook."

She put her hand on her hip. "You don't trust my cooking?"

"I didn't say that."

"Good. Then go start the grill. It won't take long for the steaks to marinade."

He sighed, then went out the back door. Des busied herself by slicing the broccoli and cauliflower, then found a pan and put the veggies in there to steam. When Logan came back in, she took the steaks out of the marinade and put them on a plate.

"How do you like yours?" he asked.

"Medium rare."

"Perfect. Same as mine. I'll be back soon."

He left with the meat, and she made the salad, then set the kitchen table, drained the broccoli and cauliflower, and seasoned them, setting them aside while she finished the salad and put it on the table. By then, Logan had come back in with the steaks.

It had all taken about twenty minutes, which was good because she was really hungry.

Logan scooped salad into a bowl, then the broccoli and cauliflower onto his plate.

"I didn't even ask you if you liked any of this stuff," she asked.

"Why would you bother to ask?"

"Some people don't like broccoli. Or cauliflower."

"I pretty much like whatever you put in front of me. I'm hungry."

She smiled at him as she cut into her steak. "Me, too."

The steak had turned out perfect, and they dug in, both of them quiet as they finished up their meal.

"I like this," Logan said.

"What?" she asked after taking a sip of her water. "The steak?"

"No. You. Cooking in my kitchen."

She laughed. "Don't get used to it. My culinary skills are limited. And you made the main course. I just did sides, and they weren't exactly complicated. But I do like to practice cooking, and it's something I'd like to do more of, so thanks for letting me play in your kitchen."

He shot her a smoldering look from across the table. "So, you like to play in the kitchen, huh?"

"Maybe." She got up and grabbed their plates, then headed over to the sink to rinse them and load them into the dishwasher.

Logan followed her, handing her the salad bowls. They got into a rhythm. She rinsed, and he loaded the dishes. Though she noticed he'd come up right behind her to hand her a dish, his body brushing against hers. She almost dropped a plate, dammit.

The man was very distracting, and her body had a mind of its own where he was concerned.

And when she took the pot from him and filled the sink with dishwashing liquid to hand wash it, he slid his hands into the soapy water, tangling his fingers with hers. His chest rubbed against her back, his hips aligned with her butt, and her brain went to mush, because he began to kiss the back of her neck and her skin broke out in goose bumps.

He slid his hands up her arms, painting a trail of soap along her flesh.

"What are you doing?" she asked.

"Playing in the kitchen. You said you liked to do that."

She tilted her head back and rested it against his chest. "Mmm. I did, didn't I?"

She loved the feel of his hands moving along her body, the slick, soapy bubbles sliding across her skin as he reached her shoulders and pulled the straps of her tank top down, then pressed his lips there. Her breath caught and held as he grasped the strap of her bra with his teeth and dragged it over her shoulder and down her arm, then moved to her other shoulder and did the same.

"Logan," was all she could manage to say, his name falling from her lips in a whimpered whisper as he drew the straps of both her tank and her bra down, taking the cups of her bra along with them, baring her to the waist. He dipped his hands into the soapy water again, this time cupping her breasts with his warm, wet hands.

She looked down to see his very tan hands cupping her white breasts, his thumbs moving lazily back and forth over her nipples. His expert fingers made her nipples tingle and her sex quiver with need. And when he flicked her earlobe with his tongue, then tugged it with his teeth and whispered, "I want you, Des," in her ear, her legs trembled. Without the sink in front of her and his body behind her to bolster her, she might have sunk to the floor.

She wound her arm behind her to cup his neck. "Yes."

He made quick work of her capris, his hands masterful in the way he undid the snap and drew down the zipper. He slid his hand inside and cupped her, his fingers warm and wet as he found her clit and touched her there with sure, masterful strokes.

"You're hot here," he said. "Wet." He slipped a couple

of fingers inside her, then used the palm of his hand to stroke as he moved within her. His other hand continued to tease her nipples until she thought she'd die from the dual sensations.

She arched against his hand, silently begging for more, the pleasure so intense she knew it wouldn't take long for her to orgasm—not when this delicious man held her, stroked her, continued to whisper dark words of sensual promise in her ear.

And when she came, she let out a soft cry, her entire body trembling with the force of her climax. Logan held her, his fingers coaxing everything she could give until she lay limp against him, fighting for breath. And still, her body continued to quake from the aftereffects.

He expected nothing from her, just held her while she kept her eyes closed and reveled in the moment. But Des finally turned around and put her mouth on his. He wrapped his arms around her and grabbed her butt, drawing her against one sizeable erection that refueled the flame within her.

She cupped his shaft through his jeans, but it wasn't enough for her, especially when he groaned against her lips. She reached for his belt buckle, making swift work of undoing it, and his zipper.

"You wanna do it here in the kitchen?" he asked, the heat in his gaze evident as he looked down at her.

"Yes. Here. Right now."

"I'll need a second." He disappeared up the stairs while Des pulled off her tank and bra, then shimmied out of her pants and underwear. When Logan returned, the smile he gave her as he looked over her body was devastating.

"Just what I wanted," he said as he stalked over to her and pulled her against him. "Dessert."

He laid a condom on the counter next to them and threaded his fingers through her hair, then laid one devastating kiss on her that ignited her desire. And when he lifted her and sat her on the kitchen island, she gasped at the cold granite under her naked butt.

But that chill quickly evaporated when Logan pulled off his T-shirt, then shrugged out of his jeans and boxer briefs. His erection sprang up, and she couldn't help her smile of pure feminine appreciation for his body. She never tired of looking at him, could never seem to get enough of his chiseled body that probably never spent a minute at a gym. His was a product of sweat and hard work earning a living, which made her admire the body she reached out to run her hands over, from his broad sculpted shoulders to his incredibly muscled biceps to his lean yet amazing washboard abs.

"You gonna stare at me all night?" he finally asked.

She drew her gaze to his face. "Maybe. Do you have a problem with that?"

"Not really. But it makes my dick hard when you do."

"Good."

He pulled her toward him and kissed her again, making her forget everything but his taste and the way his mouth moved over hers—first, a madly passionate kiss, and then, gentling, coaxing her lips to part so his tongue could slip inside. And when he lay her down on the counter and splayed his hands over her stomach, her abdominal muscles rippled at the sensation.

She was lost in his touch, at the way he gently slid his palms back and forth over her nipples, making them achingly sensitive, replacing his hands with his mouth and driving her right to the brink of madness. And then he covered her sex with his hands, enticing her right to the edge with his talented fingers.

He kissed his way down her ribs and stomach, then parted her legs and put his mouth over her clit, gently sucking until she lifted her hips, gasping at the sensations he evoked, giving her an orgasm that made her lift and cry out his name.

Shaken, her legs lax, she stared up at him, brushing a lock of his hair from his forehead.

"What you do to me," she said.

"Good?"

"Oh, yes."

"There's more." He held out his hand and she sat up. He lifted her off the counter, then turned her to face it.

Just the thought of what would come next made her burn for him. She heard the tear of the condom packet, and then he was behind her, using his legs to spread hers. He braced his hand at her back to bend her over the counter, then entered her slowly, easily, wrapping his arm around her middle to shield her body from the counter.

And when he thrust, deeply, she thought she would die from the sheer pleasure of each stroke, feeling him buried so intimately inside her. She tightened around him, gripping him, making him a part of her as he pulled partway out and sheathed himself deep once again.

"I love how you feel, Des," he said, his body aligned with hers as he pressed a kiss and a love bite to her neck. "When I'm inside you like this, I want it to last forever."

"Yes. Me, too." Because pleasure like this didn't happen all the time. A connection like they had was special. It was more than sex, and she knew it. And deep down, she knew he realized it, too.

But now wasn't the time to think about that, not when she was so close again, when his hand slid down to her clit to give her that extra stimulation she needed to reach orgasm. And when she did, he went with her, driving deep and shuddering against her as she tightened around him, both of them holding on to each other as they fell into the abyss, where nothing mattered but each other.

It was a while before she could form words. Her throat was dry, she and Logan were both so sweaty they stuck together. But she was content. And happy.

"I don't know about you," he finally said. "But I need a shower."

She smiled. "Ditto."

They disentangled and went upstairs to Logan's room and took a shower together, having fun soaping each other up and rinsing off. Logan ran downstairs to grab their clothes, and as Des climbed into hers and combed out her wet hair, he asked, "Do you need to get back tonight?"

"I can stay. If you want me to."

"I want you to."

The way he looked at her always made her feel as if she was the only woman he'd ever asked to spend the night. She was probably wrong, and it was dangerous thinking, but hell, she was already in way over her head, so she might as well enjoy the fantasy while she had it.

It wouldn't be too much longer before reality reared its ugly head.

It was still a little early, so they went downstairs into the family room. Logan brought them drinks, and they settled together on one of the sofas. Logan searched the listings on his subscription service.

"Oh, here's a movie with you in it. Something called *The Dreams*?"

Des wrinkled her nose. "Oh, God, no. The last thing I want to do is to watch one of my movies."

"I've never seen any of your movies. I want to watch one."

She turned to face him. "Really?"

"Yeah."

"Well, not that one. It's not good."

He laughed. "Fine, then. You suggest one."

She sighed. Watching herself on film was not one of her favorite things. "Okay. See if you can find *In Six Days*. It's a suspenseful, action-type movie."

He used his remote to do the search. "There it is."

He brought the movie up and it started. Des cringed when she saw herself on the screen.

"How long ago was this one made?" he asked.

"Maybe three years ago?"

"I can tell. You're younger."

She laughed. "Oh, so now I'm old?"

He kissed her nose. "Hardly. You're still a baby. But you just look a lot younger in this one."

"I was supposed to look younger. My character is nineteen."

They'd made popcorn, so they sat silently and Des ate while they watched. Okay, so she mainly snuck glances over at Logan since she knew what the movie was about, and she really didn't like watching herself all that much. Though she tried to see herself with a more critical eye now that she was forced to sit through the movie.

Not too bad, actually. A little more raw back then than she was now. She could see how her technique had improved. She grew more comfortable in front of the camera with each movie she did. This movie was about a young girl whose family is kidnapped and held for ransom, and she hooks up with a badass bounty hunter who's after the guys who are holding her family. He wants to storm in and grab the bounty, regardless of the outcome for the hostages, but she convinces him to help her save her family. It was a pretty kickass role for her in terms of physicality and weaponry. She had had a lot of fun during filming, and Bruce Leyton, the actor playing the bounty hunter, was a Hollywood legend who'd taken her under his wing and taught her a lot about filmmaking—and longevity in the business.

"You're good in this, Des," Logan said after the movie ended.

She had been laying her head on his shoulder, surprisingly engrossed in the movie. She sat up and looked at him. "You think so?"

"Yeah. I enjoyed the movie. I hadn't seen this one before. And I'm a big fan of Bruce Leyton's. But I found myself watching you. You held your own alongside him. And you were a big badass in this movie."

She laughed. "You can thank the stunt coordinator—and Bruce—for that. They were both very helpful in that regard."

"They taught you well, then." He studied her for a few seconds. "And I was wrong about your weapons skills. You're much better than I initially thought."

"Thanks. So does that mean I'm not going to need rifle training?"

"Apparently not."

"I'm sure the weapons master on this film will be relieved. And me, too, since I did a lot of training for this movie. Besides, the film is almost over, so I think we're done shooting things, anyway."

"You really love this moviemaking thing."

She shrugged and picked at a hangnail. "Sometimes."

"But not always?"

She stared at the paused screen. "Back when I made that movie? I loved it. I loved everything about it, from the grueling fight scenes to the time off-camera spent with Bruce and his wife and their two little boys to the stunt coordinator and the director."

"Not every job is going to be like that, though. Not every day in any job is going to be magic."

"That's true. And like you said, maybe I just need a vacation."

He pulled her legs onto his lap. "Maybe you do. Just a break to clear your head. It seems to me your adoring public won't forget you."

She sighed, that familiar tightening in her stomach ever present when she thought about not being in the public eye, not making multiple movies a year. "There's so much competition out there. I don't know what would happen if I wasn't working all the time. I only have a finite amount of time in this business, and then it's over."

He laughed. "I don't know about that. There are a lot of working actresses out there way older than you. And a lot of them win those fancy awards, don't they?"

"I guess you're right. But this business will make a person paranoid. So will the people we work with, like our agents and publicists and casting agents and all the media who will wonder if I'm a washout if I don't sign on for the next big movie, you know?"

"What does your heart tell you? If you're not happy, then maybe there's something else you want to be doing."

"Honestly, Logan? I haven't taken a breath long enough to even listen to my heart. So I don't have any idea what I really want to do."

He rubbed her legs. "Maybe that's your answer."

"Maybe it is."

He slid her legs off his lap and stood, then held out his hand. "Come on. Let's go to bed."

She walked upstairs with him and took off her clothes. He gave her an unopened toothbrush for her to brush her teeth, then she climbed into bed next to him, and Logan turned off the light.

"Thanks," he said as he pulled her against his chest.

"For what?"

"For letting me watch one of your movies."

"Oh. You're welcome. It wasn't as painful as I thought it was going to be."

She felt the deep rumble of his laugh.

"Logan?"

"Yeah."

"Thank you."

"For?"

"For listening to me."

"Always. I don't know that I solved any of your problems, Des, but I'm always willing to listen."

Her heart squeezed. She tried not to open her heart any more to him than it already was, but she couldn't help it.

She was in love with him, and she was never one to deny the truth. There it was, and she was just going to have to deal with it.

# *Chapter 20*

DES STOOD IN Colt's trailer with him.

"Are you sure you want me here with you?" she asked, sitting next to him on his sofa. "Are you sure they're going to want me here?"

"*They're* not going to want you here. But I do."

"Okay. But if at any time you want me to leave, just tell me and I'm gone."

Colt grasped her shoulders and looked her in the eyes. "I need your support, Des. Tony's shooting an indie movie in Colorado right now and can't be here. He didn't want me to do this alone, so I promised him you'd be here with me."

She nodded. "I'm here for you, honey. You know that."

At the knock on the door, she read the panic on Colt's face and reached down to squeeze his hand. "It's going to be all right. Just be firm. You know this is what you want."

"You're right. I know exactly what I want."

Colt went over and opened the door to his agent, Nora Pantere, and his PR rep, Stan Balleu. They weren't the same people who represented Des, but they were reputable, and they'd done a great job with Colt's career.

"Oh, hi, Des," Nora said, shaking her hand. "We didn't know you were going to be here."

"Hello, Desiree," Stan said. "I've seen some of the dailies for the movie. You and Colt look dynamite together."

"Thanks, Stan."

"Would either of you like a drink?" Colt asked.

"Mineral water for me," Nora said. "Lord, but it's hot out here. How are you two holding up?"

"Same for me," Stan said.

While Colt went to grab their drinks, Des answered. "We're handling it just fine. And the shoot's going well. Why don't you two come in and sit down?"

She led them into the living space and they grabbed a seat.

"I hope this is some announcement that the two of you are either dating or engaged," Stan said. "That would be such a stellar PR move in advance of the release of this movie."

Colt handed them both drinks. "You know that's not going to happen, Stan."

Stan, a short, stocky bald man in his late forties, sighed. "A man can dream, can't he?"

Nora laughed. "So why are we here, Colt?"

Colt took a seat on the chair next to them. Des took up position behind him.

"I'm going to come out."

Dead. Silence. Des chewed on her lower lip.

"No," Nora said.

"Absolutely not," Stan added. "It'll be the death of your career as a lead actor and you know it."

"Stan's right," Nora said. "We've discussed this before, Colt. Many actors are gay. Closeted gay. And highly successful. Some are even married. To women. You can make this work, Colt, and have years ahead of you making profitable movies. Maybe even win an Academy Award."

"But if you come out as a gay man," Stan said, taking over for Nora, "your leading man days are over. No actress will want to work with you, no studio will cast you in a leading role, and no women will fork over money to come see you. I'm sorry, but it's a fact. The American buying public is just not ready for a gay man to be a leading role in a movie."

It took everything within Des not to speak out in rebuttal. But this wasn't her show to lead. It was Colt's. And if he backed down now, he'd likely never stand up to them again.

"Sorry, but I think that's bullshit," Colt finally said.

And Des exhaled.

"I'm a bankable leading man, and you both know it. My sexual orientation notwithstanding, I can open a movie. I've been doing it for ten years, and after I come out, I'll continue to do it. I'm tired of hiding in the shadows with the person I love. I want to be able to live freely, and love the same way. It shouldn't matter who I live with, or who I love. That makes no difference in my performance as an actor."

"No, it shouldn't," Nora said. "But it will. Mark my words, Colt, it will make a difference."

Stan stood. "You're going to take a hit. A serious one. In the media as well as at the box office."

"I might take a small one. But I don't think in the grand scheme of my overall career that it'll suffer. And I don't intend to come out in a major way. I'm not going to make a major announcement. But Tony and I are going to live together, and he's going to attend the premiere of *Lost Objectives* with me."

Nora cocked a brow. "And you know with everything that's in me as your agent, I'm going to try and change your mind."

"You can try, but it won't happen. I'm committed."

Stan rubbed his temple. "You should be committed. This is a mistake. It'll ruin you."

"I don't believe that," Colt said. "I have confidence in my bankability, and in the public. In the end, it's not going to matter."

Nora sighed. "Colt, I don't like this at all. But I'll support you, and our team will do whatever damage control is necessary."

They stayed through dinner, and Des didn't leave Colt's side the entire time. The biggest thing was, neither his agent nor his PR team abandoned him, which she knew had been Colt's biggest fear. Of course they spent the entire time trying to talk him out of his decision, which Des had expected them to do, but in the end, they offered their support. She was so glad.

When Nora and Stan left around eight to catch their flight back, Colt and Des walked them to the entrance gate and waved good-bye as their SUV pulled away.

Colt turned to her and Des wrapped her arms around him.

He sagged against her, and she knew the emotional turmoil he'd been through that day had to have exhausted him.

"Jesus, that was draining," he whispered against her neck.

She brushed her hands through his hair. "I know, honey. And you can still change your mind if you want to."

He pulled back and held her hands. "I don't want to change my mind. I'm tired of being afraid that someone is going to see me with Tony, that some paparazzi are going to snap a picture of the two of us together, then blow up our relationship in the tabloids like it's some big sleazy secret. It's not sleazy. We're in love and we have been for three years. It's about time I stop living like it's a secret that I'm too ashamed to have out. I have to live honestly."

"Yes, you do. And your fans will appreciate that honesty. They love you, Colt. They love the kinds of movies you make. You're not going to be any different because you're gay."

"I know that. But will everyone else?"

"I believe they will."

He leaned in and wrapped his arms tightly around her. "I love you, Des."

"I love you, too." She lifted up and gave him a quick kiss on the corner of his mouth.

"Am I interrupting?"

Des turned to find Logan at the entrance to the gate. She smiled at him, then turned to Colt.

"Are you going to be all right, or do you need me to hang out with you?"

"I'm fine. I need a hot shower, then a hard drink. Then I'm going to make a phone call."

He kissed her cheek. "Hey, Logan. I'll see you later."

"Colt."

After Colt walked away, Des went up to Logan. "What brings you by?"

"Just wanted to see you. Was I interrupting?"

"Oh. With Colt? No."

"Looked like a pretty intense moment between the two of you."

Was he still jealous over the Colt thing? "Colt had a rough day."

"And you kiss your friends who had rough days like that all the time?"

She looped her arm in his. "Are you jealous?"

He pulled back. "Seriously, Des. Is there something going on with you and Colt?"

"Seriously, Logan. There isn't. We're friends. I've told you that before."

"I don't kiss my friends like that."

She laughed. "I would imagine you don't, since most of your friends are guys."

"I'm not kidding here."

He wasn't. He was pissed.

"Logan. There's nothing going on with Colt and me. We're friends."

"So what was going on just now?"

"I told you. He had a rough day. I was offering him some comfort."

"And you're not going to elaborate."

She lifted her chin, irritated that he would ask. "No. I'm not."

"Whatever. I'm going to head back to the ranch." He turned and walked toward the gate.

"Are you kidding me with this Neanderthal macho jealousy thing? You really don't trust me?"

He stopped and pivoted to face her. "No, it's that you don't trust me."

"Because I won't tell you every detail of what Colt and I were talking about?"

He didn't say anything.

"Some things I can't tell you. I'm sorry."

"Because your friendship with Colt is more important than what you and I have."

"Now you're being petty and childish." And she was frustrated because she held Colt's confidence.

"And now it's time for me to leave. Good night, Des."

She couldn't believe he was leaving, that he'd seen what he wanted to see, and without justification, was angry about it.

Fine. He could just leave. She wasn't going to ask him to stay. She walked back toward her trailer, determined to forget all about Logan. She had more important things to think about. Like Colt, who was her best friend and needed her and loved her unconditionally.

And her movie, which she should spend more time concentrating on instead of pigheaded, provincial, idiotic males who had their heads stuck so far up their own asses their brains were leaking out in the last century.

LOGAN SAT IN his truck, steaming mad over his encounter with Des. He popped open the top of his can of pop and drank it down in about four swallows.

It had been a brutally hot, miserable day of work on the ranch. He'd gone back to the house, ate dinner, took a shower, and the only thing on his mind after that—hell, the only thing on his mind the entire day—had been to see Des. She'd been a balm to his tortured senses from day one. Even when she teased him, she relaxed him.

Except he'd walked through the gate and had seen her in one hell of romantic clinch with Colt. And then they'd kissed, and it sure had looked a lot more than a "just friends" kind of kiss to him. The heat that had cooked his blood all damn day long had begun to boil over with a jealous rage that had taken even him by surprise.

By nature he wasn't a jealous type of guy, mainly because he never really cared all that much about any of the women he'd been with before. They'd all been casual acquaintances or occasional bed partners. So if they wanted to see other guys, that had been fine with him. He had never cared one way or another.

Except Des. Des did something to his brain or his heart or his something, because even knowing she and Colt were just friends, seeing her touching him and kissing him and being affectionate with him made him goddamn crazy.

And then he'd acted like an asshole—something he seemed to do regularly where she was concerned.

He took a deep breath and let it out. Yeah, he'd said stupid things to her and had accused her of having some kind of intimate relationship with Colt and lying to him about it.

He could lay the blame on his mother for this, but essentially, the fault was with him. Somewhere deep inside him, he was broken, and he didn't know how to fix it.

The one thing he did know was that he was going to have to face Des head-on and not let this fester. He was already miserable, and no doubt she was pissed as hell at him.

And rightly so.

He got out of his truck and went back to the gate. The

guards there knew him well by now, so they just let him through. He made his way to her trailer and knocked.

She opened the door, frowning when she saw him. "What? Did you think of a few more unsavory things to say about my character?"

"No. I came to apologize."

She paused, then held the door. "Come on in."

He walked in and shut the door behind him. Des had already walked away. She was in the kitchen, trying to open a bottle of wine.

"Here, let me do that for you."

She gave him a "drop dead" look. Undeterred, he took the corkscrew and bottle from her hands and pulled the cork, then poured her a glass and handed it to her. She took the glass and headed into the living room and took a seat.

She didn't invite him to sit. He didn't deserve it. He came in and kneeled down in front of her.

"You make me crazy. I do stupid things. I saw you and Colt holding each other tight and kissing, and it does insane things to my head."

She looked at him. "Colt and I are just friends. You know this."

"I know. But when you wouldn't elaborate, my head conjured up the two of you having secrets, excluding me from that part of your life. I don't like it. I know it's not logical, but I don't like it."

She sighed and put the glass down on the table next to her. "They're not my secrets to tell. If it has to do with my life, I'm an open book. Ask any question and I'll answer you. But as far as Colt's life . . ."

"I understand. I'm sorry I hurt you. I'm sorry I even intimated for a minute that I didn't trust you." He laid his forehead on her knee. "I'm an asshole sometimes, and I wish there was someone else to blame for that, but there isn't. This is all on me."

"You did hurt me. You've known from the beginning that I'm going to be honest with you, Logan. But as far as this? There are just things I can't tell you. Because when a friend needs you to be there for them, sometimes you have to hold their secrets."

He lifted his head to look at her, and he could see she was torn. "I'm sorry I made you feel as if you had to be in the middle between me and Colt. You don't have to be."

"He's like a brother to me, and I know that sounds icky since we do love scenes together. But we are really good friends. We're family. I love him, but not in the way—"

She stopped, and he held his breath. She stared at him for a few seconds, and he didn't know what to think.

"Not in a sexual way. Like with you. Our sex scenes are the real deal." Her lips curved.

And not at all what he thought she was going to say. "Right. So am I forgiven? Again?"

"Yes."

He rose up and brushed his lips across hers, then pulled her into his arms, dragging her on top of him onto the floor. The sweet forgiveness in her kiss was soon replaced by passion. Clothes were shed, Des grabbed a condom, and then she was on top of him, riding him to a hard and fast orgasm that left them both shattered, breathless, and perspiring.

They lay there naked, Des sprawled on top of him while he stroked her back.

"This floor sucks," he said.

Des laughed and climbed off him. They went into the bathroom to clean up and got dressed while Des fixed him a drink.

He pulled up a spot next to her on the sofa while she grabbed her wine.

"An open book, huh?" he asked as he took a sip of the pop she'd given him.

She frowned. "What?"

"You said earlier you were an open book. That I could just ask you any question and you'd answer it."

"Oh, right. That's true. So what do you want to know?"

"We've talked a lot about my family. Tell me about yours."

Des blew out a breath. "Oh. My family. Well, not much to tell, really. My dad is career army. My mom has been a stay-at-home mom her whole life in support of my dad's military endeavors. I have one older brother and one older sister. My brother went ROTC, then West Point, following in my father's footsteps. My sister is a biologist."

"So you're the odd duck."

She laughed. "Yes."

"Is your dad still in the military?"

"Yes. Currently stationed at Fort Benning in Georgia. He's a one-star general, with hopes to continue to move up the ladder."

"And what does your mom do?"

"All that stuff military wives do. I don't really know. She stays busy with all her social engagements. She's very dedicated to my father's military career. And my brother's now, too."

"How did your parents feel about you becoming an actress?"

She remembered the day she told them she wanted to be an actress, the horror on both their faces. "Both were dead set against it. My father wanted me to go to school to become a doctor."

"Had you expressed interest in being a doctor?"

"Never. I actually laughed when he said it. You do not laugh at my father. Our discussion didn't go well."

"But if it wasn't what you wanted to do, why would he be upset?"

"You don't understand. You just don't disagree with General Delbert Jenkins."

He smoothed his hand over her legs. "It wasn't General Jenkins talking to you, then, though. It was your dad."

"Yeah, well, tell him that. Anyway, I was terrible at both math and science, but he said there was nothing a Jenkins couldn't do and that I simply wasn't applying myself hard enough. That's when I told him I wanted to be an actress. He really exploded then. He told me that was the worst career choice I could ever make."

"Obviously, it wasn't."

"In hindsight, no. But at the time, it broke my heart. I had just gotten the lead in the school play and I was so thrilled. I wanted them to share my joy."

"And your mom? What did she say?"

"Nothing. She sat silently next to my dad. She was always on his side, agreeing with whatever he said."

"I'm sorry."

She met his gaze. "For what?"

"I know what it's like to not have parents on your side. Though at least I had my dad. It sounds to me like you were swimming upstream."

She shrugged. "I got used to it. He'd yell and insist, and I'd ignore him. I didn't even apply to any colleges, despite my father's vehement, very loud, very often orders that I do so. When I graduated from high school, I packed a bag and took a bus out to Hollywood. My parents never forgave me for that."

"You talk to them now, don't you?"

"They're happy for my success, but let's just say our relationship is . . . strained."

"Yeah, I know how that is." He leaned his head against his hand and played with a strand of her hair. "How about your brother and sister?"

"Teddy toes the army line, so I don't talk to him much. He's moving up the military ladder fast. Penelope and I touch base every now and then. She's as busy as I am, and she's deeply involved in biological research. But we do Skype, and she'll come out to L.A. and visit when she has a break. I'll visit her, and my parents, whenever I'm on a break from a movie."

"It doesn't sound like you're really all that close with any of your family members, Des."

She shrugged. "It is what it is. Probably out of all of them, I'm closest with Penny. But like I said, she's really busy doing research."

"Maybe you should talk to her about taking a vacation, too."

She laughed. "I probably should. Though I think she's less likely to take one than I am."

"A family trait, maybe?"

"Could be."

"Families can be the hardest on those they love the most, Des."

She nodded. "I don't doubt for a second that my parents love me. My dad just has tunnel vision. He had this very rigid upbringing. His father was military, too. He only knows one way, and that's his way. He brought that regimented military lifestyle into the home."

"And you rebelled against it."

She smiled. "I guess I did."

"Do you think that's why you decided to become an actress?"

She frowned. "You mean as an act of rebellion against my father? No. I really did fall in love with the craft. The rebellion part was just a bonus."

He laughed. "Yeah, I had that part down, too. Parents can't have all the fun torturing their kids. There has to be some payback."

"Like hiding your mom's makeup?"

"Like that. Among other things. She was so fussy she made it too easy."

"And my dad was so rigid, it was easy to get him riled up."

"Our kids will never have a chance. We're too laid-back."

She nodded. "Exactly. Plus, we know all the tricks."

"Yeah, and everyone says this, but their kids still find a way."

"True. Still, I'd like to think I'm smarter than my kids

will be, and a lot more Zen than my parents ever were about the little things. Like career. As long as they're happy, what does it matter what they want to do?"

"And getting dirty. Because aren't all kids supposed to get mud on their clothes?" he asked.

"I think so. We're going to be perfect parents."

He grinned at her, and she realized they were sitting there talking about their children. Children they weren't going to have together. But, oh, they'd have great kids. Wild little hellions who could ride horses as soon as they were old enough to be put on one. And the kids would put on plays for them in Logan's big living room. The two of them would sit on the sofa and watch them, clapping when they finished.

It was a wild, ridiculous fantasy. One that would never come to fruition, because she and Logan were going to part ways as soon as the movie finished.

But it was a fun fantasy, because so far in her life all she'd seen in her future was movie on top of movie. Never a home, never kids.

Until now.

And she liked what she saw. She wanted that future. She ached for it so much it shocked her.

"You sure went quiet. Did that whole talking-about-kids thing freak you out?" he asked.

"Actually, no." She picked up her wine and took a sip.

"Care to elaborate?"

"Actually, no." She smiled at him over the rim of her glass. "Did it freak you out?"

"No. I'm older than you, though."

"What does that have to do with anything?"

"I don't know. I guess it's time I start thinking about settling down and having kids."

"I don't believe how old you are has much to do with when it's the right time to start a family. Many people never have kids. Some have them way early, some not at all. My sister is committed to never having children."

"Why not?"

She shrugged. "She doesn't see herself as a parent—ever. Which is fine, because that's her choice to make. She's perfectly content to build a career. She says if she ever finds someone to marry, he'll have to accept that she doesn't want children."

"I guess you're right. I've known a few people—and some couples—who decided not to have kids. It comes down to a matter of choice for everyone. For me, it's a legacy thing. I want to have someone to pass down my ownership in the ranch to."

"There are your brothers."

"That's true. And they might have children who want to be a part of the ranching business. Nothing would make me happier."

"Because your kids might want to be—oh, I don't know . . . " She studied him for a few minutes.

He laughed. "What?"

"Fashion models. Or maybe sell cosmetics."

He cocked a brow. "Now you're assuming I'm going to have all girls."

"What? Guys can't become fashion models or sell cosmetics? Very sexist of you, McCormack."

"Fine. My kids can do whatever the hell they want. Even become an actor or an actress. I just hope either one of my kids, or Luke's or Reid's, wants to be a damn rancher."

"There's nothing wrong with being a rancher. If one of my kids wanted to do that, I'd be so proud of them."

He gave her a searing look. "Seriously."

"Of course. It's a tough job, but an admirable one. Look at how hard you work. And look at the results. You're building a legacy for your heirs—and for your brothers' heirs, too. Not many people are tough enough to take that on. Who wouldn't be proud to have their children be a part of that legacy?"

He pulled her onto his lap and kissed her very thoroughly. "Thank you."

"You're welcome."

"I should go and let you get some sleep. I'm sure you have a big day tomorrow, and so do I."

She stood and walked him to the door. She wanted him to stay, but they had gone through some heavy subject matter tonight. Her background, and having kids. Legacies. Their futures, both of them avoiding the topic of melding those futures together.

"I'll call you tomorrow," he said, pulling her against him to give her one last, barn-burning kiss that made her regret letting him leave.

"Okay."

He walked out and she shut and locked the door, then headed into her bedroom to wash her face and brush her teeth. She climbed into her bed and grabbed her script, intending to run through her scenes for tomorrow. But all she could think about was Logan. Each time she tried to get into character, his face swam before her eyes.

After an hour, she gave up on the script, laying it on the nightstand. She shut out the light, wishing Logan were lying next to her. The bed seemed cold and empty without his body against hers.

When her phone rang, she grabbed it and smiled.

"Didn't you just leave?" she asked.

"Shouldn't you be sleeping?"

"I was trying to study tomorrow's script. Shouldn't you be sleeping?"

"I don't like sleeping without you."

That made her smile. "Good. Because I'm not having any luck sleeping without you, either."

"Just wanted you to know I was thinking about you. I'll let you go."

"Screw that. Get your ass back over here so you can climb into my bed. I'll never get to sleep otherwise."

He laughed. "I'll be right there."

She hung up, then threw on a pair of shorts and a tank

top, slipped into her sandals and walked toward the gate. Another beautifully clear night.

She'd really miss these once she got back to the city.

One of the night security guys raised a brow at her.

"Don't even ask, Phil," she said.

Phil shook his head, but smiled. "Okay. I won't."

When Logan pulled in and came walking toward the gate, Phil opened it with a wide grin. "Evening, Mr. McCormack."

"Hey, Phil."

"Night, Miss Desiree."

"Night, Phil."

She slipped her arm around Logan's waist and they walked to her trailer.

"You didn't have to come out here and wait for me," he said.

She tilted her head back to look at him. "I wanted to."

Once inside, they undressed and climbed into her bed.

Logan grunted. "Your bed is small. We should have gone to my place."

"Quit complaining and get over here."

He tugged her against his chest and Des sighed. Perfect. Logan turned out the light and Des could already feel her lids drooping closed.

"Better?" he asked.

She yawned. "Perfect."

# Chapter 21

---

IT HAD BEEN an idyllic few weeks, but now it was coming to a close. Today, Des and Colt would shoot their final scene, and the movie would wrap.

That part she didn't want to think about, not when she and Logan had spent every single night together. As soon as she finished on set each day, she'd head over to the ranch and would either spend time with Martha until the guys came in for dinner, or if they wrapped filming later, she and Logan would spend the evening alone. She'd slept in his bed every night, had gotten accustomed to wandering around that big ranch house she'd grown to love so much.

Martha had become as much a mother to her as she had always been to Logan. What was she going to do without Martha's advice? What was she going to do without Martha's awesome food?

It was a good thing they'd filmed out here in the summer, where she sweated off a massive amount of calories working under the hot sun every day, or she swore she'd probably have gained ten pounds eating all the glorious meals Martha fixed for her. When she went back to L.A. she'd likely starve to death.

Though Martha was teaching her how to cook, so she was learning a lot under Martha's expert tutelage. At least when she went home, she'd know more than how to make a salad and steamed vegetables.

Today she and Colt were in full makeup and costume, ready for the final scene, though it wasn't the movie's final scene, because that had already been filmed prior to coming out here. The final scene of the movie was back on the planet, in a hospital room, a tender reunion scene between her and Colt. At least she wouldn't have to die in this movie, a fact that made her very grateful.

This final scene being filmed was the one before the big explosion they'd filmed several weeks ago. She and Colt were running for their lives, and the scene they were filming today had them on top of a massive rock, debating whether to jump. The stunt folks would make the jump for them, but this was where she and Colt would declare their love for each other. It was going to be a huge emotional scene, a possible good-bye, and Desiree wasn't ready for filming to finish, so her emotions were tenuous. She dug into her feelings when she and Colt stood at the edge and held on to each other, looking down into what—once CGI effects added some depth to the scene—would be a giant abyss.

"I love you—you know that, don't you?" Colt said, holding on to her as they mimicked feeling the shock waves as the aliens worked to destroy what remained of the planet.

She shook her head, the tears falling, blinding her as she kept her focus on Colt. "I'm not a goddamned mind reader. I didn't know how you felt. Why didn't you ever tell me?"

Colt looked away, then back at her. "Because I'm a coward, Lacey. Because I was afraid you didn't love me back. Because I thought you still mourned Brace."

She pulled him to her, kissed him, then squeezed his

hand, all the while mimicking trying to hold her balance as the planet fell apart around them. "Brace was a long time ago. And it was never him, Deacon. I've always loved you. Since we first met, since you made that cocky remark to me. You were mine. You'll always be mine."

Colt swept his fingers across her jaw, and she gave him her deepest look of love. "Let's make this jump and get the hell out of here. Together."

They hovered on the brink of the precipice, looked into each other's eyes one last time. Des nodded at Colt, and then—

"And, cut." Theo stood, and the crew clapped. "That was as damn perfect a scene as any the two of you have shot. We have a location wrap."

Des smiled and swiped at the tears. Colt hugged her and kissed her cheek.

"Fucking finally," Colt said.

Des laughed. "Seriously."

It was done. They were finished here. As she watched the crew start pulling the sets apart and wrapping up wires and equipment, she looked toward the far corners of the ranch. She was going to be leaving all of this.

She was going to be leaving Logan.

"Tell him how you feel, Des," Colt said as they walked back to their trailers.

"Tell who?"

Colt rolled his eyes. "I'm not the only one who needs to live an honest life, you know."

"Oh. Well, you know. We've had fun, but there's no future for the two of us. He's here, and I'm there and, yes, I have feelings for him, but it would only end in disaster, with us hating each other. I don't want that when we can end it friendly."

"Already deciding how he feels without asking him?"

They stood at the entrance to Colt's trailer. Des had no answer to that. She was brave—fearless, really—in so many areas of her life. But this? This scared the hell out of her.

"Just talk to him, Des. Don't walk away without knowing what might be between the two of you."

"I guess so."

He kissed the tip of her nose. "Don't guess so. Just do it. You kicked ass in that last scene, by the way. You nearly had me crying."

She laughed. "Thanks. I'll see you at the wrap party later."

She showered, changed clothes, then headed over to the ranch. She walked into the house, the smell of something delicious coming from the kitchen.

"Hi, Martha."

Martha gave her a bright smile. "Hi, sweetheart. I just pulled a couple peach pies from the oven."

"I smelled them as soon as I opened the front door. The scent is to die for."

"Thank you. They're for my church group. And how are you doing? Did you finish the movie?"

She pulled up a seat at the island. "We did. Finally."

"Congratulations." Martha poured her a glass of iced tea. "And did it all go well?"

"I think so."

"You must be so happy to be finished."

Des took a drink of tea and nodded. "Yes. I guess so."

Martha loaded a few things into the dishwasher, then wiped her hands on the towel and refilled her tea glass and came around to the other side of the island to take a seat. "You're going to miss the ranch. And Logan."

"Yes."

"Have you told Logan that?"

"No."

"Why not?"

Des laughed. "Now you sound like Colt. He told me the same thing today."

"Maybe Colt's suggestion makes sense. You two are never going to figure out what you both want if you don't communicate with each other."

"I don't know, Martha. I can't see how this could ever work."

"Unless you talk to each other."

She sighed. "I know. I'm afraid, though. He's so reluctant about relationships, and ours has been perfect because there've been no promises. No ties."

"Well, a relationship has to either progress or it dies. I think it's high time to figure out where yours is going, isn't it?"

Martha made a lot of sense. Which didn't comfort Des all that much. "You're right, of course."

Logan came in the door a short time later, his face darkly tanned, rivulets of sweat running down his temples. He took off his cowboy hat. His hair was matted to his head and soaking wet. So was his T-shirt, which was so wet it outlined his chest and abs to perfection. He looked utterly miserable, and absolutely, breathtakingly sexy.

When he looked up at her, he straightened and smiled. "Hey. Didn't expect to see you here today."

"We finished up early, so I thought I'd surprise you."

"I'm surprised."

Martha filled up a giant glass of ice water and handed it to him. "It's over a hundred degrees out there today. Drink this."

Without a word, he accepted the glass from her and downed the contents. "Thank you."

"You look exhausted," Des said. "And fried."

"It's okay, just hot out today." He came over and brushed his lips over hers. She tasted sweat, and something purely elementally male that never ceased to turn her on.

"Still, you'd probably like to take a shower and put your feet up in the cool air-conditioning for the rest of the day."

He leaned against the counter. "What's going on, Des?"

"A wrap party tonight. But you don't have to come if you don't want to."

"You inviting me?"

"Yes."

"Then I want to come. What time?"

"Eight thirty."

"I'll be there."

She grinned. "Good. And thank you."

"Now that that's settled," Martha said. "We're having salmon steaks and asparagus for dinner, along with fruit salad. Are you staying, Des?"

"I'd love to, Martha. Can I help?"

"Everything's already done, except for the salmon, which we're fixing on the grill tonight."

"Sounds great. And, Martha, you and Ben are also invited to the wrap party tonight. If you'd like to come."

Martha's smile was as wide as the state. "I'd love to come. How thrilling. How do I dress?"

"Just as casual as you'd like. There'll be drinks. And we're letting the press in. It'll be a free-for-all. Should be a wild and crazy night."

"Oh, boy." Martha's eyes gleamed with excitement. "I'm going to head home to pick out somethin' to wear."

"Leave the fancy furs in the closet, Martha," Logan said. "It's a little warm for those."

"You hush. And see what Ben's up to. I'm sure Desiree is hungry."

"Yes, ma'am."

After Martha left the room, Des slid off the barstool and went over to him, sliding her hand into his hair.

"I'm hot, I'm sweaty, and I stink," he said.

"I don't care. Kiss me."

He tugged her close and put his mouth on hers, kissing her with that same familiar hunger that never failed to drive her desire to feverish levels. She whimpered and raised up on her toes, molding her body to his. He grabbed her butt, then pulled away, his breath coming out in harsh gasps.

"Martha will be back any minute. Their house isn't that far away. We need to stop."

"Or, you could take me upstairs with you."

"You're a bad influence."

"Not the first time I've heard that."

He took her hand and pulled her upstairs, then shut the door to his room and headed into the bathroom.

She took a seat on his bed. "Where are you going?"

He paused and turned around. "To take a shower."

"You think I mind a little sweat?"

"Babe. I've been out in the pasture all day. Trust me, I'm not pleasant."

She kicked off her sandals and slid out of her capris. "Come here and make love to me, Logan."

She heard the low rumble of a growl somewhere deep in his chest, but he jerked his T-shirt over his head and unzipped his pants, toeing out of his boots at the same time. Soon, he was beautifully, gloriously naked, and she looked her fill.

He grabbed her ankle and pulled her to the edge of the bed, grasping her panties and drawing them down. Her tank went up next, followed by her bra, baring her breasts. And then his mouth was on her neck, licking and sucking it before moving to her nipples, the scratchiness of a day's growth of beard across her skin only making her writhe with pleasure.

She wanted him, and the clock was ticking down to her departure. She wasn't going to wait when her need was so great. She wrapped her legs around him, loving the weight of his body on top of hers, the way he surged against her, making her body quiver in all the right places.

"Logan, please."

He grabbed a condom and put it on, then slid inside her, holding himself off of her with his hands as he lifted, then thrust deeply. She swept her hands over his muscled arms and shoulders while he drove within her, then rolled his hips over the most sensitive spot until she arched, crying out for more.

And when he gave her more, she splintered, so ready for him, so needy for this moment that she couldn't hold back the orgasm that rushed through her like an eruption of the sweetest pleasure. Logan cupped her behind and held her close while he shuddered with his release. She held tight to him, licking away the salty sweat on his neck as he rode it out.

Panting, he pressed a kiss to her brow. "Now you need another shower."

"It's summer. I can always use another shower."

He smiled down at her, kissed her, then dragged her up and into his bathroom. She grabbed one of the hair clips she stored in his drawer and stepped into the shower, washing quickly, then stepping out while Logan took his shower. She dried off and got dressed, then went downstairs and poured another glass of tea.

Martha showed up a few minutes later to find Des sitting at her same spot at the island.

"Did you find something to wear?" she asked.

"I did. Sorry I was gone so long. Where's Logan?"

"He went up to shower."

"Uh-huh." Martha gave her a strange smile. "Well, Ben's starting the grill, so we'll get the salmon going."

"Great."

Logan came down a few minutes later and gave her a sexy half smile.

"Ben's going to grill the salmon," she told him.

"Okay." He bent to kiss her cheek, then whispered in her ear. "You have a hickey on your neck."

Her eyes widened and she slapped her hand over her neck as she pivoted to look at him. "Seriously?"

"Would I joke about something like that?"

"Uh, excuse me. I'll be right back." She dashed into the bathroom, and sure enough, there was a mark at the bottom of her neck. And more spots than that, obviously because he hadn't shaved before they made love. Dammit. So much for thinking they had pulled something over on Martha. No wonder Martha had given her that knowing smile.

She came back out and Martha was busy setting the table, so Des dove in to help.

Nothing was said about the mark on her neck. Thank God. She was certain Martha wholeheartedly approved of her relationship with Logan, but she didn't think she'd survive discussing her and Logan's sex life with a woman she considered Logan's mother figure.

Ben brought in the salmon and they ate. Logan and Ben spent most of dinner discussing something cattle-related, while she and Martha were focused on the wrap party, so she didn't get to listen in to Logan's conversation. But Des knew Martha was a little nervous, especially since the press was going to be in attendance.

"It's not those jerks that have been hanging out at the gate for the past couple of months, is it?"

Des shook her head. "No. These are press correspondents from various reputable outlets, unlike paparazzi who are just looking to take photos and sell them to the highest bidder."

"Okay. I don't like those paparazzi people."

"I don't either, Martha."

"What kinds of questions will the press people ask you?"

"They mostly ask about the movie, though more often than not they segue into personal relationships. It's like they can't help themselves. But we choose to answer the questions we want to. And they're limited to being on set only the first hour. Then we kick them off so we can relax without worrying about every word we say and every move we make being scrutinized or misinterpreted."

"Oh, that's good. So you can have fun."

"Exactly."

After dinner, she helped Martha with the dishes, then said she had to go get ready. Logan walked her out.

"I'll see you there?"

He pulled her close. "Yeah. I'll be there."

She laughed. "You sound thrilled."

"I'll be there."

"Okay." She kissed him, then climbed into the SUV

and drove back to the set to get ready for tonight. For the first time in a long time she was actually excited.

Tonight, after the party, she was going to tell Logan how she felt about him.

And then they'd talk about where they went from here.

With a renewed confidence, she went to figure out what she was going to wear.

# Chapter 22

MARTHA INSISTED LOGAN dress up. Which for Logan, meant his clean jeans and a dress shirt, and his newest boots. That was as good as it was going to get.

Martha wore her nice slacks and a pretty blouse, and she made Ben wear his khakis. They drove separate cars in case Martha and Ben wanted to leave before he did.

When they got out of their trucks, Logan turned to Ben. "Right after this, you can go to church, seeing as how you're already dressed for it."

"Shut up," Ben said, frowning and tugging at the collar of his button-down shirt.

"Enough, Logan. We have to dress nice. And I can't believe you wore jeans."

"It's a wrap party. On the ranch. Not exactly the Academy Awards, Martha."

"Still, It wouldn't kill you to dress up for the girl, would it?"

He looked down at his white button-down shirt and dark jeans. "I wore my new jeans and my best pair of boots."

Martha rolled her eyes. "Come on, boys."

Though as they passed through the security gate, Logan noticed most of the set was gone, replaced instead by billowing white tents and a wood floor. And lots of food, drinks, and waiters.

Fancy.

There was already a crowd of people, too. Some pretty dressed up. Okay, so maybe he was underdressed. Then again, no one was going to be interviewing him, so he could fly under the radar. This was Des's gig, not his.

There was some kind of champagne fountain, and a bar set up where people could get drinks, and a whole buffet of all kinds of food Logan couldn't even identify.

"Wow," Martha said as they walked past the buffet table. "If I'd known there was going to be food like this, I wouldn't have bothered to make dinner."

"I can still eat," Ben said.

"Of course you can. All right, let's grab a plate, and then we'll go find a table in the corner somewhere where we can observe and I can sneak photos. You coming, Logan?"

"I'm going to see if I can find Des. I'll catch up to you later."

They waved him off and went in the opposite direction. Logan stopped at the bar and grabbed a beer, which he didn't have to pay for. Nice. He took a long swallow, and after today, the cold brew tasted great. He wandered around, seeing a crowd and a lot of noise, so he went to investigate.

And there she was, in the middle of a throng of press. Des was dressed in something red and sparkly—and short, her legs looking sexier than he had ever seen because she also wore killer high heels. Her hair was curled and partially piled up, and she had makeup on—not on-the-set makeup, but getting-her-picture-taken-by-professionals kind of makeup, with her lips all glossy and kissable.

He'd never seen anyone look more gorgeous.

"So tell us, Desiree, how did the shoot go?"

"It went well. Colt and I worked incredibly well together, as always." She turned to the side, and the dress bared her shoulders, and her back. All of her back.

Christ. She was just . . . So. Damn. Sexy.

"And how did you handle the Oklahoma heat? It's one of their hottest summers."

"I managed just fine. There's a lot to like about the land here. And with all the trees, there's plenty of shade."

"But we heard the shoot was pretty brutal. No trees on the barren landscape of Quazena, the post-apocalyptic planet where these scenes were set."

She turned and smiled at the cameras, and the effect was devastating. "That's true. But the crew takes very good care of us, and Theo Winfield is a very generous director who doesn't overwork his actors."

Logan wanted to laugh. Des was the one who was generous, considering how much of an asshole Theo was. Theo should consider himself lucky she hadn't thrown him under the bus and told the press what a womanizing, cheating prick the guy was.

"Any on-set romances brewing? Like between you and your costar, Colt Stevens?"

She didn't even hesitate. "Colt and I have been friends for many years. That's all it's been between us, though I feel we have wonderful chemistry on film. You'll see that when *Lost Objectives* releases in two weeks. I hope you'll all be there to see it. It's a great movie. I think it's one of Colt's finest performances."

Des was in her element, fielding questions easily, deflecting those she didn't want to answer without insulting the press.

This was what she was born to do. She took his breath away. No wonder she loved this acting thing so much. Not only was she good at sinking into a part, but there was a glow about her when she was the center of attention. Not that there was an ego involved, because as far as he'd seen, she didn't have any. But she was an entirely different person now that she was dressed up, fielding questions, and talking about her craft.

The press ate it up, snapping pictures, asking her questions, and surrounding her.

She was a goddamned movie star.

And as he watched her playing to the press, he realized he had no choice.

He had to let her go. She no more belonged in his world than he belonged in hers.

The thought of it caused an ache in his chest, as if someone had reached in there and snatched out his goddamned heart.

Maybe they had. Des had.

He'd thought tonight they could talk about a way that they could possibly make this relationship between them work. Because he couldn't imagine her leaving this ranch and him never seeing her again.

But now, watching her tonight, he realized she would never be satisfied with someone like him, living in a place like this. The L&M ranch could never hold her, would never make her happy.

They might have fun for a little while. Just like his mom and dad had. But eventually, she'd be gone, craving the limelight and adventure, needing more than dust and cow shit and miles of nothing but land.

This wasn't the life for her.

And he wasn't the right man for her. She needed someone like Colt, who dressed up nice and made movies like she did and looked good standing next to her. Not a dusty cowboy who knew nothing about this business.

When she finished with the press, she stopped and said hello to a few people, then made her way over to him.

"You look good," she said. "I want to kiss you, but the press is still here and I don't think you want to be on the front page of some entertainment website tomorrow."

"No, I don't. And you look gorgeous."

She smiled. "Thank you."

"You really know how to handle the press."

"Thanks. Years of experience in learning what to say and what not to say. And typically, they ask the same types of questions over and over again, so it's just a matter of knowing the right answers."

"You did well."

"Did you get something to eat? They catered in a bunch of fancy food."

"I'm still full from dinner."

"Okay. Once the press leaves, I want to talk to you about something."

"Yeah, I want to talk to you, too."

She grinned. "Hopefully it's the same thing."

He doubted it, but still, he didn't want to ruin the high she was obviously on, so he smiled at her. "I'm going to let you mingle with the important people. I think I'll track down where Martha and Ben wandered off to."

She laid her hand on his arm. "I'll catch up with you in a bit?"

"Yeah."

He started to wander off.

"Logan?"

He stopped. "Yeah?"

"Thanks for coming tonight. It means a lot to me that you're here."

He nodded, gave her a smile, and walked away.

Her sweetness, her trust in him, that was going to kill him, knowing what he was going to do later.

DES WAS SO tired of smiling for the cameras, of having to answer the same questions over and over again about the movie and her personal life and whether or not she'd talked to James lately and how she and Colt were getting along and if they had started up a romance. It was like the press had a wish that every leading man and leading lady who were single were going to have a romance. She understood it was a Hollywood thing, but how many times did she have to tell them that she and Colt were just friends? She was ever so grateful when the press's time was up and they were escorted off the property.

The best part of tonight was that Tony had come to be here with Colt. It was the beginning of the two of them being together in the open. Colt had decided he wasn't going to make some grand announcement, he was just going to start being with Tony, living with him, and at some point in an interview, he'd mention how long they'd been together as a couple and leave it at that. And then maybe it wouldn't *be* such a big thing if he didn't make a big thing of it.

Des hoped so.

Colt and Tony sat together at a table in the corner. She waved as she walked past them. Colt blew her a kiss and Tony smiled and waved.

Theo's wife was in attendance tonight, so he stuck to her like glue, on his best behavior for the press. He'd stood beside her and proclaimed the shoot had gone smoothly and that both his leads had performed to perfection. While barely standing within two feet of Des.

Ha.

She found Logan at a table near the bar, sitting with Ben and Martha. Martha's cheeks were pink with excitement, and every time one of the actors walked by, she'd snap a picture. Des wandered over.

"Oh, Des, you look so beautiful tonight," Martha said. "Like a true movie star."

"You do clean up pretty," Ben said.

"Thank you both," she said, sliding into a chair.

"Are you finished with all your work for the night?" Martha asked.

"Yes."

"What can I get you to drink?" Logan asked.

"A club soda with lime would be great."

Logan stood. "Anyone else?"

"Oh, we're fine here, I think, Logan, but thank you," Martha said.

While Logan wandered over to the bar, Martha asked, "So what's next for you?"

"There's a premiere of my next movie in a couple of weeks. Plus, I have to do some finishing work on this one at the studio. So I head back to L.A."

Martha took her hand. "We're going to miss you."

"I'm going to miss you, too."

"When do you leave?"

"Tomorrow."

Martha's eyes brimmed with tears. "Oh, so soon?"

"I'm afraid so." Des fought back tears of her own.

"Will you come back and visit us sometime?"

"Well, I have been invited to Emma and Luke's wedding."

"Oh, it'll be so wonderful to see you again. But I'm hoping you'll be back before then."

She sighed. "We'll see. I hope so, too." Her fingers were crossed she'd be seeing a lot more of Martha and Ben.

"Here you go." Logan handed Des her drink.

"Thank you. All that talking I had to do made me thirsty." She took a few sips of her club soda.

"I think we've had enough of all the partying," Martha said. "I'm going to wander through the crowd, snap a few more photos, and then we're going to head out for the night."

Martha and Ben stood.

"Thank you for coming."

Martha scooped her into a hug. "You're welcome here anytime."

"Thank you for making me feel so at home, so much like a part of your family."

Martha kissed her cheek, then Ben hugged her and they left.

"That was hard."

"What was?" Logan asked.

"Saying good-bye to Martha and Ben."

"Oh. Well, you have a lot of things to do back in L.A. Soon you'll forget all about us here."

She frowned. "I don't think so. This place has become like home for me."

He laughed. "The way you're dressed tonight? You couldn't be further from looking like you belong here."

"That's just for show. I'm way more comfortable in a pair of jeans and tennis shoes than I ever am dressed up like this."

"You look like you should be dressed like that all the time, Des. You look amazing."

"Thank you. But this isn't who I am. This is just an act."

He didn't say anything more to that, and then they wandered through the crowds, stopped and visited with various members of the crew.

"There's Colt," Logan said. "I didn't know your friend Tony was in town."

"He is."

They went over to their table.

"Hey, Logan," Colt said. "Why don't you two take a seat?"

Des and Logan sat.

"What brings you back in town, Tony?" Logan asked.

Tony looked over at Colt, and Colt nodded.

"I wanted to congratulate my boyfriend on completing his movie."

Logan looked over at Colt, who was smiling at Tony. It didn't take Logan more than a few seconds to make the connection. He looked at Des, who nodded.

"Oh. I didn't know."

"No one did. Until now," Colt said. "I'm not making an announcement. Tony and I have been together for a long time. I'm just tired of hiding it."

"Why should you hide it? You should be with whoever the hell you want to be with. I wish you two the best of luck."

Des watched as Colt visibly exhaled. "Thanks for that,

Logan. You don't even know how much that means to Tony and me."

Tony nodded. "Agreed. Seriously, man. Thanks."

Logan shrugged. "You're welcome, but I don't know why anyone would make a big deal over who you love. I know they do, but it's bullshit and none of their goddamn business."

Colt looked over at Des. "Why can't everyone be like Logan?"

"Why not, indeed?" She grasped Colt's hand. "It's going to be okay."

They ended up staying to hang out with Tony and Colt until the party started breaking up. Then Des went to her trailer to change into a sundress and sandals, taking her hair down and brushing it out. She washed her makeup off and felt normal again.

She'd told Logan she'd come to his house after she changed, so she hopped into one of the SUVs and drove over to the ranch. Her stomach tightened when she drove up to the big white house, knowing she was leaving tomorrow and how much she was going to miss this place that she now thought of as hers. Ridiculous, of course. It wasn't her home.

She got out of the SUV and saw all the dogs running over to her. She was going to miss them as much as everyone else.

"Hi, babies." She knelt down and petted them. She stuck her face in their fur and hugged them close.

Logan was on the front porch waiting for her as she climbed the stairs.

"It's like seeing Cinderella poof into the scullery maid at midnight."

"Hey. I take exception to that. Are you intimating that I'm dowdy now?"

He laughed. "You could never be dowdy. Now you're just regular beautiful instead of glamorous beautiful."

She walked up to him and twined her arms around his neck. "I'll accept that as a compliment."

"Good. Because it was intended as one."

They went inside and to the living room. She led him over to the sofa. "So I have a question to ask you."

"You're not gonna get down on one knee and ask me to marry you, are you?"

She laughed. "No, cowboy. I might be a little unconventional in some areas, but in that, I'm traditional."

They took a seat and she turned to him. "So the premiere of the last movie Colt and I made together is two weeks from now. I want you to attend with me."

He frowned. "Like a big movie premiere in L.A.?"

"Yes."

He shook his head. "I don't think so. Thanks for asking, though."

"No, you don't understand. It's a really big deal. We'd dress up, you'd get to wear a tux, I wear a fancy dress. We watch the movie, then there are parties."

"Yeah, Des. I do get it. And that's not my thing."

She stared at him. "What do you mean that's not your thing?"

"I mean this is where it ends for us. Hollywood is your life, not mine."

She felt like a knife had been stuck in her heart. *This is where it ends for us.*

"Surely you don't mean that. Yes, the whole Hollywood thing is a part of my life. Movie premieres are such a small part, though. But you've become a large part of it, and I thought you might want to share it with me."

"My life is here on the ranch. It always was and always will be."

"So what does that mean? That we're through?"

"Yeah, that's exactly what I mean. I can't be a part of your Hollywood life."

She wasn't going to just give up. Not without a fight. "You need to learn to bend, Logan, to be flexible. You know what we have together is worth it."

He stood. "We don't have anything together, Des. We

had fun while you were here, and now it's over. Your life is traveling all over the world, and going to those movie premieres, and standing in front of the press being a star. My life is here on the ranch, standing ankle deep in cow shit. And this is where I'm content to be. I wouldn't be happy in a tux attending your movie premiere."

She lifted her chin. "So you'd be unwilling to bend, just a little, so we could be together. You couldn't be even a little bit flexible."

"You know what? I'm the most goddamn flexible person I've ever known. I've bent to everyone else's needs my entire life. It's about damn time someone bent to my needs and my wants."

"Really. And what is it that you want, Logan? What is it that you feel you need that you're not getting?"

He didn't answer, and then she knew.

"I see. You want me to give up my dreams for you."

He shot her a look. "Absolutely not. I'd never ask that of you. And that's the problem. You and me—we don't fit together. We never have. And all the wishing in the world isn't gonna make it happen. Give it up, Des."

She stood. "I didn't ask you to change your life for me, Logan. I would never do that. I thought you and I had something together. That we could figure out how to merge our lives together and make it work."

She paused, then looked at him. "I'm in love with you. The thought of walking away from you hurts my heart and tears away at my soul. So I wanted to share a piece of my life with you by asking you to be my date at the movie premiere. Not to leave your life but to invite you to glimpse a piece of mine. If you can't even bend a little for that, then you're right. We have nothing together, and we never did."

She grabbed her keys off the coffee table and walked out. Tears pricked her eyes, blinding her as she made her way out the front door and into the SUV. She started it up, a part of her hoping and wishing that Logan would come running out of the house after her.

She wasn't surprised when he didn't.

She drove back to the set and made her way back to the trailer, forcing back the pain and the tears that threatened to tear her apart until she got into her trailer and shut and locked the door.

Only then did she give in. She went into her bedroom and curled up on the bed, grabbed her pillow, and sobbed.

LOGAN SAT ON the sofa, unable to move. It wasn't in him to deliberately hurt someone the way he'd hurt Des.

But hadn't that been what he'd done to her over and over again since they'd been together? He'd hurt her. And the last thing he wanted to do was keep hurting her.

Seeing the pain in her eyes when he'd said the things he'd said nearly tore him apart. He almost changed his mind right then, nearly pulled her into his arms and told her that he was lying, that he loved her and would move heaven and earth to keep her in his life.

But that wasn't what was best for Des and he knew it, so he'd lied and told her he didn't care enough about her to do whatever it took to make it work.

Now his heart was in shreds and the woman he loved had just walked out of his life.

And his house was emptier than it had ever been before.

He walked through the house and turned out all the lights, then headed upstairs to bed.

Alone.

He was used to that, had done it for years. It had become his comfort and his solace.

It had become his hell.

Until Des had come into his life and changed it all.

But now he was alone again.

And hell had moved back in.

*Chapter 23*

A WEEK AND a half after Des had left, Logan took an uncharacteristic night off and headed to his friend Bash's bar. It was a quiet, middle-of-the-week night and all he wanted was to watch some baseball and drink beer.

The one thing he could count on when hanging out with Bash was quiet. He could drink beer, they'd watch sports together, and they wouldn't have to talk about anything.

Or at least that's how it used to be.

"So how are things going with you and the hot actress?" Bash asked.

"That's over."

"Sorry to hear that. I thought you two had something that might last."

Logan took several long swallows of beer before answering. "Not sure why you'd think that."

"Because everyone in town talked about the two of you and how you and Des seemed like such a good fit together."

"Yeah, well, you can't believe everything you hear."

An hour later, his brother Luke showed up.

Logan sighed. "What are you doing here?"

"Saw your truck outside, thought I'd have a beer with you. You got a problem with that?"

"Nope."

Bash sat a beer in front of Luke.

"Have you heard anything from Des since she left?" Luke asked.

"No." His *no* had come out sharper than he'd intended.

"I see."

Logan grabbed his beer and finished it, then signaled Bash for another. "No, you don't see anything. No one sees anything. Why is everyone trying to push Des and me together?"

"I don't think anyone tried to do that, but the two of you were together a lot when she was here. I think it was a given you were a couple."

He shrugged and took a long swallow of beer. "Well, we aren't now."

"And you're obviously not happy about that."

"I'm just fucking fine."

Luke laughed. "Yeah, you're fine all right. What happened, Logan?"

"She's all Hollywood glamour and traveling all over the world. And I'm . . . here. Anyone with two eyes can see that we're not meant to be together."

"Or was it just you who saw that? You dumped her, didn't you?"

He stared down at the bottle of beer. "Maybe."

"You are such a dumbass. She was the best thing that ever happened to you. I've never seen you so full of life as you were when you were with her. She really did bring out the best in you—if there is such a thing."

"She'd have ended up hating me. And hating the ranch."

"She's not Mom, Logan. And she loved the ranch. Tell me what happened."

"She invited me to her movie premiere. I broke things off."

"Because you're afraid to try and make it work with

her. God forbid you actually take a chance on loving someone, right? Because it might actually work and you'll have to admit that someone could actually love you—and love the ranch. You have to stop letting that fear rule your life. It's taking away every chance you have at happiness."

Despite the six beers Logan had had, Luke's words sank in. Not that he hadn't heard them before, but he'd never been so crazy in love like he was now. And he'd never lost a woman he loved. He'd lain awake every night since she'd left his house, unable to sleep. He'd walked out onto the deck, thinking about how he'd shared the deck with her, wishing she was there with him and missing her so much even his bones ached.

"What do you think, Bash?" Logan asked as Bash cleaned away the empty beer bottles.

Bash laughed. "I'm the last one to give love advice, man. It didn't work so well for me. But if you love her, don't let dumb shit like geography and career get in the way. Go get your woman back."

He did want her back. But had he done too much damage to make that happen? Because Luke and Bash were right. Des loved him. And she loved the ranch, too. And if he couldn't give a little, then he didn't deserve her.

"I've had too many beers to drive back to the ranch," he said to Luke. "Give me a lift?"

"Sure."

"Thanks. I've got a few phone calls to make."

And he hoped like hell it wasn't too late.

# *Chapter 24*

---

IT WAS PREMIERE night for *Lost Objectives*. Des was both excited at the prospect of having critics and fans see the movie she and Colt had filmed last year, while simultaneously dreading going to the premiere.

"I've got a date lined up for you," her agent, Jennifer Simonds, had told her earlier in the day.

"Oh, God, Jennifer. I don't need a date. Going solo works just fine for me." The last thing she needed to deal with was being matched up with some up-and-coming actor who needed the exposure.

"You do need a date. It looks better for the press. And I think you'll like this guy."

"Who is it?"

"I've got another call, honey. He'll meet you at the premiere. Talk to you soon."

Jennifer hung up.

Des stared at her phone. Great. Just great. Now she had no idea who her date even was. If Logan hadn't been such a disappointment, he could have been her date. But that would have required him to meet her halfway, and God forbid he do that.

Her stomach tightened, the pain since she'd walked away from him ever present. She'd misjudged him, and how she'd thought he'd felt about her.

But she couldn't worry about him anymore. He was out of her life, and she was going to have to get used to it. He hadn't called her, hadn't texted, and he had obviously moved on.

So would she. And eventually she'd stop thinking about him.

Like today, when there were so many other things to attend do. She'd left her condo and booked a room at a hotel near the movie theater. There, her makeup and hair team would attend to her, and her dress was being brought in.

Colt had stopped by, pacing back and forth in her room, obviously anxious because he was taking Tony to the premiere tonight as his date. They'd moved in together and had been out and about together in town. Photos had been taken and it seemed the cat was out of the bag because all the gossip sites had photos of the two of them together. But so far, Colt had remained mum about his sexual orientation. Tonight, it would become official.

"Are you nervous?"

"Terrified."

She hugged him. "It's going to be fine. You and Tony are going to be fine. And you're both going to look incredible, so the public is going to go crazy over both of you."

He grinned. "We do make a dynamic couple, don't we?"

"Yes. Now go get beautiful while I do the same."

"I've heard your agent set you up with a mystery date tonight."

She rolled her eyes. "Yes. Exactly what I don't need. Some needy wannabe star trying to shove me out of the way so he can get his photo taken at all the right angles."

He kissed her cheek. "Don't even worry about your

dipshit date for the night. Concentrate on the movie and smiling for the press. I'll be there for you, honey."

"Thank you. And I'll be there for you and Tony, too."

Des showered, then her makeup and hair people showed up, and it was a flurry of activity as she was primped and readied, her hair styled in a messy updo to go with the beautiful white strapless gown she'd chosen for the night. The jeweler came by to present the lovely necklace and earrings she'd wear to go with the gown. They were stunning diamonds and teardrop earrings, and worth a million dollars. Expensive jewelry always freaked her out. It just wasn't her style, but it went with the whole movie-premiere thing, so she'd do whatever was necessary.

By the time she was dressed, it was nearly five, so she slipped on her silvery heels and looked into the mirror. The dress fit her perfectly, the bodice a corset fit to her hips, then flared out in a beautiful, flowing shape. And the diamonds were a perfect touch—not too much, but just enough bling.

She thanked her team profusely for getting her ready. They left, and she put the finishing touches on her lip gloss, then headed downstairs to her waiting limo.

The lineup for the premiere was long, but as she got to the front, she pasted on her best smile, excitement running through her. She couldn't wait to get out on the red carpet.

She couldn't wait to get this over with.

She got out, and a hand was there to help her out. She turned to smile at the person assisting her, and her heart thudded against her rib cage.

"Logan."

Dressed in a tux, he folded her hand in the crook of his arm.

"What are you doing here?"

"I'm your date."

"But—"

"Not now. Your public's waiting for you, Desiree."

He led her to the red carpet, where fans screamed, the click of cameras was deafening, and all she could think about was the man she loved was here, at her side.

Except as soon as they hit the press line, he took a step back and let her have the limelight.

She turned to look back at him. He looked amazing. Tall, lean, tanned, and the tux fit him perfectly. He had to be so damned uncomfortable in that tux, and yet he smiled at her, shoved one hand in his pocket, and nodded while she turned to answer questions in the press line.

"Des, who's your date tonight?"

She took a deep breath. "That's Logan McCormack, the owner of the L&M ranch where we just finished filming. It's my treat to him for allowing us to film there."

"Is there any relationship going on with Logan McCormack?"

"Logan is the owner of the L&M ranch, where we just finished filming. Next question."

She fielded many of the same questions and moved on, grateful to reach the end of the press line, where Logan was there to once again take her hand.

Then she was off to take photos with Colt. "How are you holding up?" she asked him.

"Not too bad. They've noticed Tony and are asking a lot of questions. I'm telling them my personal life is not the subject to be discussed today, but I'm happy to answer questions about the film."

"Good for you. Let them think what they want while you go about living your life. And in the meantime, you and Tony are free to do what you want. People will figure it out. When the time is right, you can do whatever article you want discussing the two of you."

"*Out* magazine has already asked if I'll do an article."

"Are you going to do one?"

He turned to her. "I think so."

She squeezed his hand.

"And I see you have an interesting date tonight."

"I don't know how that happened."

Colt gave her a half smile. "Yeah, me either."

"It was you?"

He kissed her cheek. "See you inside."

She met up with Logan again. "I can't believe you're here."

"You invited me. And you didn't answer questions about us."

"It's not the media's business. Besides, I don't really have answers, do I?"

"I guess you don't. But you will."

Curious, she let him lead her inside, where they took their seats.

The movie was wonderful, and Des was proud of the work she and Colt had done on this film. It was a drama about a drug-addicted wife and how she drags her husband and family through her agonies. The movie received tons of applause at the end, and Des thought Colt, as the tortured husband, had delivered an amazing performance.

They both received cheers when they left the theater. Des smiled, and Logan never left her side. They went to one of the after parties, where the media took photos of both of them. They even asked Logan questions.

"I'm just a rancher, happy to be invited here to see one of Colt and Desiree's movies. This was a great one, wasn't it?"

That was the standard answer he gave to every question the media asked.

When Des pulled him aside, she told him, "You're very good at this PR thing, considering you have no training."

"Like you said, it's none of their business."

"But you were polite. Which isn't really in your nature."

He arched a brow. "Are you saying I'm a rude sonofabitch?"

She quirked a smile. "Sometimes."

"How much longer do you have to stay here?"

"I've put in the appropriate amount of time."

He took her hand. "Good. There are some things we need to settle between us."

They got into the limo and took it back to her hotel. Des opened the door.

He stepped into the spacious living room, complete with fireplace, two sofas, and multiple chairs. The living room doors opened onto a balcony that overlooked Hollywood. "Fancy. Very you."

"Not really. You should see my condo. You'd be very disappointed. It's not movie-star quality at all."

"I'd like to see it."

"Maybe I'll invite you over, once you tell me why you flew all the way out here. Surely it wasn't just to watch a movie."

"No. It wasn't. Not that kind of circus, with all the media that seems to follow you everywhere."

She walked up to him. "Then I hope you have good security at the ranch, because it's going to be like that if I come live with you."

"I don't recall asking you. Yet."

She put her hands on her hips. "Really. Then what the hell are you doing here if you aren't here to tell me what a colossal asshole you've been, what a mistake you made by letting me go, and then to tell me you love me madly and ask me to come live with you?"

Logan sighed. "Goddammit, Des. You are the most frustrating woman I've ever known. Mind if I do things on my own timeline without you telling me how I'm supposed to feel?"

"Fine. You do it."

He pulled her toward him and kissed her, that melt-her-panties kind of kiss that never failed to explode a few brain cells in the process. And when he pulled away, he said. "I love you, Des. I flew out here and put on this stupid tux because I love you. I stood in front of all those cameras and answered dumb questions because I love you. Because I sure as hell wouldn't do it for any other reason than love."

Her heart melted. "I love you, too, Logan."

He pulled her down on the sofa, then sat next to her. "I'm sorry. You're right. I acted like a complete moron and I let you go. I hurt you and I hurt myself in the process. But when I saw you the night of the wrap party, dressed up and looking fancy, it made me feel like we were too far apart to ever end up together. And instead of talking to you about it, I backed away."

She sighed. "You know there's nothing you can't talk to me about."

"I do know that. But you know where I come from. And I'm scared of making the same mistakes my parents made. Every goddamn day I'm afraid of the past repeating itself."

She swept her fingers through his hair. "I know you are. But I'm not going to hurt you."

"I know you're not. It's taken me a long time to come to grips with that reality, but I've finally let go of the past and I'm ready for the future. And that future doesn't mean anything to me unless you're in it. Please come to the ranch and live with me. Even if that means you have to live there only part-time when you're not making movies, that'll be enough. We'll figure out a way to make it work, but I need you in my life."

Des felt as if she were soaring three feet off the ground. "I love you and I love the L&M. I loved that ranch the minute I stepped foot on it. And like it or not, Logan McCormack, I'm moving in with you. Me and all my girlie things and my scripts are going to be a part of your life. I'm going to take some time off and learn this whole ranching thing."

He cocked a brow. "Is that right?"

"Yes. It's high time I take a vacation, kick back and relax a little."

"You do realize that ranching is not relaxing."

"To me it is."

"Well, I've been giving some thought to this whole vacation thing. I've never taken one, and the Caribbean sounds good. I'd like to see you in a bikini. Or out of one."

She grinned. "I can arrange that."

He leaned in, but she laid her hand on his chest. "One more thing."

"Okay."

"And occasionally, when I go on a location shoot, you're going to have to learn to let go a little and take some time off, because you're coming with me."

He looked at her, then nodded. "Okay."

She stared at him. "Just like that? Okay?"

"It's the new me. I'm learning to bend a little."

She threw her arms around him and kissed him, so filled with love and joy and the prospect of making a life with him that it overwhelmed her. And when he kissed her back, she felt the love in his kiss.

She pulled back and gazed into the eyes of the man she loved.

"Take me home, cowboy."

TURN THE PAGE FOR A PREVIEW OF
JACI BURTON'S NEXT HOPE ROMANCE

# Hope Burns

**COMING SOON FROM HEADLINE ETERNAL**

**THIS WEDDING WAS** going to be a disaster.

Molly Burnett didn't know what had possessed her to agree to come back to Hope for her sister Emma's wedding. Love for her sister, of course. But she knew what was at stake. She never came home, hadn't been home since she'd left when she was eighteen.

That had been twelve years ago. She'd moved around from town to town, state to state, never setting down roots. Permanence just wasn't Molly's thing. And she sure as hell had never once come back to her hometown.

Until now. Even as she drove past the city limits sign her throat had started to close up, her breathing becoming labored. If she hyperventilated, crashed the car, and died a week before Emma's wedding, her sister would never forgive her.

Then again, with all the sputtering and coughing her ancient Ford Taurus was doing, it might just do itself in before she had a chance to crash it into anything.

"Come on, George," she said, smooth-talking the car.

"Hang in there." She didn't have the budget for a new—or a newer used—car. Old George, currently age fifteen and she hoped heading toward sixteen, was just going to have to suck it up and keep working.

At the next stop sign, George shuddered and belched rather loudly, making the two little kids sitting in the backseat of the car next to her point and laugh. She gave them a smile, then gently pressed on the gas. Obviously having cleared his throat, George lumbered on and Molly sighed in grateful relief. Gripping the steering wheel and forcing deep, calming breaths, Molly drove past the First Baptist Church, her favorite donut shop, the florist, and Edith's Hair Salon. So many places still stood, all too familiar.

So much had changed in twelve years. So much progress, so many new businesses had cropped up. New restaurants, the hospital was bigger than she remembered, and they'd widened the highway. When she'd lived here before, there'd been only one shop to stop at for gas and sodas along the main road. Now there was one at every corner.

She purposely turned off the main road, determined to avoid the high school. Too many memories she wasn't ready to face yet. She headed toward the main strip of town. There was a new bakery, and on impulse, Molly decided to stop and buy some goodies for the family.

She headed inside, the smell of sugar and baked goods making her smile.

After buying a box full of croissants and cream puffs, she made her way outside, stopping short at the sight of a very fine ass, bent over, inspecting her car.

"Can I help you?"

He straightened and turned, and Molly almost dropped the box of baked goods.

The last person in Hope she wanted to see today stared back at her.

Carter Richards, her first and only love, and the main reason she'd left Hope all those years ago.

"Hey, Molly."

"What are you doing here, Carter?"

"My auto shop is just a few doors down. I saw you get out of the car."

Recovering, she walked over to the driver's side, placed the box on the hood, then opened the door. "And you thought this would be a good place for a reunion? Really, Carter?"

She hoped he wouldn't notice her hands shaking as she slid the box onto the passenger seat and climbed in, shutting the door.

He leaned his forearms inside the car. "That's all you have to say?"

"I think we said all we needed to say to each other twelve years ago."

She turned the key and winced at George's attempts to fire on all cylinders. She tried again, and this time the car started. Sort of. It mostly wheezed. And then died.

Dammit. *Come on, George. I just need you to start this one time.*

"Let me help you with that."

She shot him a look. "I don't need help. I can do this."

She tried again. No go.

"Molly."

Carter's voice was deep and low, causing skitters of awareness to race down her spine. She wanted him to disappear. She wanted to pretend he didn't exist, just like she'd tried to erase him from her memories for the past twelve years. She wanted to be anywhere but here right now.

"Slide out and let me give it a try."

With a resigned sigh, she opened the door and got out. Carter slid in and fiddled with the ignition.

"George is a little touchy," she said.

He turned to face her. "George?"

Crossing her arms, she nodded. "Yes. George."

His lips curved, and her stomach tumbled. God, he was

even more good looking now than he'd been in high school. Thick, dark hair, and those mesmerizing green eyes. He wore a polo shirt that stretched tight over his well-muscled biceps. Why couldn't he have turned out bald and fat and hideously ugly? Not that it would have made a difference anyway, because it still would have been Carter.

When George's engine finally turned over, tears pricked Molly's eyes.

Carter got out and held the door for her. "There you go."

"Thanks."

He shut the door, then leaned in the window again. "Molly . . ."

She looked up at him. "Please don't."

He nodded and backed up a step so she could back out of the parking spot, which she did with a little too much fervor. As she drove away, she saw him watching her out of her rearview mirror.

She forced a tight grip on the steering wheel and willed the pain in her heart to go away.

It was in the past. Carter was in the past, and that's where he was going to stay.

CARTER WATCHED MOLLY drive away, that old junker she drove belching out smoke and exhaust like it was on its last legs.

He shook his head and leaned against the wall of the bakery, needing a minute to clear his head before he went back to work.

He'd been thinking about Molly for a while now, knowing she was coming back to Hope. She had to, because she was in Luke and Emma's wedding. He hadn't expected to see her today, though, when he'd stepped out front of his auto body shop to take a breath from all the damn paperwork that was his least favorite part of being a business owner.

He'd always liked watching the cars go by on his breaks.

When he'd seen an unfamiliar one—an old, beat-up Taurus choking out a black trail of exhaust, then wheezing as it came to a stop in front of the bakery—he couldn't help but wonder who'd drive an old piece of shit like that. Surely the owner had to realize that poor junker should be shot and put out of its misery.

His heart slammed against his ribs when a gorgeous brunette stepped out of the car. She had on shorts, a tank top, and sandals, and she was hurrying into the bakery like she didn't want to be recognized. She even kept her sunglasses on, but there was no mistaking who it was.

Yeah, like he could ever forget the curve of her face, the fullness of her lips, or her long legs. It might have been twelve years, and she might have changed from girl to woman, but Molly Burnett was someone Carter would never forget. His pulse had been racing and he knew damn well he should turn around and go back to his office. But for some reason his body hadn't been paying attention to what his mind told it, and he pushed off the wall and started down the street toward the bakery.

He debated going inside, then thought better of it and decided to figure out what the hell it was she was driving. So he'd walked over and studied the car.

A '99 Taurus. Christ. He wondered where Molly was living, and how the hell that car had made the trip. It had dents all over, the muffler was nearly shot, and the tires badly needed replacement—like a year ago.

In retrospect, he should have let her be, should have kept his distance from her. But when he'd seen her, he'd closed his eyes for a fraction of a second, transported back in time to the last time he'd heard her voice. It had sounded hurt and angry. The last words they'd said to each other hadn't been kind ones.

And maybe he'd wanted to change all that.

But it hadn't gone at all like he'd planned. She was still hurt, still angry with him, even after all these years.

Carter dragged his fingers through his hair, pushed off

the wall, and made his way down the street toward the garage, then back to his office. He shut the door and stared at his laptop, but all he could see was Molly's long, dark hair pulled up in a high ponytail, and her full lips painted some shimmering pink color. She was tan, and her body had changed over the years. She was curvier now, had more of a woman's body.

But she was still the drop-dead gorgeous woman he'd fallen in love with all those years ago.

He'd thought he was over her, that what he'd once felt for her in high school was long gone. But they'd had a deeper connection than just being first loves.

And seeing her again had hurt a lot more than he'd thought it would.

*Once passion ignites, you can't stop the flames...*

From *New York Times* Bestselling Author

# JACI BURTON

# *Hope Flames*

Emma Burnett once gave up her dreams for a man who did nothing but hurt her. Now thirty-two and setting up her veterinary practice in the town she once called home, she won't let anything derail her career goals. But when Luke McCormack brings in his injured police dog, Emma can hardly ignore him. Despite her best efforts to keep things strictly professional, Luke's an attractive distraction she doesn't need.

Luke knows the only faithful creature in his life is his dog. After an ugly divorce that left him damn near broke, the last thing he needs is a woman in his life. Fun and games are great and, as a divorced man, the single women in town make sure he never lacks for company. But there's something about Emma that gets to him, and despite his determination to go it alone, he's drawn to her feisty spirit and the vulnerability she tries so hard to hide.

## PRAISE FOR JACI BURTON AND HER NOVELS

"Jaci Burton's stories are full of heat and heart."
—Maya Banks, *New York Times* bestselling author

"Passionate, inventive...Burton offers
plenty of emotion and conflict."
—*USA Today* Happy Ever After blog

Jaciburton.com
facebook.com/AuthorJaciBurton
facebook.com/eternalromance